"My lord, we must converse on a most important matter.

"I would have you know that though we are wed and I am forced to accompany you to your lands…I do not intend to be your wife in any other sense."

Benedict's brows rose in shock. She had come right out and denied him her bed.

"You seek to send me from you?"

She bit her lip with uncertainty, but there was defiance in her eyes. "I do."

He shook his head in disbelief. "You have no right to do so. I am your husband."

"You will not be so lest you force me."

He moved toward her, his anger a tight ball in his belly. "What makes you think I would force you?"

Her gaze widened. "I…I simply assumed…"

"I have never forced myself upon any woman—never had to." His gaze raked her meaningfully.

Dear Reader,

Spring is in full bloom and marriage is on the minds of many. That's why we're celebrating marriage in each of our four outstanding Historicals romances this month!

We are delighted with the return of Catherine Archer, who captures the essence of our theme with *The Bride of Spring,* book two of her outstanding SEASONS' BRIDES miniseries. Filled with emotion and wry humor, this medieval tale highlights intrepid heroine Raine Blanchett, who, realizing she must marry to protect her young brother, decides to have some say in the groom. She cleverly orchestrates a "forced" marriage, unaware that the man she has chosen, intriguing knight Benedict Ainsworth, will become her true love.

Another heroine who knows her mind is Lady Sara Fernstowe in Lyn Stone's *My Lady's Choice,* in which Sara determines to wed the semiconscious and oh-so-handsome warrior she's just saved from near death. Award-winning author Cheryl Reavis brings us a powerful story about a second chance at love and marriage in *The Captive Heart.* Here, a British officer's wife is imprisoned by her husband, but rescued by a Native American frontiersman.

And don't miss *Tanner Stakes His Claim,* book two of Carolyn Davidson's terrific EDGEWOOD, TEXAS miniseries. It's a darling marriage-of-convenience tale between a squeaky-clean Texas sheriff and the amnesiac—and pregnant—saloon singer he can't stop thinking about.

Enjoy! And come back again next month for four more choices of the best in historical romance.

Sincerely,

Tracy Farrell,
Senior Editor

THE BRIDE OF SPRING

CATHERINE ARCHER

HARLEQUIN®

TORONTO • NEW YORK • LONDON
AMSTERDAM • PARIS • SYDNEY • HAMBURG
STOCKHOLM • ATHENS • TOKYO • MILAN • MADRID
PRAGUE • WARSAW • BUDAPEST • AUCKLAND

ISBN 0-373-29114-0

THE BRIDE OF SPRING

This edition published by arrangement with Harlequin Books S.A.

® and TM are trademarks of the publisher. Trademarks indicated with ® are registered in the United States Patent and Trademark Office, the Canadian Trade Marks Office and in other countries.

Visit us at www.eHarlequin.com

Printed in U.S.A.

Available from Harlequin Historicals and
CATHERINE ARCHER

Rose Among Thorns #136
* *Velvet Bond* #282
* *Velvet Touch* #322
Lady Thorn #353
Lord Sin #379
Fire Song #426
† *Winter's Bride* #477
† *The Bride of Spring* #514

* Velvet Series
† Seasons' Brides

Please address questions and book requests to:
Harlequin Reader Service
U.S.: 3010 Walden Ave., P.O. Box 1325, Buffalo, NY 14269
Canadian: P.O. Box 609, Fort Erie, Ont. L2A 5X3

This book is dedicated to all of my readers.
Thank you so much for your letters and for making it possible for me to do the work I love.

Chapter One

England, 1461

Raine Blanchett waited among the courtiers gathered outside King Edward's audience chamber. She, unlike the other finely garbed nobles, was not here to see the king.

Raine was in search of a husband. The knowledge that she must find one soon was beginning to press more firmly upon her with each passing day. Yet the long month she had been at court had seen no development as far as her hope of finding a husband was concerned.

Coming to court had seemed such a grand notion when she had told her brother, William, and their childhood nurse, Aida, of the decision. Arriving here had shown her that even the best propositions are not always simple to carry out in practicality.

Raine was honest enough to admit that it was her own fault that things were not going well. She did not want just any man. A handsome face and a witty tongue would not suffice. She wanted a man who would look after her eleven-year-old brother and his estates until he came of age. She wished for this man to do so without succumbing to an unacceptable urge to "dip into the pot."

What he looked like, his age—naught mattered but that he would be fair and honest and strong. Strong enough to keep Cousin Denley from thinking he could continue to harass them. In the last weeks before her decision to come to court, his persistent offers of marriage had changed to clumsily veiled threats to force her, should she not come around.

Raine knew that William would not fare well under such as he. It was no secret that the dull-witted Denley wanted to marry her so that he could gain control of the vast holdings her brother had inherited six months ago, when their father died.

The thought of her father's death brought a now familiar ache to her chest, but Raine refused to give in to her sorrow. She knew her father had wanted her to go forward, to look after her brother and his heritage. Though neither of them had ever spoken of his utter despair after her mother's death, her father's dependence and trust in Raine had begun that day. She had the sense that he would want her to do whatever she must in order to see that William and the lands were taken care of. Raine meant to do just that.

When she had first arrived at court, Raine had gone about the usual method of meeting prospective grooms. She had made herself presentable in the beautiful new gowns she and her ladies had fashioned. She had smiled and danced, and tried to seem appealing. The problem was not a shortage of male interest. It was the sort of males she had attracted.

Each of the three that she had taken a particular interest in had ended in disappointment, including Lord

Henry Wickstead, whom she had thought far beyond a greed for lands and money at his great age. He, like the others, had proved to be far from her ideal. When she had made an effort to find out about them and their situations, she had learned that each was in financial difficulty and in search of a wealthy bride. It did not seem to trouble them that Raine, though not unprovided for, was no great heiress. It was clear that they looked to all that young William possessed, and rubbed their hands in glee.

Yet precious weeks had been wasted in discovering these would-be suitors' true intentions. She had realized that she must find some method of learning something of a man without expending great amounts of time. It had been one week ago that Raine had hit upon the notion of going directly into the king's audience chamber and finding out exactly what each courtier there hoped to gain from him. Surely that would reveal much about a man's financial situation, at the very least. No one seemed to question Raine's presence each day, appearing too occupied with his own concerns. Her method had certainly proved efficient, but it also gave her to understand that the task she had set herself was a difficult one.

No one had, as yet, passed this preliminary test.

Only desperation kept her from tucking her tail between her legs and going home. She could not count on Denley to continue to heed her refusals of his suit. Raine feared that he would not hesitate in forcing her to marry him, or worse yet, doing some harm to William in order to inherit the estates. As their second cousin and only living relative, Denley stood to gain all if something were to happen to her brother.

Quickly Raine pushed that thought away. Nothing

could happen to William. With their father gone, he was all she had left.

She cast another hopeful, and admittedly desperate, glance over the courtiers who were gathered in the waiting area, then sighed.

It was only a moment later that the king's steward opened the door of the audience chamber and pushed it wide. He bowed to those gathered. "You may go in now. His majesty King Edward will see you, each in turn."

As Raine entered with the others she looked toward the dais, where the lavishly dressed Edward was seated, his direct gaze assessing those gathered. Not for the first time she wondered about the young king. There were those who said that though he was endowed with intelligence and sense of purpose, he lacked his father's strength of character. Raine knew that only time would tell. He was barely twenty. Did he miss his own father, who had died not so very long ago as a result of his efforts to gain this very crown? Or had the responsibilities of his position robbed the dark-haired young man of his freedom to grieve, much as her own change in circumstances had done to her? Looking into the young monarch's already wary eyes, Raine felt they must.

Yet Edward and his grief, all else, must fade in the wake of her own need to care for and protect William.

The hours of the morning dragged on, and as each man present submitted his case to the king, he removed himself from possible consideration as a husband. Some were married; others, well…they were simply not suitable.

Raine was beginning to believe that she must abandon hope of finding a likely candidate for another day when there was a slight commotion at the door behind them. Though she was very close to the back of the chamber, she could not see the cause of the disturbance over the heads of the men, who craned their necks in order to discover what was going on.

It was only when King Edward stood and smiled with a pleasure and enthusiasm he had not shown in the past that she realized anything of real import was occurring. The young king waved a beringed hand. "Come forward, Benedict."

Many gazes, including Raine's, swiveled to follow a head topped with coal-black hair and a pair of very wide shoulders encased in burgundy velvet. The unknown man seemed to fairly glide through the crowd as he went forward with easy grace. Raine raised up on tiptoe, yet could still see no more of this man than his shoulders and the back of his head, even when he gained the dais and Edward reached out to offer him his hand. At the king's welcoming gesture, those in front of her craned their necks even more in order to see.

For a moment King Edward and the man he had addressed as Benedict spoke quietly to one another. Suddenly the king frowned with concern and stood, drawing him to the side of the dais. There the two men continued to converse quietly.

A subdued murmur of what Raine could only describe as envy rippled through the crowd.

A thoughtful frown creased her brow as she wondered who the newcomer might be. What manner of man could consider himself friend to the king of England? For that was what their relationship appeared to be.

Raine tried to press forward, but could get no closer to the front. The crowd was too dense.

She heard a tall, blond, haughty-faced young man to

her right snicker aloud to his equally haughty companion. "Arrogant bastard." Both were garbed in scandalously short houpellands.

Raine, concealing her own opinion on who seemed arrogant, asked, "Who is he?"

The blond man looked down his long, aristocratic nose, and there was no mistaking the disdain in his voice. "Benedict Ainsworth, Baron of Brackenmoore. He was a great friend to Edward's father and quite instrumental in aiding him in his bid for the throne."

Raine nodded, her voice unconsciously weary as she said, "And very well rewarded for his troubles, no doubt." She had seen much of greed in this chamber over the past days, though 'twas often couched in clever terms and a humble countenance.

The young man shrugged. "Not to my knowledge, though who can say? It is rumored that he and Richard of York were great friends as boys and that Ainsworth supported him out of friendship. But, as you say, it is likely that he did seek some personal gain even if the reward is not widely known." His face showed how little impressed he was by this Ainsworth.

But Raine herself was intrigued by his disclosure that the man had gained nothing from the crown. Perversely, she found herself arguing the point she herself had introduced. "But as you said, no one speaks of any gain he has made from his support of Richard. Perhaps he simply did do so out of friendship."

It was only then that the young noble seemed to truly look at her, his curious gaze running over her fine, ermine-trimmed velvet gown and jewels with appreciation. "And what care would you have for such things, my young beauty?"

Raine turned her head so he would not see her roll

her eyes at his all too obvious avarice. "I was but curious to know of one who would be so heartily welcomed by the king. Is he wed?"

The young man smiled with deliberate charm. "I think not, but have no care for that. I am Sir Robert Fullerton and I am not wed. I would be most interested in conversing with you on matters more interesting than Ainsworth...."

"Yes, perhaps later at table." Raine nodded absently, putting him from her mind. She was already thinking about how to find out more about this Benedict Ainsworth, though she hardly dared think—

"Your attention!" King Edward spoke then, drawing her gaze back to the dais. She raised her head to hear what he had to say. He smiled out over those gathered. "I offer my regret to you all, but I really must attend a very important matter at this time. I must ask you all to leave now. I will hold open court again on the morrow."

Raine felt disappointment wash through her. She had so wished to hear why the man had come to King Edward. Now she would never know, for they meant to send everyone from the room, including her. There was nothing she could do.

She turned with the others to make her way from the chamber. She heard the mutterings of displeasure that came from either side of her and sighed. Clearly she was not alone in her disappointment at being sent away, though she doubted the motives of the others were the same as her own.

Frustration and a desire to try to get one clear glimpse of the man slowed her steps. Raine allowed herself to fall to the back of the crowd. But before she had an opportunity to turn and actually get a look at Benedict

Ainsworth the steward was calling for everyone to make haste.

Raine scowled. If only she could make herself small, so small that she could do as she wished and not be noticed. Her shoulder brushed the heavy, red-velvet drapes that hung along the stone walls to keep out the chill. And as it did so, an idea came to her.

Perhaps she could not make herself so small that she was invisible, but she might be able to disguise her presence. Quickly, not giving herself time to consider, Raine ducked behind the drape. She held her breath, waiting for a damning voice to signal that her action had been noted, even as the heavy velvet settled in thick folds about her.

Benedict Ainsworth, Baron of Brackenmoore, faced King Edward with resolve as he waited for the other nobles to leave the chamber. He knew that the decision he had made before coming to Edward would cost him in goods. Maxim Harcourt was indeed dead, and at his brother Tristan's own hand. There was no denying it, or the fact that Maxim's own brother, whom no one Benedict knew had ever so much as seen, felt that he was owed some retribution.

Benedict also knew that there had been very good cause for Tristan having killed Harcourt. Yet Benedict was prepared to make the reason for the man's death known to none save the king himself. That was why he had taken the audacious step of requesting this private audience with Edward, would never beg such favor for any lesser reason. He was not unaware of the weighty glances that were cast his way as the room emptied.

When the last of the courtiers had filed from the

chamber, Edward turned to his steward. "You may leave us as well."

The man looked at Benedict with an assessing frown. Ainsworth said nothing. The steward's opinion of him mattered not in the least. He had more important things on his mind.

When the steward had gone, Edward swung around to face him with a smile. "Shall we sit?"

Benedict sat in one of the chairs Edward indicated, to the left of the dais. The young king took the other. "You have expressed your desire to speak with me in seclusion. What is it you would like to say to me?"

Benedict leaned back in his chair, looking closely at this young king. He was somewhat like his father in appearance. Whether or not he would ever attain Richard's wisdom and devotion to England could not yet be known.

Benedict gave himself a mental shake. Assessing the king was not why he was here. "Your majesty—"

The king interrupted him. "Please, you were my father's friend and seemed like an uncle to me when I was a lad. Do not stand on ceremony now because of that," he said, gesturing toward the velvet-draped throne beside them. "You may address me as Edward, as you always have."

Benedict nodded. "I think I must not be too presumptive, your majesty. Your father and I were friends, but that does not mean you owe me any more familiarity than other men. You are king of England now."

Edward smiled at him. "I am king, but I hope that you will remain friend to me in spite of that, as you would have to my father had he lived to take the throne."

How could Benedict do other than bow his head in

acquiescence? "I would feel privileged to count myself that, sire. But I must keep this meeting upon a more formal footing because of its nature. As I said when I arrived, I would ask a boon of you, my lord."

Edward nodded, obviously seeing the seriousness of his intent. The grave expression of ruler settled on his intelligent young face.

Benedict went on. "Some months ago, my brother Tristan slew Maxim Harcourt."

Edward propped his fingers together thoughtfully. "I have had some correspondence with his brother, Alister Harcourt, on this matter."

"As have I, sire, though I did not know that the fact of his having a brother was more than rumor until the man's first letter arrived. He is, understandably, angry at what Tristan has done, as you must know from your own contact with him."

Again Edward nodded as Benedict continued. "Clearly he feels himself justified in his anger, and due to the circumstances, I would not fault him on that. Yet I must tell you, your majesty, that he does not know the full events that led up to his brother's death, which, I feel, exonerate Tristan."

"Why do you not then apprise him of the facts?"

Benedict hesitated. "The situation is…well, delicate. You see, it involves my brother's wife, Lillian Ainsworth, formerly Lillian Gray."

Edward shrugged, though the name did not seem new to him. Benedict was beginning to realize that the king was not quite as oblivious concerning this subject as he had first appeared. He probably did indeed know a great deal of the facts. Yet when he spoke it was still in that same unconcerned vein. "Harcourt's letters have contained some mention of this woman and that she was his brother's intended bride. He seems to be of the opinion that your brother Tristan spirited her away, thus bringing about the conflict in which his brother died.''

Benedict was very glad that he was not attempting to get anything past this young king. Young he might be, but dim he was not. ''That is, in part, true. Yet there are mitigating circumstances that, as I said, exonerate Tristan of any real wrongdoing in this.''

Edward sat back with raised brows. ''Again I say, why do you or your brother not simply make his reasons known?''

Benedict frowned. ''That would mean telling Alister Harcourt a very involved and extremely private tale. He could then relay the story to any who would heed him. Knowing nothing of his character, I hesitate to give him the power over my brother and his wife that knowing their secrets might afford. You see, sire, Lily and Tristan had been lovers three years before her engagement to Maxim, and there is a product of that union. My niece, Sabina.''

Edward leaned forward. ''I begin to see. You would not have this bandied about by those he might tell.''

''Aye, sire. Lily and Tristan have been through enough. They had never intended for the child to be born out of wedlock. Due to an accident, Lily and Tristan were separated. When she awoke, she recalled nothing of Tristan or the babe. Her family felt it best to keep her past from her. It was not until Lily was on her way to marry Maxim Harcourt that Tristan saw her and kidnapped her, completely unaware that she recalled nothing of her past with him. Although I would not follow my brother's method, I do understand his actions. He and Lily did have the prior commitment. Maxim Harcourt was killed in fair combat against Tristan.''

Again Edward nodded. "So what is it you ask of me, Benedict? Do you wish for me to make an explanation to Alister Harcourt that would disabuse him of his perceived grievance with you and your family?"

Benedict shook his head. "As I have told you, knowing nothing of the man's character, I have no wish to tell him anything of my family's misfortunes. Neither would I ask the crown to place itself in the position of contriving some excuse for me. What I would propose is that I pay a penalty to him by way of lands and monies. In that way he would feel that his perceived wrong had been avenged in some small way."

Light dawned in Edward's eyes. "And you wish for me, as the king, to oversee this transaction?"

"If you will be so kind as to do so. It might then seem as though you had set the penalty yourself. I would also have your approval of the transfer of the land and keep. You would not appear to be showing me any undo favor, as your father's friend, and I would have no need to explain to Tristan what I am about. He is a proud man and would certainly rather take care of this matter himself, if he knew of it. And would do so quite well, I am certain. I simply wish to see that he and his new bride have some peace in their lives now. As I said, they have faced much to find a new life with one another." Benedict was not unaware of the slightly wistful quality in his own voice when speaking of their love, and was surprised at it. Though he was very happy for the couple, he had no real desire to experience such an all-consuming love.

Brackenmoore and his family were his passions. And that was the way he wanted it. Perhaps it was the recent wedding and all the joyous emotions around it that had left him with an uncharacteristically romantic bent.

He focused his attention on Edward, who looked at him thoughtfully for a long moment. The king smiled. "Have you considered coming to live at court, Benedict? We can make use of such a diplomatic mind as yours."

Benedict shook his head. "I am much too occupied with running my estates, your majesty. I will leave the life of diplomacy to those who seek it."

Edward smiled again, this time ruefully, and pulled on the tasseled cord beside the dais. Immediately the steward entered, through a door partially hidden behind the throne. "Your majesty?"

Edward addressed him. "Fetch me a clerk."

The man bowed and left as Edward rose and moved toward the table near the window. He poured wine from a gold pitcher into two ruby-colored glasses, then turned to hand one to Benedict. "Just out of curiosity, am I prepared to be generous toward Alister Harcourt?"

Benedict smiled for the first time. "Oh, reasonably so, my lord, reasonably so." He raised his glass to drink.

Raine had heard every word as the clerk came and then went again, though she could see nothing from behind the heavy drapery. The more she heard, the more she wished to learn about Benedict Ainsworth, wished to see him. Yet she dared not risk looking out from her hiding place, for as the men talked she had begun to realize that she had indeed risked much in secluding herself in order to overhear the private conversation of a king.

Few would believe that she had done this in order to discover all she could about a man she did not even know, even if she could explain her reasons to them.

Yet Raine did not wish to worry about the possibility of being found out. All she had heard of Benedict Ainsworth had made her even more intrigued by him. He seemed a good, decent man, willing to give up his own property and money to protect the reputation of his brother's wife and her child.

As Raine listened to Benedict give the specifics of what he was willing to offer, she was again moved by his care for his family. If only she had a man to look after her in that way, someone like Ainsworth! Things might have been different for her if only there had been someone who felt a family affiliation to herself and William.

But there was only Denley, and he cared nothing for them. Of that she was sure. He pretended a great interest in herself, but Raine knew of his longtime mistress, of their children.

He kept them openly at his own home. Raine was somewhat surprised that he would not expect her to have had word of them. Perhaps he simply gave it no thought whatsoever. Many men kept both a mistress and a wife, though not nearly so openly.

If Raine were ever to marry a man with the intention of actually living with him, she would never allow herself to be so blatantly dishonored. If she were not required to wed for the sake of protecting William and his lands she would... Her thoughts trailed down a list of qualities she would desire in a man.

He would favor her with a modicum of respect.

He would be kind.

He would have his own wealth and thus would not wish to take what was William's.

He would behave with honor.

He would understand the meaning of family.

Again she found herself becoming aware of the two men's voices. She could not help noting that Benedict Ainsworth's seemed somehow deeper and richer than the king's. At the same moment she realized that they sounded closer than before.

Obviously the men were coming toward her. She strained to see through the dense velvet. If only she could give face to the voice she heard! Surely they were too intent on their conversation to pay her any heed. Moving ever so carefully, she peeked out from behind the curtain.

And realized that the two men had moved even nearer than she had imagined and were standing mere feet from her. The heaviness of the drape had muffled the sound of their voices and made them seem farther away. She quickly drew back, but not before she had glimpsed the face of Benedict Ainsworth. It was an arresting face, with kindness, warmth and firmness of character displayed in the smooth wide brow and the slight lines around his eyes. It was also a handsome face, with its pleasantly modeled and strong features, including a regal, straight nose and a pair of intense eyes of a startlingly deep cobalt-blue. Those direct and compelling eyes were surrounded by thick black lashes the same color as his raven hair.

Raine's heart felt like a throbbing drum in her chest, even though she was sure they had not seen her, for neither had been looking in her direction.

Under no circumstances did she wish to be caught. Again she asked herself who would believe that she had hidden herself here for the reasons she had. Even if they would, she would not wish to admit her motives to either Edward or Ainsworth himself.

At the thought of Benedict Ainsworth, another image

of that pleasing face flashed though her mind. In spite of the risk, she felt a compelling desire to look at him again, to see if she had only imagined such an attractive visage.

Benedict and Edward looked up at the same moment as the steward appeared in the door once more. "Your grace, an envoy has arrived with a reply to your message to France. I have taken him to a private chamber as you requested me to do upon his arrival."

Edward was very suddenly a king again as he replied, "I come."

He nodded to Benedict, who bowed deeply even as Edward left the chamber. The steward, taking care to pretend that he was not watching Benedict, moved to tidy the glasses they had used.

Benedict turned to go. He was finished here, for the moment at any rate. Edward had voiced surprise at Benedict's generosity in the keep and monies he would provide to Harcourt's brother, but he had given his approval to the transfer of goods.

It was as Benedict swung around to go out the far door that he noted the presence of two small, dark green slippers just visible beneath the edge of the scarlet drapery. The fact that the intruder was female seemed apparent and kept him from being overconcerned. Yet he grew very still, and a pensive frown creased his brow even as he saw a pale face surrounded by a cloud of auburn hair appear at the edge of the drape. A pair of golden eyes widened in horror as they met his own.

The face was definitely that of a woman. And an extremely pretty one. Surprised, Benedict started toward her without thinking.

The steward chose that moment to turn back to Benedict. He spoke with just the proper degree of deference, though it seemed obvious that he would prefer for Benedict to be on his way. "Is there something wrong, my lord?"

Benedict halted, his gaze searching the female's eyes, now filled with panic.

"My lord?" The steward spoke again, more insistently.

Her gaze darkened with pleading even as her hands came up to cover her pink lips. For a moment as he looked into those eyes Benedict felt as if he had fallen into a vat of liquid gold that swirled around him as he floated effortlessly in its warmth.

Something, an urge he could not name, made him close his lips on the words that would expose her position. Instead he cast the mysterious female a warning glance. Her face disappeared behind the curtain again as he turned to the steward. "Nay, I was just leaving. I was wondering if you might tell me where my horse will have been stabled?" Benedict knew it was a poor excuse. Never would he allow the stallion to be stabled without knowing the exact conditions, but the steward was not aware of this.

Benedict waited as the servant moved to join him at the door. He knew the woman could not escape from her hiding place until the steward left the chamber. Still, Benedict did not know why he would aid the unknown woman; he simply could not seem to do otherwise.

The man nodded, saying, "As you will, my lord," and led him from the room. Although he had a nearly overwhelming urge to do so, Benedict did not look back over his shoulder for fear of giving her away.

Her heart pounding like a drum in her chest, Raine escaped from behind the curtain as soon as the men were gone. Why had she given in to the urge to look at Benedict Ainsworth one more time? She had convinced herself that he would be too occupied with King Edward's leaving to heed her. She was shocked at her own lunacy. Even more confusing, why had the baron, a stranger, helped her? She could think of no ready answer and could only feel grateful that he had done so.

Now more than ever she felt intrigued by the man named Benedict Ainsworth. Recalling the fathomless depths of his dark-lashed eyes, which seemed far too blue to be real, she felt just the slightest bit attracted to him, as well.

Instantly Raine halted herself, feeling nothing but misgivings over such a thought. She was not interested in him or any other man in that way. She knew what she was looking for and why. Nothing else, no other consideration, must be allowed to interfere in her plans. To allow any other thought was to open herself to possible disaster. William's welfare must come first and last with her. If there was a possibility that Benedict Ainsworth was the right man to protect William, then she must meet with him, speak with him.

As she considered how best to try to come into contact with the man again, she felt a strange thrill ripple down her spine. There was no denying that he was the most fascinating man she had ever seen, not just because of his handsomely chiseled face or his obvious physical presence and vigor. The man exuded an air of quiet strength that drew her as a cricket is drawn to the scent of rain.

Again she told herself she could not allow such a thing to sway her. That having been decided, Raine felt much easier in her interest in the man. She *was* doing this for William. With a sigh of resolution, she went directly to her assigned chamber. The very tiny room had no window and one large bed with threadbare velvet hangings that might once have been gold but had yellowed to an uninviting shade. It was not an attractive or even a comfortable room, with its well-worn stone floor and roughly made furnishings—a table and two hard benches pulled close to the narrow hearth, which smoked profusely each time it was lit.

Raine could have been housed with some of the other ladies of the court, but she had not wished to be separated from her brother or Aida.

They looked up the moment she opened the door. Taking a deep breath, Raine informed them, "Well, my loves, I have just seen our most promising prospect yet."

Predictably, Aida got to her feet and began to pace, wringing her hands. "Dear heavens, Lady Raine, are you sure that this is what you should do? 'Haps we should forget all of this talk of finding a husband and go home to Abbernathy Park, leave things as they are."

Raine felt herself stiffen. She above all people would like to go home and pretend that everything was well, that they would be fine. That option was not available to her, for Denley would certainly be there the moment she arrived.

Someone had to see to the future, and she was the only one who could do so, no matter how difficult it might be. But they had been over all of this before. She took a deep breath and let it out slowly. "Aida, please, let us not discuss it all again. I need you to help me now."

William, who had been reading a book, laid it gently

on the table and fixed her with a thoughtful gaze. "Who is he, Raine? What is he like?"

Being a newborn babe at the time, he had no memory of the terrible months after their mother's death. Their father had been so deeply lost in his grief that Raine had been forced to act far beyond her eight years. But William did have some understanding of why she was so determined in this now. He had been at their father's bedside the night he'd died, knew how serious he had been in his request for Raine to look after everything. None of them had ever expected the elder William to go when his son was so very young. Their father had been in the prime of his life, strong and seemingly invincible in Raine's eyes. The illness that had taken his life had come on so rapidly that none of them could ever have been prepared for his death.

And since that time Raine had not allowed herself to feel her own pain, had taken all her anguish and turned it into an unshakable determination to take care of William as her father wished. Her brother was not a robust boy, though he had a soundness of character and intellect that more than made up for it in her eyes. His physical vulnerability only made her all the more resolved to do what she must.

Quickly Raine told them what had happened in the audience chamber.

Now William seemed as concerned as Aida. "You hid behind a curtain and eavesdropped upon the king of England and this man? Raine, have you gone completely mad? What would have happened had you been caught? You could have been accused of spying or treason, or…"

She went to him and laid a comforting hand upon his arm, her tone contrite. "I was not caught." She suddenly realized how terrible it would have been for him if she had been arrested and accused of some wrongdoing. Who would have seen to William's interests then?

"But you could have been. And you say this man saw you? He might still decide to tell someone you had been there." William's green eyes revealed concern and a clear sense of his protectiveness toward her, giving her a hint of the fine man he would grow to be.

Raine spoke with a conviction that came from some inner knowing she could not explain. "Ainsworth will tell no one."

Aida's rejoinder was filled with fear. "How do you know this, Lady Raine? You just laid eyes upon the man."

Raine was unable to meet the maid's searching gaze as she said, "He will say nothing." That inner knowing seemed only to grow each time she considered the matter. Benedict Ainsworth would not betray her.

Chapter Two

Raine readied herself for the meal with even more care than she had shown on previous occasions since coming to court. She was determined to make herself known to Benedict Ainsworth, and prayed he would appear in the hall.

That she must explain her presence behind the curtain in the audience chamber, she knew. Somehow she would think of something. Her real purpose, that of discovering whether or not Lord Ainsworth would be a suitable guardian for William, was foremost in her mind.

Raine entered the splendor of the great hall with mixed feelings of dread and anticipation. She paid scant attention to the lush tapestries that lined the walls, the dark beamed ceiling overhead or the elegantly garbed courtiers, who crowded about the tables consuming roast meats, stews, fowl of various varieties, fine bread and copious amounts of wine and ale. She did note, though, that Edward was not in attendance at the high table, for his heavy, carved chair stood empty. Raine felt unaccountably relieved at this, though she was quite sure that Ainsworth had not told him of her presence in his chamber.

Her mind was firmly fixed on the matter at hand. The thought that she might actually be nearer to accomplishing her goal of finding someone to give William the protection of his name—a husband—was both terrifying and strangely exciting. It was especially so when she recalled how tall and handsome the man under consideration was.

Raine pushed this last thought away. She could not think about such things. To do so would be to risk allowing them to cloud her judgment about Benedict Ainsworth being the right man to protect William and his lands. And that was all he need do. She had no desire for a true marriage. She had Abbernathy and her brother to look to.

She squared her shoulders beneath the heavy sapphire velvet of her gown and let her gaze sweep the room. When she did not immediately locate the baron among the throng, she took a deep breath and searched again, more slowly. There was no sign of those unmistakable broad shoulders, nor his raven hair.

Disappointment made her own shoulders slump. Even though she had known there was no guarantee of his attendance, she had not actually believed Lord Ainsworth would be absent.

Benedict had considered the notion of joining his men at the inn in which they were staying. There he could dine and drink in relaxed company. He disliked court life at the best of times.

Yet something made him remain at Westminster. He could not stop thinking of the young woman whose presence in the king's chamber he had concealed. The more he thought about her, the more he knew that he must discover what she had been doing there. Surely he had been quite mad to shield her as he had.

His doing so made him responsible for finding out what she had been about. He wanted no crime against the crown upon his conscience. For that was the only purpose he could imagine for her being there, though for some reason he was fairly certain that was not why she had been.

A sudden notion struck him as he paused in the doorway of the great hall. Perhaps she was infatuated with Edward.

Benedict was surprised at how much this thought displeased him. He told himself it was because she had seemed, even in the moment that he had looked into her eyes, to have an air of innocence about her. She would not retain it long were she to become involved with the king of England. Edward was already known for his way with women.

Benedict shrugged, albeit stiffly, as he entered the crowded chamber. If that was where the woman's interest lay, the outcome was her own quandary. He meant only to learn if she had been up to some other devilment.

He had no trouble finding her among the throng. Though her back was to him, and he had seen her only once, he would recognize that red hair anywhere. Tonight it was escaping her blue pearled headdress. She was seated some distance from the head table, which implied modest status. Again curiosity gripped him.

A strange anticipation filled him as he made his way among the tables to her side. Benedict stopped beside her and she looked up at him, those golden eyes of hers widening in surprise and, dared he believe it, pleasure.

He found himself thinking of his first impression—that she was quite pretty. He realized that he had been in error there. She was far more than pretty with those surprisingly dark lashed, golden eyes. Her nose was straight and aristocratic, her chin firm but not stubborn. Her mouth was pleasingly curved and lovely, and as she began to smile, it turned up slightly more on one side than the other in a way that he thought amazingly endearing.

An odd warmth suffused him and he found himself simply standing there, staring down at her like a besotted calf. His confusion over his unprecedented reaction made him speak with more gruffness than he intended. "May I sit here with you?"

Her smile faded somewhat and a pensive frown marred her brow. "You are welcome to do so, my lord."

He realized that he had been less than civil, but concentrated on his desire to learn why she had been in the king's chamber. Once he had taken the place on the bench next to her, Benedict found the proximity to her slightly unnerving. For he could not move without his own shoulder brushing against hers. And each time it did so he knew a far too heady sense of his own masculinity in comparison to her delicate womanliness.

Because of his own disturbance he lost no time in getting to the point. "My lady?"

She looked up from contemplation of her glass. "My lord?"

Again he was struck by the color of those amazing eyes of hers. He looked away, forcing himself to concentrate on the matter at hand. He kept his voice low. "I have come here this evening in hope of finding you so that you might have opportunity to explain why you were in the king's chamber this morn, when he had expressly sent everyone away."

Her voice was eager as she said, "Oh, of course, my lord. I have no wish to hide anything from you, and I do hope you realize how very grateful I am for your discretion this morn." Her lids fluttered down over those incredibly beautiful and ingenuous gold eyes.

"Well?" he prodded, not pleased with his thoughts.

She spoke softly. "Firstly, please allow me to introduce myself, my lord. My name is Raine Blanchett."

He made no reply to this, though he could not help thinking that the name Raine somehow suited her perfectly. He was immediately and unaccountably reminded of the last time he had seen his father. The six Ainsworths had been standing on the docks beside the ship that would take his parents to visit his mother's sister in Scotland. It had been raining, and his father had reached into his pouch and removed a gold coin. That coin had glistened in the rain as his father said, "Take your brothers about the town before you go home."

His mother had showed concern. "Should he do so, Benedict? The younger boys can be quite unruly."

His father had smiled and put an affectionate hand on her shoulder as he'd met his namesake's gaze. "Aye, Leticia, I trust him to look after them in my stead."

Benedict had never forgotten that moment, nor his father's faith in him. He was not sure why the color of Raine's eyes reminded him of it, or why that was so unsettling.

Raine had gone on at his silence. "Allow me to admit I should not have been where I was. It was completely foolhardy of me. I had hidden behind the curtain because I was attempting to avoid someone who would not cease in his efforts to speak to me and then..." She stared down at her hands. "I could not very well come out while you and King Edward were... What would he have thought?"

Benedict felt slightly uneasy with this almost too earnest explanation. He scowled. "Your words seem somewhat strained to me. I begin to think I may have good cause to go to King Edward on this matter."

She looked at him then, her eyes wide with horror. "No, please, my lord. I beg you not to do that. I swear on my own father's grave that I meant no harm to king or crown by my actions. I have no interest whatsoever in any of the king's business."

Now Benedict believed, There could be no doubting her sincerity this time. Whatever had brought her to commit such a rash act, it had not been treason.

For some reason he breathed an inner sigh of relief. He told himself it was because he was glad to have had no part in any plot against the king. But he found himself paying undue attention to the way a stray curl brushed the side of Raine Blanchett's cheek as she looked down.

His gaze moved over her pearl-dotted headdress, then down the sleeve of her matching gown of blue velvet. Obviously the woman was not suffering financial lack. He recalled the fine green slippers she had worn earlier in the day. He would likely never forget the surprise of seeing those unmistakably female feet peeking out from beneath that curtain. He suddenly realized he was smiling.

Instantly he schooled his expression to a more grave one. There was certainly no reason to smile over what she had done. He felt he must warn her to try to think about the consequences of such acts. "I will take your word, Lady Raine. But I suggest you mind your ways in the future. Should I learn you have ever again done such a thing, I will go to King Edward. And make no mistake, my departure from court two days hence will not prevent me from hearing.''

An unfathomable expression of disappointment seemed to pass over her features as he finished. She said only, ''Oh, thank you, my lord, you are the most kind and chivalrous of men. I will do nothing to betray your faith in me.''

Her vow, though spoken in a low voice, was so heartfelt he found himself touched by it. He was also slightly overwhelmed by her seemingly genuine flattery of himself. Why, she did not even know him. What an enigma she was, this Raine Blanchett. Benedict realized that his brief acquaintance with her had certainly been interesting—more interesting than any such acquaintance in his memory.

He caught himself immediately. He had no need of interesting things to occur in his life. He was quite busy enough running his estates and caring for his family. It was all he had done in the ten years since his parents had died, and all he wanted to do.

Raine was more impressed with this man by the moment, though his revelation that he was leaving in two days was not encouraging. He had certainly seen through the lie she had told him about hiding from the unwanted attentions of a would-be suitor. Yet he had believed her when she'd spoken of not wanting to bring any harm to the crown. How very astute he seemed.

She could not help smiling with secret approval as she looked up...and saw Denley Trent standing at the end of the room. Her pleasure turned to a groan of despondency. Denley was the last man she expected or wished to see.

Her pained gaze trailed over him. He was dressed in what was obviously a new scarlet velvet houppelande of the type preferred by the more daring of the courtiers. 'Twas short to the point of indecency, and the long dagged sleeves seemed too feminine against his large hands. The lumbering Denley was not made for such fashion.

His very presence was like a weight upon her shoulders. What manner of man was he to follow her here to court? Indeed, where would he stop in his persistence to see both herself and William beneath his thumb?

Raine glanced up at Benedict Ainsworth. How different he was from Denley. Having a man such as him at her side would surely make her cousin reconsider his dogged determination to have her.

But Ainsworth was now talking with the nobleman to his right. Though she had gone to great trouble to make herself appealing, he seemed interested in nothing save her intentions toward King Edward. Now that she had made herself clearer to him on that score he appeared to have lost interest in her completely. And with Cousin Denley having arrived, what was she to do?

Her desperate glance raked the crowded chamber as if seeking some answer to the problem of Denley Trent. In all the weeks she had been at court, Raine had not found one man, other than Benedict Ainsworth, who even appeared to come close to what she was hoping for.

Her gaze went back to Denley. He was looking about as if searching for someone, and even as a frown marred her brow, his gaze came to rest upon her with obvious relief.

Raine sighed with frustration and despair as he then stalked toward her like a bull in a cow pen, resolution written upon his heavy features. She bit down on her lip as she moved to rise. She did not wish to face Denley here, in the midst of this company. There was no telling what he might say about her having left Abbernathy without informing him. He had taken to visiting her almost daily after her father's death and had surely been shocked to arrive there and find her gone. Especially as she had instructed that no one was to tell him whence she had gone.

Her efforts to leave the hall before he could reach her were thwarted. The benches were pressed too closely about the tables, and with her heavy skirts slowing her efforts, she could not get to her feet quickly enough. Denley reached her side before she was able to extract one leg.

He spoke in a voice loud enough to draw the attention of those sitting near her, including, she noted out of the corner of her eye, Benedict Ainsworth. "Raine, I have been looking for you."

She glared up at him. "Denley, what a surprise."

The man scowled. "It should not be so great a surprise. Any man would be concerned about his future bride. You disappeared from Abbernathy without warning."

Utter and complete frustration colored her tone as she leaned back, putting her hands to her hips. "I am not going to marry you. That is my final word on the subject."

He reached down to grasp her arm in a tight grip. "Do not be ridiculous. Of course you will marry me. Has some court dandy been filling your head with nonsense? I will persuade him of his error soon enough."

Raine leaned farther away from him, but there was only so far she could move in the circumstances. She was infinitely aware of the rock solid breadth of Benedict Ainsworth's shoulder beside her. Denley pulled her toward him.

She knew they were creating quite a display, and kept her gaze trained on that of her nemesis to keep from having to look at anyone else. She must extricate herself from this situation as quickly as possible. This would in no way help her in her efforts to attract the baron.

It was with utter mortification, and surprisingly, an undeniable trace of happiness, that she heard the deep and unmistakable voice of the man she so wished to make a favorable impression upon. "Your pardon, sirrah, this lady does not appear to welcome your attentions."

Her gaze fixed on his darkly handsome face. He was watching her cousin with disdain.

Denley frowned at Benedict as he said, "I do not see that this is any business of yours, my lord, and would warn you to mind your own affairs."

Benedict turned to Raine. "Are you bound to this man?"

It was a long moment before she could reply, for the gentle regard in those dark blue eyes seemed to make her heart beat just a bit faster than was usual. At last she replied, "Nay, he is but my cousin. The notion that we are to be wed is purely his own."

Benedict reached out and put his own hand over Denley's on her arm. Even as embarrassed and exasperated as she felt, Raine could not help noting that as large as Denley's hand was, Benedict's was larger, and more sun bronzed. His fingers were longer and more supple and obviously stronger as they gripped her cousin's.

Benedict spoke with quiet but unmistakable command. "You will unhand this lady, now. This is not the time nor the place to discuss such matters and you should certainly take them up with her guardian rather than humiliating her in company as you have."

Denley seemed, for the first time, to realize that they were being closely observed by those around them. He had the grace to flush and let go of Raine's arm, though the fact that he did so under duress was clear in his angry expression as he stepped back. He sputtered, "As her only living relation, I am her guardian."

Raine shook her head. "He is not. My father died some months gone by, but did not name Denley as guardian. As I said, he is my cousin, nothing more."

Denley grimaced at this but seemed to have nothing more to say, since Benedict obviously would not heed him in the face of Raine's objection. Yet Raine cared nothing for what Denley thought. She had no more interest in him for the moment.

She looked at Benedict, who was watching her closely. His concerned expression brought about a strange fluttering in her chest. It had been many years since anyone had shown such an interest in looking after her. Raine was accustomed to being protector and caretaker to Will, Aida and all the others who resided on the estate.

The sense of being cared for, if only on the most superficial level, was unexpectedly enervating. She felt sharp tears sting her eyes, but she refused to shed them.

She did not need anyone to care for her, but for Will and his inheritance. She dragged her gaze from Benedict, taking in those around them with a wave of mortification as she noted their interest and speculation.

She told herself it must surely be her shame that Denley had brought this public display upon her that made her react with such weakness. Raine knew she could face no more in this moment without crumbling. Again she moved to extricate herself from the table. When Denley stepped forward to help her, Benedict Ainsworth forestalled him by standing.

Raine could do no more than cast Benedict a brief and grateful glance as she at long last freed herself and rose. She was aware of the eyes upon her back, knew that people would be thinking all manner of things. She had heard them speak of the goings-on of others often enough. But she did not run as she so desperately desired to do. She squared her shoulders and forced herself to walk away with her head high.

After a long and sleepless night, Raine knew that she had to act without delay. Denley had traced her all the way to court, had made a terrible scene before everyone within earshot, with no thought to her own feelings or those of others.

Benedict Ainsworth had certainly come to her aid without hesitation, but he had clearly failed to note her feeble efforts to attract him.

Perhaps, she realized with a heavy sigh, he simply did not find her appealing. The thought was not an encouraging one, for how else was she to get him to wed her? She did not require him to care deeply for her. Love was something she had determined to live without when she'd decided to marry solely for the purpose of protecting William.

It was, in fact, best for all concerned if the man she married was not in love with her. Especially as she had no intention of living with him, but meant to go home to Abbernathy as soon as the marriage was settled.

There had been a member of her family living at Abbernathy since before the time of William I. She would not be the first to abandon her birthright, but would hold it in trust until her brother was able to take up his own duties. If her husband wished to come to Abbernathy, then he was welcome to do so.

Again she reminded herself that going home could come only after a marriage had taken place, and no husband had yet been found.

For a moment despair made a lump rise in her throat. She was glad that she was for once alone in the tiny room that had been allotted them, Aida and William having gone for a walk about the castle grounds. Raine had no heart for such distractions, and she would not wish for either of them to know how worried she was.

At that moment a knock sounded on the door, causing Raine to give a start. She told herself she was getting far too anxious. Nothing would be gained by becoming so overset that she could not reason clearly. Quickly she rose from the bench beneath the window, taking a deep, calming breath before going to answer it. She had no idea who it might be, as William and Aida would simply enter.

Seeing Denley Trent on the threshold when she opened the door did nothing to soothe her already tattered emotions. Immediately she moved to close it.

Denley stopped her by stepping into the opening, effectively forcing Raine backward. She faced him with bravado, though the way he smiled at her as he came farther into the chamber and shut the door behind him gave her a definite sense of unease.

She pointed toward the closed portal. "I want you to remove yourself immediately."

He grinned. "Oh Raine, is this the way you hope to win me? By ever playing hard to get?"

She threw up her hands in exasperation. "I am not trying to win you. I wish that you would go and never again darken my stoop. Can you not understand that?"

For a moment Denley seemed uncertain, and she felt a budding hope that she had finally made him see. But his uncertainty was soon replaced by a lecherous smile that she realized he must think charming. He came toward her with outstretched arms. "There is no need to be frightened, Raine. I will not hurt you. I know well how to please a woman."

Raine found this difficult to believe. Surely in order for that to be true, he would need have more sensitivity than he had ever displayed in her presence. Not that she had any experience with such things, but she preferred to live by her own misjudgment than for Denley to prove otherwise.

But she had no time to discuss her preference now, for he was still moving toward her. The intent in his brown eyes was more than evident.

Trying hard to hide the anxiety that rushed through her in a sickening tide, Raine took a step backward. She shook her head. "Nay, Denley, do not touch me. You cannot."

He shrugged. "I simply mean to show you that there is no need for so much maidenly fear on your part. Once the deed is done you will see that there is nothing to be afraid of and we can be wed without delay."

Anger flared in her like a burning torch. "I will not allow you to pretend that you are attempting to do me some courtesy by forcing yourself upon me. If you touch me it will be rape and nothing less."

He faltered only briefly. "We both know that our being together—our marrying—would be for the best."

"For you, perhaps."

Denley did not hesitate again, but continued toward her with obvious purpose. Raine was brave, but she was not a fool. She realized that retreat would be better than valor at the moment. She dodged around him and ran toward the door.

Denley Trent was a big man and by no means light on his feet. He reached out to grab her, getting hold of the sleeve of her amber gown, as he cried, "I have you now."

But the stitching on her shoulder gave way and she pulled free, losing only a small amount of momentum, as she replied with relief, "Nay, sir, you have not." She managed to get the door open and race out into the hallway before her cousin could prevent her from doing so.

He followed close behind, though he cast a glance about the hall. She wondered if last eve's debacle had made him slightly more reticent about creating a spectacle. She could only pray that was so.

"Come now, Raine, need we continue with these childish games?" he whined. "You only put off the inevitable."

She did not dally about to discuss it, but hurried toward the more public rooms of the castle, holding her torn gown in place. To her relief, Denley made no move to follow her.

Yet as she reached what she considered a safer location, blending in with the milling courtiers in the hall, she knew that she had only effected a temporary solution. Denley had not finished with her. Nothing she could do or say made the least impact on him. He was so set on meeting his own ends that he would not heed her, nor anyone else, and had clearly convinced himself that she was only resisting him out of some maidenly fear of marriage. Clearly he would stop at nothing to see them married, even if that meant he must resort to rape, a scenario she had only suspected before.

Raine knew that she had to do something. The time for indecisiveness was past. Last night Benedict Ainsworth had revealed his plan to leave the court within the next two days, and he was her only hope.

Under no circumstances could she allow William to fall into her cousin's hands while there was a possibility of doing something to prevent it. The question remained, just how far was *she* willing to go to meet her ends?

Aida, who had slumped down on the end of the bed as Raine began to tell her of her plan, shook her head in disbelief. "My lady, we cannot do this. What if you are found out?"

Raine stood her ground. "We will not be found out, at least not until it is all over and I am safely married. If we follow the plan I have devised, no one will have time even to question what is occurring."

The terror in the maid's green eyes would have been enough to give a less determined woman pause. Raine was not such a woman. "I told you what Denley attempted to do in this very chamber today. You saw what he did to my gown when I broke free of him. I can delay no longer. I must protect Will from Cousin Denley. Father would never forgive me for allowing that madman to gain control of his lands."

"But, Lady Raine, I do not think...I do not understand how you could ever have the courage to...do what you mean to do. Nor how I can have a hand in this scheme. He is a nobleman.''

Raine rolled her eyes in exasperation. ''You really have no need to do aught but get what we need from the castle kitchens, keep William from our chamber for the night and then to shriek as if you'd been cast into the fires of hell when you come into the room in the morning. It is really very simple on your part, Aida. I am the one who must get him here and manage all the rest of it.''

Aida continued to look anything but certain of what her mistress was proposing.

Raine felt her own certainty lag for a brief moment, but she braced herself firmly. The dread of what might happen if she fell into fear and indecision was too great. She knew all she could do was keep moving forward. From the moment this notion had popped into her head she had done just that.

She turned to the maid. ''Aida, you will help me to dress and arrange my hair for this evening. I must look the very best that I possibly can, though judging from what has gone forth so far I do not know how much that might aid me with Benedict Ainsworth.'' She tried not to hear the regret in her own voice. ''Still, I must consider every possibility. Our success hinges on my getting the man to this chamber.''

She moved to the chest containing the new gowns she had made up in the hope that looking well would help her find a husband. Unfortunately, as she had already told Aida, after Benedict's reactions to her last eve she was not sure that her appearance would make any difference whatsoever. What would be accomplished in fussing over such things would be in keeping the frightened maid occupied until she must go down to dine.

And herself as well. Raine did not want to think about what might happen if Benedict was not there. Nor did she want to think about what would happen if he was not willing to come to her chamber. She simply could not allow herself to dwell upon the impossible.

Several hours later, Raine paused at the chamber door and looked back at William, who sat upon the bed watching her. He had come in from the stables some time past, his gaze assessing as he saw that preparations were already underway for her to go down to dine. Yet he said nothing, though she was sure he could not have failed to note Aida's anxiety. Raine realized that the maid was ofttimes agitated of late, and was grateful that he did not seem to put any particular meaning upon it now.

Raine did not want William to know what she was about. She wished to save him the burden of worrying about her, for she knew he would certainly do so if he knew. His guilt at her having shouldered the responsibility of caring for him had been apparent to her on more than one occasion.

In spite of his desire to spare her, there was nothing he could do. He was only a boy, albeit a good and loving one.

Her informing him that he and Aida would sleep in the hall with the servants this night had understandably brought comment. But Raine had told him only that she was required to share the room with another lady who had just arrived at court.

She hated to lie to her brother, but could not tell him the real reason she needed to be alone. Aside from wishing to protect him from any unpleasantness in this Raine also knew she could not summon the fortitude to convince one more soul of the soundness of her logic.

Or perhaps she was afraid that if she discussed the matter more, she would not have the courage to follow through with it. Perhaps she was afraid that her own fears would make her think of justification to stop now before it was too late. Hurriedly she left the room.

The hall was crowded, as it was every night. For a brief moment, as she stood in the entrance, Raine was again beset by fear that Benedict Ainsworth might not be there, that he might have gone home already. She well recalled his remarks to King Edward about his dislike of court life.

His sentiment, in that area, matched her own very well. She greatly missed the hills and dales of home, her duties about the keep, her own folk.

With a sensation of both dread and relief, she saw him, seated not far from where he had taken his meal the previous night. Drawing a deep breath, Raine moved among the crowded tables, not hesitating until she reached his side. There, not knowing what else to do, she simply waited for his attention.

She stood for only a brief moment before he looked up with an expression of surprise. "Good evening, Lady Raine."

She nodded. "My lord." Raine gestured about the room. "I would beg your indulgence. I see that the tables are quite full. Is there any possibility that room might be made for me here?"

Raine did not allow herself to even stop to consider her own audacity. For in truth there was no more room at this table than any other. She was quite aware that he, too, must know this. She simply had no time for subtlety and would not be sure how to go about displaying it if she did.

If Benedict Ainsworth was aware of her forwardness he gave no indication of it. He spoke to the man next to him. "I am certain that we can find room for one small woman, can we not, Lord Longly?"

The elderly nobleman bowed his white head politely. "Of course." He waved a frail hand toward the space they had made on the bench.

Raine seated herself quickly as the men went back to their conversation. Neither appeared to take any further interest in her—a fact that did not bode well for her plans.

She had no real heart for the food that was piled on the platters, but she knew she must go through the motions of appearing to eat, at the very least. She was not happy to see how badly her hands were trembling as she took a small portion of the savory roast fowl and bread.

Far from being appealing, as it was meant to, the rich scent of the meat nearly made her choke as she took a bite. Raine was far too conscious of what she was attempting to do, too conscious of the sheer temerity of her actions.

She could feel the heat of Benedict Ainsworth's body, hear the deep sound of his voice as he spoke to the man on his other side. Ainsworth had been kind to her, had defended her against Denley last eve when no other man present had so much as spoken a word. There was something very comforting about having him near her. All she had learned of him showed him to be a strong and honorable man.

Raine suddenly wondered if, in the event that she

succeeded here, she would be doing this decent man a grave wrong.

Immediately she told herself that she had no choice. The qualities that caused her to hesitate over going forward were the very reasons she had chosen him. She had run out of time, and Benedict Ainsworth seemed to be exactly what she had been looking for—was in fact the only possibility.

It was Denley Trent who was to blame in this. He had forced her hand. For her brother's sake, she could not falter now.

With that thought uppermost in her mind, Raine waited for a lull in the men's conversation, then turned toward Benedict as he tore a section from his bread. "My lord?"

He stopped and looked at her, his expression expectant, and she thought perhaps somewhat leery. "Aye."

Although she told herself that she must surely be mistaken, Raine had a sudden urge to run screaming from the hall, but knew she could not. In spite of the reticence she perceived in him, she smiled with what she hoped was appealing flirtation. "My lord, I wish to thank you again for your aid last eve."

His face was unreadable as he lifted a dismissive hand. "There is no need to thank me. I would not have such a lout accost any woman."

Raine smiled again, dropping her gaze and looking up at him from beneath her lashes as she had seen other ladies about the court do. "Yet I do wish for you to understand how grateful I am, Lord Ainsworth, for your chivalrous behavior. You have done me no small service. My cousin has plagued me greatly for some time and refuses to heed my rebuffs even yet."

She was not displeased with the look of concern that

passed over Ainsworth's face at her words. He spoke somewhat roughly. "You mean he has accosted you again?"

Raine raised her wide gaze to his. "Oh yes, my lord. Why, this very day he came to my chamber when I was alone. If I had not barely managed to escape him I fear he might have..." The truth of what she said lent an air of fear and desperation to her voice, even though she was telling him all of this with deliberate intent.

Chapter Three

In spite of the fact that Benedict had spent the whole of this day attempting to put Raine Blanchett from his thoughts, he had not been as successful as he wished. His reluctance to dwell on her was brought on by the great certainty that to allow himself to be entangled with her, no matter how lovely she might be, would open himself to all manner of unpleasantness. Though it might indeed be through no fault of her own, chaos appeared to follow Raine about, beginning with his first glimpse of her in the audience chamber. She had claimed she was hiding there from an unwanted suitor, and now she was beset by another.

As he listened to her, he felt a great swell of sympathy for this delicate young woman. It was not her fault that he had been thinking of her, of the way he had felt when he looked into her eyes.

Even now he found himself looking into those unforgettable golden eyes and replying gently, "If there is aught I can do to aid you I will gladly do so. Though I am at court for only another day, perhaps I could bring your situation to the ear of the king?"

She shook her head quickly, appearing distraught for

a moment, before giving him a reassuring smile. "Nay, my lord. There is no need. I would not wish for King Edward to appoint Denley as guardian over us. And being our only living relation, Denley might convince him to do so. He has a quick tongue when need be."

Benedict could only look at her in surprise. He would not have described the lout as quick-tongued. He had, in fact, seemed something of a dullard, yet she did know him best. And had not the very man that Tristan had been forced to kill, whose brother now sought revenge, managed to retain favor at court in spite of his multitude of shortcomings? Benedict shrugged. "As you wish."

Her expression was tinged with uncertainty. "There is one small thing you might do to aid me. If it would not trouble you overmuch I would be grateful for your accompanying me to my chamber. I am certain my cousin would not dare to press himself upon me in your presence."

Benedict found himself noting that those golden eyes were flecked with even deeper bits of gold. Huskily he said, "I will be happy to perform such a small service for such a beautiful lady." He realized even as he spoke how unlike him it was to make such a romantic declaration. Yet how beautiful she was! Perhaps being around the deeply in love Lily and Tristan was making him fanciful.

Not for the first time he found himself glad that the unpleasant business with Alister Harcourt would soon be resolved. This very morning he and King Edward had drawn up a final draft of the offer to Harcourt. The king had spoken of his own certainty that it would be eagerly accepted, appearing as it did to come from the crown itself.

Perhaps Benedict's oddly fanciful feelings had to do

with relief at having it all settled. He would soon be on his way home to Brackenmoore.

Yet looking at Raine, he could not deny that for once home was not uppermost in his mind. Again he found himself noting how very lovely she was, with her rich auburn hair framing the fine-featured face beneath her intricate head covering of gold wire over ivory velvet. The heavy gold and ruby necklace she wore could not hope to rival the creamy skin of her throat for luster. The rich gold on her cap and the fur trimmed gold gown only made her eyes all the more startling and compelling. As on the previous day, Benedict suddenly felt as if he were falling into those eyes, and a strange dizziness seemed to take him.

He dragged his gaze away, raking the room, searching for something, anything, that might capture and tame his wayward attention. What the devil was he thinking? He was staying for one more day and had no time for thoughts of a distressed young damsel, no matter how comely.

At the moment, what with Tristan and Lily's difficulties and his brother Marcel's troubling and unexpected departure on one of Benedict's own ships, he simply could not see his way to even considering his own future.

He would certainly not contemplate one with a woman he knew nothing about. His unwillingly appreciative gaze swept Raine again. Again he reminded himself of how she seemed to be fraught by ill fortune.

Never would he focus his regard on a woman such as Raine Blanchett, no matter how bemused looking into her eyes made him feel. He would have a more tranquil maid.

He made an effort to attend the meal, which had now

cooled before him. He could not help noting that Raine's own food had apparently received even less attention.

Glancing about them, Benedict realized that most of the other diners had finished eating. The room had not yet cleared, though, as many lingered for the dancing and socializing that went on each night. He hoped, now that he had agreed to take her to her chamber, that Raine Blanchett would not care to stay on in the hall. He wished to get her safely to her room as quickly as possible.

Benedict spoke more abruptly than he intended. "Whenever you are ready, I will accompany you."

She looked up at him with what he interpreted as an anxious but relieved expression. He could only think that she must fear her cousin's putting in an appearance in the hall this night as she asked, "You are not going to remain in the hall for a time?"

He shook his head. "Nay, I am not one for dancing, nor making small talk."

She shrugged. "Aye, I understand."

Benedict could not help being surprised. He would have expected her to revel in being in company, and said as much. "I would have thought you would enjoy having the attention of all the young men."

Quickly she shook her head. "I can assure you, I do not. I much prefer being home at Abbernathy. The men at court, they want what is not mine to give." Flushing, she looked away.

For a brief moment, Benedict wondered why she was at court. He wanted to ask, but did not wish to get more embroiled in her life. Her remarks about the courtiers must mean that, like her cousin, they pressed her for intimacy. Benedict stood, holding out his hand to her. "In light of your own feelings, then, shall we go?"

Raine seemed to hesitate, her gaze uncertain as it met his. Then she put out her hand. Those long slender fingers felt delicate in his, and he wondered at their coldness even as their touch brought a compelling warmth to his own body, brought thoughts of how they would feel against his heated flesh. He found it hard to concentrate on her words as she said, "Thank you, my lord." Benedict realized that, in spite of telling himself that an attraction to Raine was completely unsuitable, he seemed unable to control his reaction to her as he wished to.

Once she was standing he released her.

Benedict was relieved that Raine did not seem to note his reluctance to touch her. Appearing quite preoccupied, she fell into step with him as they left the hall.

Benedict felt slightly and unexplainably perturbed by her lack of attention. He told himself that it was very likely brought on by her concern over a possible confrontation with her cousin. That eventuality was, he reminded himself, why he was accompanying her.

He had already established the fact that he was not interested in this far too chaotic young woman. There were no more words exchanged between them until they actually arrived outside a door in a narrow hallway quite some distance from the main part of the castle.

Raine hesitated as she reached for the latch, then peered up at him, biting her lower lip. "I thank you so very much for your kindness. I would ask just one more moment of your time, if I may, to ascertain that my cousin is not within."

Benedict could not mistake her anxiety and was

moved by it. Devil take any man who thought to force himself upon a woman. His own ward, Genevieve, had barely escaped such a situation at the hands of her own cousin, who happened to be Maxim Harcourt. Benedict could not mourn the man's death even though it had brought more troubles.

He had no sympathy for those who preyed upon others, and this Denley Trent was no exception. Deliberately Benedict shrugged, attempting to keep both his manner and tone unconcerned in aid of soothing Raine's fear. "I do not mind. One more moment will make no great difference to me."

She nodded with relief, but he saw that her hand was trembling as she reached for the latch.

Raine took a deep breath and pushed open the door. The sight that met her gaze could not have been better geared to the satisfaction of her plans.

For there in a chair pulled close to the fire was none other than her cousin Denley. He could not have been more obliging had he tried, though she had made no effort to get him here. Surely she was doing the right thing. It was all falling into place. She nearly sighed aloud in relief as she turned to Benedict Ainsworth. "You see, my lord. He will not leave me be."

Benedict frowned with unmistakable anger as he addressed the other man. "Have you gone mad that you cannot heed this lady's request to cease in your pursuit?"

Denley lumbered to his feet with a gasp of outrage. "How dare you, sir? You know nothing of this situation."

"I know that she has made her wishes quite clear, and that is all I need to know."

Driven beyond caution, Denley moved to stand before Benedict with balled fists. "Is it possible that you wish to have her for yourself? I must tell you that I will not sit idly by and allow you to dishonor my cousin."

Benedict Ainsworth's black brows arched in amazement. "You will not sit idly by and allow *me* to dishonor her, sirrah! Have you no sense whatsoever?"

Denley faced him without flinching. "You heard me."

Suddenly Benedict's expression took on a new and deadly seriousness that caused Raine to shiver in spite of the fact that it was not directed toward her. "I have afforded you all the patience I possess. I now suggest that you leave this chamber and do not, unless she give permission, ever speak to this woman again."

Raine watched with horror as Denley swung one large fist. A heartbeat later she realized that she need not have worried. Though he was nearly of a size with Benedict Ainsworth, he was not nearly as agile nor as strong.

The black-haired man caught her cousin's hand in his own. Denley's gaze widened in shock for a brief moment before he jerked away. He lifted his fist again.

Benedict did not raise his voice, but there was cold hard steel in it. "Do not."

Denley hesitated and in that instant lost any hope of following through. He turned and stumbled from the room, obviously not having the courage to face the other man. Raine's lips thinned. Her cousin was the kind who only had the nerve to browbeat women and children. Or perhaps he would have withstood a lesser man than Benedict Ainsworth.

Her gaze swung to Benedict who stood staring at the open portal with a frown. Indeed, she had chosen well in him. Never had she imagined that there would be an actual confrontation with Denley this night, but it had proved to her that Ainsworth did have both the mental and the physical strength to protect William.

Quickly Raine went and closed the door. She could not allow him to leave.

Her gaze flew to the pitcher on the table, the two glasses, which, thankfully, had remained untouched by her cousin. Aida had known when she set them out that only one of the glasses would ever be used.

Did Raine have the courage to follow through? She did, because she must. Denley's presence in her chamber this night had convinced her of that.

Raine went forward and poured some of the wine into one of the cups, then moved to Benedict's side. He looked down at her, his gaze taking in the offered wine. "Nay, I should be on my way now."

Raine spoke too hurriedly. "Please, do not go yet, my lord." She glanced toward the closed door. "I...my cousin might return and I would not be here alone."

Her fear seemed to affect him, for he said, "I will remain for a moment longer, just until you feel safer. But I do not think he will return this night, and you must remember to bolt the door when I am gone."

She nodded vigorously, anything to get him to drink the wine before she lost her nerve. "I will do so."

Raine watched with horrified fascination as he took the cup from her hand, raised it to his mouth and drank. A silent but heavy sigh escaped her heart.

It was done.

She was set on this course now, could do nothing to stop it. Once Benedict had fallen under the influence of the sleeping potion she would have no way of getting him from her chamber without bringing attention to them and thus the consequences of their being alone and unattended.

She felt both relief and regret when he said, "The wine is very sweet. Are you not having any?"

Raine shook her head. "Nay, not this night."

He seemed little interested in her reply as he looked toward the door, clearly eager to be away. But Raine was no longer anxious on that score. She need delay him for only a few more moments now. He would soon be unconscious. Aida knew how much to give, being quite skilled in the art of herbal medicine. "Would you care to sit for a moment?"

He shook his head as if it were feeling very heavy. "Nay, I must..." His gaze seemed to focus on her briefly and he whispered, "You are so very...lovely...."

The words sent a strange tingling through her. She closed her eyes, telling herself that she must keep her mind centered on the work at hand. The drug had made him fanciful. She could not allow herself to think of this man as anything but a means to an end.

She took a deep, calming breath and with it a sort of fog seemed to descend upon her, a fog of unreality and numbness. It was through this fog that she saw Benedict's gaze widen in confusion, saw him put his hand to his head, saw him stumble and drop the cup to the floor.

He tried to focus on her again. "What...?"

She moved toward him and took his arm. "Let me help you." In spite of her resolve she could hear the regret in her voice as she led him to the bed. Raine knew that she must put aside her own feelings, keep her mind centered on what she must do. She needed him on the bed and would not be able to move him once he was asleep.

Benedict was so far beneath the influence of the potion that he made no effort to resist her. He barely made it to the edge of the bed before he groaned and fell backward upon the coverlet, unconscious.

Raine breathed deeply as she looked down at the man, who seemed more large and imposing than ever. His shoulders alone would surely take two strong men to lift. Or one very determined woman, she told herself firmly.

Yet as she bent over him, Raine recalled that she must disrobe him first before getting him beneath the cover. And she was not at all sure about how she was going to accomplish such a feat.

Yet this, as the other difficulties, must be overcome. Raine climbed up onto the bed. She would begin with his houppelande and tunic.

'Twas not nearly so bad as she had imagined. Until she actually got his golden chest bare, that was.

Though she told herself she would not touch him more than she absolutely must, she soon found her palms flat against the molded wall of his chest. Her busy fingers slowed as if of their own accord and she realized how very smooth that golden skin was, how very male and different from her own in the most...

A soft groan escaped him and she started, a deep flush heating her neck and cheeks. Whatever was the matter with her? She had no interest in this man. He was nothing more than a means to an end.

She closed her eyes firmly before finishing disrobing him. Even when she moved to tug off his hose, she first draped the sheet across his body. Raine told herself that she did so out of sympathy for his vulnerable state, not because she had any interest in looking at *that,* and certainly not because she was afraid to do so.

Then she was able to put all her concentration into rolling and tugging until she got him into the bed. The last thing she did was empty the small vial that Aida had hidden beneath the top corner of the bed.

The maid had said there must be blood in order to make the scene complete, yet Raine again felt the heat rise to her face as she sprinkled the chicken blood over the sheet.

"It is all for William. It is all for William," she chanted silently as she did the deed, then threw the empty vial into the fire.

She turned and looked at Benedict then, his handsome face seeming troubled as he lay against the pillow. Quickly she told herself that she was simply being foolish. He knew nothing of what was going on. She must not allow guilt to make her fanciful.

She had only done what she had to do.

With grim resolve she began to remove her gown.

Raine was still lying there awake, her burning eyes staring up at the ceiling, when she heard the chamber door open the next morning. She did not move.

Just as they had planned, Aida approached the bed and pulled open the heavy draperies. First she glanced at the sleeping man next to her, then met Raine's gaze with silent entreaty.

Raine shook her head. There was no going back now.

Aida nodded and opened her mouth wide, emitting a screech that would have wakened the very dead. The sound was so loud that it startled Raine, who had fully expected to hear it.

The unfortunate Benedict Ainsworth had not expected it. Even with traces of the sleeping potion still befuddling his mind, he reared straight up in the bed. It was a moment before his startled gaze could focus on Raine's face. Shock became confusion as he frowned, looking down at himself, then took in their positions in the bed.

"What..." he sputtered.

And all the while Aida continued to scream, intermittently adding statements such as, "My lady, my lady, my poor despoiled lady."

Even though Raine knew that this noise was indeed a very important aspect of her plan, that someone must come and see her here with Benedict, she wished above all things to tell Aida to cease in that caterwauling. She was so very tired from lying awake the whole long night, from being ever so careful not to actually brush up against the strange and oddly fascinating form of the man next to her.

More than once she had been forced to stop herself from reaching out to touch his smooth golden skin as she had while undressing him. Yet she had done so. How she felt about Benedict Ainsworth had no place in this.

For her to have perpetrated this hoax against him for any reason other than to protect William would be completely despicable.

Even as these thoughts were passing through her mind, Benedict moved to the edge of the bed. He was watching Aida with that scowl still firmly in place, and it became more intense with each shrill syllable she uttered. He stood, dragging the linen sheet with him as he shouted, "Why do you not cea—"

He was interrupted by the appearance of an obviously hastily clad older gentleman, whom Raine had seen going into the chamber next to hers on more than one occasion. "What is going on here?" the newcomer bellowed.

Only then did Aida stop screeching. The sudden silence was somehow almost shocking in its intensity. Benedict and the man exchanged bewildered and slightly relieved glances before the man looked to where Raine still sat in the bed. The gentleman's gaze then went to the sheet Benedict clutched about his lean hips as he obviously searched for his garments, which Raine had put in the chest at the end of the bed.

Her attention followed the older man's, and she saw the scarlet stain that had spread over it. Her gaze widened with horror. She had had no notion that the small vial of blood would look like so much upon the sheet.

She blushed, but forced herself not to cower. She had done this to herself.

Several more folk appeared in the open doorway as Aida spoke in what Raine considered a far too dramatic tone. "He has deflowered my mistress."

All eyes then seemed to focus on the bloodied sheet, before turning to Raine. She felt herself blush even more deeply, from the roots of her hair to her feet, though she knew that no one else would know this as she had the coverlet pulled all the way to her chin.

Sweet Saint George protect her. She had indeed done this to herself, yet she had not expected the sight of that blood to be so very humiliating.

Aida had insisted upon it, though, if she were to have any part of it. She had asked Raine how, without any evidence, anyone was to be convinced that she was no longer a virgin and that Benedict was responsible. Raine had had no rebuttal.

As if reading her thoughts, Benedict looked down at

the bloodstained sheet at that very moment, seeing what they were looking at with a gasp of amazement. He swung around to face Raine. When she saw the expression of suspicion that was beginning to replace his confusion she returned it with defiance.

An elderly woman stepped into the open doorway, where a crowd was rapidly becoming larger. She spoke to the older gentleman. "Ulric, this man is obviously a brute as well as a knave. I have never seen so much blood. You must do something."

Raine had not known that it was possible for her cheeks to heat any more than they already were. Yet they did so.

The man, whom Raine believed to be the lady's husband, answered, "I will, my dear, as soon as I am able to ascertain exactly what has gone on."

Benedict gave Raine one last long measuring look, then swung around to face the others. His voice emerged as a command. "I will see to this now. You may all go."

The elderly lady sputtered. "I think you have a—"

Benedict interrupted, albeit politely. "Your pardon, my lady, I wish to cause you no insult, but this is between the lady and myself."

She turned up her rather long narrow nose and reached for her husband's arm, dragging him with her as she flounced out. "Come, Ulric. We shall see about this."

Benedict moved toward the door, looking far more imposing than Raine would ever have imagined a man clad in nothing but a sheet could. All the others who had gathered there backed away as he moved to close the door.

That was, all but Aida. She stood nearby, wringing

her hands. Now that she had accomplished what Raine had asked of her she had reverted back to the anxious demeanor she had adopted when Raine's father died.

Benedict paused in the act of closing the portal, looking at the maid with impatiently arched brows. She stared back at him. He indicated the narrowed opening. "Would you excuse us, please?"

She started, her gaze going to Raine. "My lady—"

"Will be fine." His tone, though still low and calm, brooked no argument.

Aida scuttled toward the door. As she passed within inches of him on her way out, he leaned over and spoke in a confiding tone. "That was a very fine performance you gave, if I do say so myself."

She raised horrified eyes to his now grim face. "My lord, I—"

"Out!"

Benedict slammed the portal behind her and took a deep breath, hoping to ease the pounding blood in his head before turning to face Raine.

She tilted her chin. "You will please refrain from harassing my maid. She has been with us since my mother died. She is certainly flighty at times, especially so since father's death, but loves us as if we were her own."

He looked at the woman in the bed for a very long time. He was somewhat moved by her concern for the maid when she would be wiser to concern herself with the trouble that might come to her own pretty head, but had no intention of letting her know that.

He could actually see very little of the wench with the coverlet pulled up the way it was, but he was able to read the determination and defiance in her eyes. Benedict was quite aware of the fact that he had been duped by this woman and her servant. Why, he did not know, but he had every intention of getting to the bottom of it, no matter how reluctant this red-haired she-devil might be to share her motives with him.

Though he had never been with a virgin, Benedict was quite aware that there was far too much blood here. And that screeching the maid had done had certainly been in aid of bringing as many witnesses as possible. He could still feel his ears ringing now that she was gone.

And Raine Blanchett was the one who could answer why. He approached the bed with deliberation.

Raine drew back as far from him as she could. "Do not touch me."

He could hardly believe the audacity of her to tell him not to touch her after what she had done. Benedict was not a violent man where women and children were concerned. But this damsel had driven him beyond all reason and restraint.

Without pausing to think, he reached out and grabbed her arm, half dragging her across the bed. "You are not in a position to give any orders here, madam. *I* will do so, and the first order of the day is for you to tell me right now and in full detail why you have concocted this elaborate scheme to make it appear as if I have bedded you!"

Only the delicate flaring of her nostrils as she met his eyes, her own wide with feigned innocence, gave away her agitation. "But you did bed me, my lord. You have the proof of it there."

He was only slightly mollified that she had the grace to blush as she indicated the bloody sheet. He shook his head. "There is enough blood here to have butchered an ox in this bed." It was an exaggeration, he knew, but as likely as the explanation she suggested.

He could see the wheels turning in the wench's mind. Benedict stopped her before she could even try to prevaricate. "And make no mistake, you will not convince me that I have caused you to bleed so profusely. I have never in my life bedded any woman and hurt her thus, nor have I ever been completely oblivious of such an event afterward. The last thing I recall was becoming dizzy after taking the wine you insisted I drink. I am not so great a lover that I am able to perform while unconscious."

A scarlet-faced Raine looked down at her tightly folded arms. Benedict waited.

At last she raised her head and met his gaze. He was not pleased at the way his chest tightened at the tears glittering in her golden eyes. "You are right, my lord. I did trick you. I did drug you and you did not touch me."

The utter defeat in her tone only served to move him further as she went on. "I will tell the truth to all who saw us here this morn."

Not only was he moved by her despair, Benedict was also shocked at her complete capitulation in telling him the truth. In spite of his warning for her not to prevaricate further, he had fully expected her to try to defend her actions, at the very least.

He ran a hand over his face and up through his hair. His jaw was covered with rough stubble and he was sure he must have looked like a madman to the folk who had gathered in the door of the chamber, standing there in a blood-covered sheet, his hair, unruly at the best of times, standing on end.

Yet that was the least of his worries now. He sank

down on the end of the bed. "Tell me why you did this."

Raine raised her chin. "I felt I had no choice. I tried to gain your attention in the usual way but you seemed to have no interest in me."

Benedict gave a rueful laugh. He had been attracted to her, but he had no wish to admit as much. "Why me? I am not the sort of man who would draw the interest of a beautiful young girl."

She looked at him with obvious surprise and finally said, "Why do you think that I would not be interested in you? You were everything that I was looking for—strong, honorable, kind. I needed someone who would see to my brother and his interests without fear of supplanting him, or worse, which was exactly what Cousin Denley would have done. William's holdings are the reason for his diligent pursuit of me. And what I told you of his attempting to force himself upon me yesterday—" her contrite and open gaze met his "—that was truth. It made me realize I could not continue to hope I would find a man who would afford me the protection of his name, and thus William, before it was too late."

At her open admission of wanting him for what she considered his more noble qualities alone, Benedict felt an unexpected regret. He gave a mental shrug. He had not expected a young and lovely woman like her to have become infatuated with him for any personal reason.

He brushed such thoughts aside. "Again I ask, why me? What made you think I would look after you and your brother without taking something for myself?"

"I lied, you know, when I told you that I had been closed inside the king's chamber inadvertently." In her agitation she rose up on her knees, her fiery auburn hair tumbling about her slender white shoulders in wild disarray, and Benedict was hard-pressed to recall the fact that she did not want him in any personal way.

He was not surprised to learn that she had lied to him, but continued to be somewhat shocked that now she had been found out, Raine was eager to admit it all, and so openly. It was almost as if she could not stop herself.

What a strange, impulsive creature she seemed. Exactly the opposite of the woman he had imagined for himself—for Brackenmoore.

He forced himself to attend what she was saying. "You were so worried about the honor of your brother's wife that day, protective of her and her child. I wanted someone who would look after William that way. You see, he is gentle and small for his age. Besides needing someone to look to his lands until he is old enough to do so, he also requires gentle guidance. I felt you might be the one to give it. But I am no fool to believe the words a man speaks to a king. I talked with others, asked questions of all who knew of you, and none had a thing to say about you that contradicted my initial impression. Some said you were overstaid and responsible, but that did not trouble me."

Benedict's brows rose at what he felt was a less than flattering description of himself, but he made no comment. "I still do not see why you did not simply ask for my help. Why go to all of this effort at deception and cause us both such great embarrassment?"

She shrugged, with a frown of chagrin. "I did not think of it, never considered that you would help a strange woman with no familial ties to you. I knew only that I could not allow Denley to rape me and thus force a marriage. I could not allow him to gain control of all that my father had entrusted to me when he died. And truth to tell, I do not believe I would have asked that of you if I had considered it. Denley would have felt free to press his suit as long as I was unwed.'' She shrugged again. ''I do not know how you can doubt me on that score after having met him, seen his determination.''

Benedict grimaced. He could not argue the point. ''The man does seem completely blind to all but the way he wishes to view things.''

Raine nodded. ''Precisely.''

Though he did agree with her on that one matter, Benedict could not allow her to think he was dismissing the sheer madness of her actions. ''Even saying that, I cannot forget your own disregard for the feelings of others, namely myself.''

She had the grace to flush scarlet, though he could tell by the way she tilted that finely shaped nose of hers that she resented his words. ''Disregarding your feelings is not what I was trying to do.''

''Yet you did do it and we now find ourselves in this predicament.'' His gaze went to the closed doorway. In spite of his sending all of them away, Benedict knew that there were questions that would need be answered in order to have any hope of salvaging Raine's honor. No matter what he or she said now, things would never be as they had been. Too many people had seen them here together, witnessed the blood on the sheet.

Most of them would not stop to think about the ludicrous amount of blood, nor any other facts, even if the truth were told to them. But that was not his fault. It was not he who had brought this upon Raine's head. She had.

Hadn't she?

He stood and looked about the chamber. ''Where are my clothes?''

She frowned and pointed toward the chest at the end of the bed.

He was somewhat surprised to see how neatly she had folded them atop her own equally neatly kept garments. He would not have thought her so tidy.

Immediately Benedict began to dress. He paid no attention to Raine other than turning his back. Any further show of modesty would be pointless. He was certain that she was the one who had undressed him, so there was really no point in attempting to hide himself from her.

He heard the rustle of her movements as she rose from the bed behind him. She did not speak until he had finished putting on his houppelande, which told him that she had made note of his progress in dressing.

When she addressed him, the regret in her voice made him turn and look at her bent head closely. ''I am very sorry, my lord, for the trouble I have brought you.''

She then raised her gaze to his, even as she wrapped her arms all the more tightly around the waist of the green velvet robe she had donned. ''Yet I must admit that I would do it all again. I love my brother and promised my father that I would look after him no matter what. Given my thought process, I could not have done other than what I did.''

Benedict sighed, sympathy for her again rising inside him in spite of the fact that she was at fault here. He was distracted from having to answer by a soft scratching at the door.

His gaze met Raine's as she called out with forced composure. ''Who is there?''

A hesitant voice replied, "William."

The regret that stabbed him as chagrin and sadness filled her golden eyes surprised and worried Benedict. Wanting to give himself anything to think about other than his disturbing reaction, he strode forward to open the door.

Chapter Four

The first thing Benedict noted about the young boy standing there was his heavy thatch of dark brown hair, which bore definite auburn undertones. It made his pale face, dominated by a pair of green eyes, seem somewhat small. Those eyes, though not nearly so translucent as Raine's, made Benedict realize this could be none other than her brother. The lad's hesitant but clearly concerned gaze first raked Benedict with uncertainty, then searched out his sister. When he saw her there in her robe, he pushed past Benedict to her side.

Benedict closed the door, then turned to watch the two. Raine avoided looking at him as she put her arms around her brother. Quickly the boy pushed back, his eyes searching hers as he murmured, "Oh Raine, is it true what people are saying? That you…"

She met his gaze unflinchingly, clearly putting aside her own concerns in an effort to soothe her brother. As she spoke, Benedict felt an unexpected stirring of respect. "Do not worry about what others say, but always first ask me for the truth. Besides, the opinions of these folk matter not in the least to us. We will soon be gone from here."

The boy peered up at her, and Benedict could hear the relief that he tried to hide beneath a manly pose as he said, "I do not care what they might think. I was worried for you." Then he added, his relieved tone giving away his youth and anxiety, "We are going home to Abbernathy?"

She ran a hand over his hair. "Aye."

Benedict could not but be moved by this exchange. The love and care between them was more than obvious. He went toward them, speaking evenly. "You must be young William."

The boy squared his slight shoulders, his gaze assessing. "And you are the man everyone is saying—"

Benedict interrupted wryly. "Yes, I suspect I am."

William frowned, glancing at Raine. "Is it true what they are saying? That you and…this man—"

Again Benedict interrupted him. "Benedict Ainsworth."

The boy nodded stiffly. "My lord Ainsworth." His gaze met and held Benedict's directly. "I hope you have not…the stories they are telling…Raine is my sister."

Benedict could not fault him for his protectiveness toward Raine, but he had no wish to become involved in a conflict with the lad when he had committed no fault in this. He spoke evenly. "You must address me as Benedict."

The young man frowned in frustration. His troubled gaze went back to Raine's face. "Well, is it true what they are saying about you and Lord—you and Benedict?"

Meeting his gaze directly, she shook her head. "Nay, it is not, William. He did not touch me. Though I—"

For reasons that he could not explain, Benedict forestalled her. "Raine and I have done nothing untoward here. I simply had too much wine and fell asleep." He was not certain why he felt the need to say that, to protect her. He'd simply had the feeling that she was about to reveal the whole of her crimes to her younger brother, and unaccountably, Benedict felt the need to spare her that. He told himself that there was no reason for the boy to know all. It could gain him nothing.

Glancing at Raine, he saw that she was watching him with surprise and, he thought, gratitude. When she noted his interest in herself she quickly turned to her brother. "You see, William, there is nothing to be concerned about. It has all been a misunderstanding."

The relief on his young face could not have been more obvious. And Benedict was gladdened that he had acted upon the impulse to spare the boy. When Benedict's parents had died on the return journey from visiting his aunt in Scotland, the raising of his own brothers had fallen to him. He had been eighteen, and the youngest of the three of them had been around the same age as the lad before him.

Benedict looked at Raine, who seemed determined to change the subject now as she asked, "Have you eaten, William?"

William flushed, glancing at Benedict and away. "Please do not fuss over me, Raine." He shrugged, his gaze meeting the man's then as if their maleness forged a bond between them. "She's always wanting to know if I've eaten, thinks I'm too small." He finished with a trace of defiance.

Benedict could see what this admission had cost him. He murmured, "One of my own brothers was quite small when he was your age. He's nearly of a height with me now."

William looked up at him in amazement. "Truly?"

Benedict nodded. "But it is also true that he has ever shown a hearty appetite. He would no more miss breaking his fast than a day of hunting, which I may tell you is no small matter in his mind."

He could see that this information was being taken into account most seriously. William looked down at his own spare frame. "As you see, my lord, I am somewhat lacking in size, but you give me hope that it will not always be so."

Benedict asked, "Was your father a small man?"

A shadow passed over the lad's face at this mention of his father, but he answered evenly. "Nay, my lord, he was a tall man, though not so large in form as you."

Benedict smiled with certainty. "Then all you need do is eat. Nature will see to the rest."

The boy frowned thoughtfully. Glancing over his head, Benedict saw that Raine was watching him with an equally thoughtful and surprisingly disappointed expression of her own. Yet what had she to be disappointed about? Other than her failed plans to force him into marriage with her.

Apparently William had read his sister's expression as well, but interpreted it quite differently, for he said, "Enough of this talk of me. What are we going to do, my lord? Even if we leave the court, everyone believes you and Raine..." He looked toward her with a protective grimace.

Benedict shrugged. "I do not know, lad. Perhaps we will be able to devise some way to make all understand that she has done nothing to deserve their derision."

William sighed, his wary gaze going to the bed, and Benedict wondered if someone had mentioned the bloodied sheet within his hearing. The fact that Benedict did not see the offending item told him Raine had surely stashed it out of sight while he was dressing. He was not sorry.

As the boy spoke softly, Benedict realized that her having done so had not lessened the damage that had already been done. "I do not think anyone will believe you now. They are saying that they saw—"

Benedict halted him. "As I said before, you need not trouble yourself. Things are not as they appeared."

His face told Benedict that William desired, above all things, to believe him. But there was uncertainty in his eyes as the boy watched Raine sit down on the end of the bed, her gaze dark with sorrow. Benedict somehow knew she was far more concerned about the harm she might have done her brother in this than what would be said of her. He believed her assertions that she had done all of this in a misguided attempt to find a protector for the boy.

That did not excuse her actions.

But are you not a man, a soft voice exclaimed within, *with the strength and authority to rebuke any who might attempt to dominate you? She has no such power.*

William went on, and Benedict found himself listening to the young man very carefully. "It has been so hard these months since Father died."

Hurriedly Raine interrupted him. "You need not bore the baron with our troubles, William."

Benedict surprised himself by saying, "On the contrary, William. I find myself quite interested in what you have to say. Please continue."

In spite of his sister's disapproving expression, William did go on. It seemed almost a relief to voice his worries aloud. "Raine has tried her utmost to take care of us all, and when Denley would not leave be, she decided we should come here to court. She said we would find a man who would help us.'' He met Benedict's gaze directly, displaying a straightforwardness he could not help but respect. Benedict had never cared much for beating about the bush.

More and more was he impressed with this manchild.

Raine was now staring at the gray stone floor. She seemed impatient and flustered at William's refusal to remain silent. Benedict could also see the unmistakable traces of disconsolation in the downward curl of her lovely mouth, no matter how she tried to hide it.

Clearly Raine worked very hard to keep her brother from knowing how uncertain she was. Her bravery in the face of the difficulties she and William had faced did her credit. Obviously their father had done his best to raise his children well. It was apparent in their manner and care for one another. They had simply been left alone too soon, with one inexperienced girl to choose their path.

Loyalty and care for others were qualities that he had always expected in the future bride of Brackenmoore. He continued to study the dejected Raine. Knowing what had brought her to such desperate means made him feel differently about what she had done. Although there was no question her efforts to force him into a marriage had been wrong.

He sighed heavily. He could not simply abandon these two to their fate. Raine, however misguided in her actions, had been doing her utmost to take care of her only sibling.

Benedict realized that he was thinking of committing the first, and he hoped only, hastily considered act of his life. But there was little time to contemplate. He must return to Brackenmoore this day. He had left his youngest brother, Kendran, alone too long already. Lily and Tristan were away at Tristan's hunting lodge, Molson, and he could not have asked them to come home without mentioning some reason for his visit to court.

He looked into William's eyes. The lad was so young. Benedict turned to Raine, saw the vulnerability she tried to hide in the dejected pursing of her mouth.

It must be done now, or not at all.

He spoke with quiet resolution. "William, would you be so good as to leave us for a while? There are some things I would like to discuss with your sister."

William studied him for a long moment. "Aye, Benedict, I will leave you." He leaned close and whispered so that his sister would not hear. "She is really not so very contrary and wild as she seems, you know. She's just so afraid sometimes that if she stops to think she won't have the courage to do what she believes she must."

Benedict nodded, his gaze going to Raine, where she perched on the bed watching them. It was a very perceptive and likely accurate assessment, he thought. Bringing Raine into his life would not be without possible consequences to his peace of mind.

Then, surprised that he would even entertain such a thought, Benedict squared his shoulders as he watched William go to the door. No green female would be allowed to destroy his peace. He would simply have to make it clear that he would not tolerate such behavior in future.

When the door closed behind William, Benedict turned to the now scowling Raine. She had her arms folded across her chest and her tone was less than eager. "What more could there be for us to say, my lord? I believe you made yourself clear before William arrived.''

He scowled back at her. She was not making his inclination any easier to live with, yet his understanding that she would protect William at all cost to herself drove him on. He had felt that way about his own brothers when they had been left in his care.

"There is just one thing to say, really," he told her. He went and stood before her, his gaze intent.

As if sensing the import of what he had to say, Raine became very still. Holding that troubled, yet brave golden gaze with his own, Benedict spoke in a tone of firm decision. "I ask you, Raine Blanchett, to be my bride."

Her mouth formed an O and she stared at him in amazement. "Do not jest with me, Benedict Ainsworth."

His mouth twisted in a wry grin. "I assure you that I am not jesting."

Raine could only look at him for a long, long moment. At last she said, "Why are you so suddenly willing to do this? I have told you that I will reveal the truth of what happened here to all."

He shrugged, his expression maddeningly unreadable. "Suffice it to say that I am willing."

From deep inside her the reason came. It was because of William. Meeting him had made her brother's predicament clear. She had seen for herself that Benedict Ainsworth was a man who cared much for the plight of others. How many men would secretly enlist the aid of the king of England for the sake of giving his newly wed brother some peace?

Though she had wanted nothing but the protection of his name, she felt almost deflated at understanding the reason for his proposal. Taking a deep breath, she looked down at her hands and replied, "For the sake of my brother I will accept the protection of your name, Benedict Ainsworth." She raised her head, attempting to imbue her expression with gratitude. "I thank you for your kindness. I vow not to trouble you greatly from this point onward and will leave you in peace." And she meant it. Once back at Abbernathy, she and William would do quite well with this powerful man's name to protect them from harassment from Denley and those of his ilk.

This seemed to please him, for he smiled at her then, his white teeth flashing, and for a breathless moment her heart stood still. Though she could not quite fathom the degree of her reaction to a simple smile, she had a difficult time concentrating as he said, "I am so very gratified that you see there is cause for that statement. It encourages me."

Raine nodded, glad that she had, at last, done something, however paltry it seemed, to please him. And she did mean what she had said. She intended to be no trouble at all to her new husband.

Raine felt a strange numbness as she folded the last of her garments into the chest. From the moment Benedict Ainsworth, Baron of Brackenmoore, and now her husband, had smiled at her, a sense of unreality had settled upon her. It had all happened too quickly to be real. Yet it was real.

She was well and truly wed to Benedict Ainsworth.

The marriage had taken place in one of the king's private chambers, with none other than Edward himself in attendance. He had spoken only a handful of words to Raine, for which she was grateful. She was far too dazed by the haste and efficiency with which Benedict had been able to arrange the union to make polite conversation with a king.

Why, it had been only hours ago that she had stood in this very room with Ainsworth and heard him ask for her hand. The marriage had been accomplished and Raine shown back to her room without her new husband having uttered one word of a personal nature.

His request that she pack in preparation of leaving had been brought by one of his men. Far from being irritated by Benedict's autocratic manner, she had been glad of something to occupy her. Raine was quite eager to take herself away from court. Her duties at Abbernathy beckoned.

And now the packing was done, her own men summoned to await her in the courtyard. William and Aida had already gone down to see to the loading of the small wagon.

The maid had been as shocked as Raine at the baron's proposal. Surprisingly enough, William had not seemed to be. He had simply hugged her and told her that he thought Benedict a very kind man. Raine could only agree.

Even so, as she made the final preparations for the journey, Raine did not understand why she did not feel more cheered, why there was this odd sense of regret in her belly. She had found a husband, one who would serve her purposes very well indeed, and one who was kind, as William had said. For how else could she describe a man who would go so far simply to aid her and William?

Yet he had not said one word of goodbye. Quickly she told herself that he had done far more than she had a right to expect. Why would he further trouble himself with them?

She sighed and closed the lid on her chest just as the nobleman who so occupied her thoughts entered the chamber. Raine stood immediately, distantly noting as she did so that she was now smiling.

Benedict stood in the doorway, his large frame filling the opening, and nodded with approval as he saw what she had been doing. "Good, you are ready. My men are as well."

She frowned, surprised at his words. "Do you mean to escort us home then?"

He frowned back at her. "Do I mean to escort you? If that is what you wish to call it, aye. Why would I not accompany you to Brackenmoore?"

Puzzled, she took a step backward. "Brackenmoore?"

Benedict put his hands to his hips. "Aye, it is home."

"Your home!" she murmured, bewildered.

"Our home," he replied with conviction. When she continued to frown at him, he closed his eyes and took a deep breath, before murmuring, "I am beginning to have a growing suspicion that I am not going to enjoy this conversation. So much for not causing me any difficulty."

Raine stiffened from the top of her head to the tips of her toes as she laid a determined hand upon her chest. "Somehow I have not made myself clear. I...we...William and I are not going to Brackenmoore." She had indeed told him she would cause him no further distress, but she had not meant to imply that she would simply put aside her own responsibilities if he wished her to.

He was clearly aghast at her words, even though she

was certain he had known they were coming. The man was obviously too full of himself to believe that she would actually oppose him. His tone was incredulous. "Of course you are going to Brackenmoore. It is my home. Your home now that we are married."

Raine shook her head, attempting to clear it of some of her outrage, realizing that she had indeed been lax. "I realize that a terrible error has been made here." She tried her utmost to maintain a semblance of reason even as she understood how great an error indeed. "The wedding took place so very suddenly and we had no opportunity to discuss any of this properly, but I never intended to go with you to Brackenmoore. I ask your pardon for any misunderstanding I may have caused, but I am going home to Abbernathy. I am needed there. The head woman's grandchild will be born soon and I must be in attendance at a castle birth, as have all the women in my line for hundreds of years. The planting must be done, the spring cleaning of the keep." She threw her hands in the air in frustration. "All those tasks and more must be seen to. I cannot simply abandon my brother, the folk who rely upon me."

Benedict sighed as if with great relief. "I see the cause of your concern, but you need not worry. William will come with us to Brackenmoore. And as far as the other things are concerned, I will send a man to oversee Abbernathy. I have other estates besides Brackenmoore and they are well tended with my supervision, but do not require my residence." He added, with a trace of humor, "You may be assured that the man I have in mind will acquit himself well, though he may be of little use at a birthing."

Ignoring this attempt at jesting, she shook her head again, her gaze meeting his with absolute resolve even though she knew that what she was about to say would not be welcome. "I cannot leave the running of Father's estate, William's and my home, to a stranger."

His displeasure with her statement was betrayed only by the slight narrowing of his eyes, but betrayed it was. And she suddenly became aware of the fact that this man, as her husband, had more power over her than she would wish. Without conscious thought she found her uncertain gaze falling to the wide expanse of his chest. Benedict's size and height were imposing in spite of the fact that she did not wish to be intimidated.

"Your home is Brackenmoore and that, Wife, is where you go," he stated.

Raine knew that she had brought this upon herself. Benedict did have a right to expect her to accompany him. She tried again. "I am very sorry for what has happened here. It was all so very fast. I never meant to conceal my intention to return to my own home from you. You have, by any standard, shown me the greatest kindness this day. But I must ask one more boon. I ask that you forgive me in this and offer my most heartfelt invitation for your coming to Abbernathy with us."

His gaze widened. "That is impossible."

She shrugged. "Then we shall certainly part ways. For I tell you that I cannot go to Brackenmoore."

He glared down at her. "You have abused my goodwill overmuch this day, madam. You will come to Brackenmoore."

She raised her chin, determined to defy him in spite of the fact that she was grateful for what he had done. Yet as she looked up into those ice-cold blue eyes she felt a growing realization that he was the one in control here.

She pulled the cloak of bravado about her stiff shoulders. "I will not." What was the matter with him that he could not see reason? Had she not explained all?

His voice did not rise, holding a cool certainty that only served to further infuriate her. "You shall, and mark me, I will have no compunction against forcing you, should you attempt to defy me. You initiated this marriage. You will live by your desire."

Desperation made her incautiously frank. "I never intended to abide with you."

He leaned ever closer, forcing her to bend her head back to keep contact with those blue eyes. "That, Lady Ainsworth, is your own dilemma. I never intended for you to do otherwise. And mark me well, you will abide with me. I will personally carry you to your horse if you do not do as I have said. To salve your pride and reputation I have married you. You will not refuse to live as my wife."

Before she could so much as say another word, he spun on his heel and exited the chamber.

Raine felt her hands curl into fists at her sides, rage and frustration making her feel as if she were about to explode. The blackguard. How dare he demand this of her, then turn his back as if she were no better than a servant?

Knowing that her anger would gain her nothing, Raine took deep, even breaths to calm herself. She must try to think of a way to make him see that she could not go with him. Yet even when the pounding of her blood eased she could see no way out of this situation.

Grateful as she was to him, Raine could not accept this command, nor Benedict's assessment of the situation, with good grace. He had not married her in order to salve her pride. She was quite aware of the fact that it had been for William's sake. In spite of her anger and resentment it still gave her an unexpected twinge of regret.

For the longest moment, Raine considered going on to Abbernathy as she had planned. Her own men were waiting in the courtyard. She could go down right now, mount her horse and be gone before Ainsworth could prevent her. This last chest need not be taken. The possessions it contained would be a small price to pay for her independence.

But something would not let her act upon this impulse. Perhaps it was the memory of how Benedict had so easily bested Denley. Perhaps it was because she knew instinctively that he was not a man to make idle threats. In no part of herself did she doubt that her husband would indeed carry her out before the whole court if he felt the need to do so.

Or come after her if she attempted to escape him. She could have no hope of outdistancing him, for it was obvious that he, too, was ready for the journey.

She could see no way out of doing as he said. For the moment, at any rate.

Seething with indignity, Raine marched to the door and jerked it open. Aida and William stood in the hallway. There was uncertainty on William's face as he said, "Raine, Benedict just came out to the courtyard where we were waiting and informed us all that we would be accompanying him and his men to Brackenmoore. Is it true?" The anxiety on his face made her understand that she could not share her own rage and frustration over this with him. He had been through too much in the last months, and as ever, she was determined to keep him from suffering the fear and anxiety she had known after their mother died.

She spoke with deliberate calm. "Aye. We will be

going to Brackenmoore.'' At his surprised expression, she added, "For a time.''

Benedict stared unseeing at his serving of roast meat and bread that his men had readied for the evening meal. His stomach was in too tight a knot for him to even consider eating it.

He was angry. Angrier than he cared to admit. What manner of woman had he married that she thought she could treat him as she had?

She had never intended to abide with him, indeed!

As he had reminded her, it had been Raine herself who wanted the marriage. He had agreed for her sake. And the boy's.

His gaze went to William, who sat close to the fire, talking animatedly with Benedict's knight, Sir Peter. William's six men sat nearby. After a brief initial surprise they had accompanied Benedict's party with good grace, and seemed a decent lot.

He looked again at William, who smiled as Sir Peter waved his hand in the air to illustrate some point he was making. The lad did not appear to be as distressed at going to Brackenmoore as his sister. In fact, he appeared less troubled by the weight of his future than when Benedict had met him that very morn. This encouraged Benedict to hope he had done the right thing in marrying that hellion.

Although she had said not one more word of dissent to him the whole of the day, her anger was still apparent. It continued to burn in those golden eyes of hers each and every time he had so much as glanced in her direction.

His gaze went to the tent that had been erected a few feet away. A scowl darkened his brow. He had seen no sign of either Raine or her maid since it had been set up soon after their stopping for the night.

Benedict told himself that that was all well and good with him. He did not need her to acknowledge his presence. All he required was her obedience in the matter of her going with him to Brackenmoore. His marriage was of great impact as far as the estates were concerned.

Go with her to Abbernathy, indeed! She was quite mad.

He could not allow her to do aught but accompany *him*.

He felt the heavy weight of frustration upon his chest. As he had been since his parents died when he was eighteen, Benedict was responsible first and foremost for Brackenmoore and its inhabitants. Yet he had jeopardized the peace of his home in marrying Raine Blanchett.

Now Benedict realized that he had arranged the wedding too quickly. His decision to have her had been made without his usual deliberation. Yet he had not been able to walk away from the boy—or truth be known, Raine. They needed someone.

In all honesty he was willing to be that someone still. He must simply make her see that his actions and hers had consequences. When she had married him she had married Brackenmoore, which was more important than any one individual, including one headstrong and impetuous damsel. Raine was clearly confused about her own obligations. As a woman it was her duty to bring her loyalty to her husband and his lands once she was wed.

Surely, if he could only explain this to her, she would see reason. Her loyalty to her brother, her concern for his estate, did in fact do her much credit, and told Benedict that she did indeed understand the concept. She would simply need to understand that as his bride she was now a part of Brackenmoore, with ties to her former home, yet no longer an integral part of it.

His bride.

The words brought an unexpected tightening to his lower belly, in spite of all that had occurred this day. With the sensation came an awareness that he might not have married Raine solely for the sake of rescuing her.

She was a very beautiful and desirable woman. And was it not right that he should desire his own wife? Their joining would, with God's blessing, result in an heir for his lands and heritage.

This was his wedding night. What was he doing sitting here on a stump like a green boy?

Surely he could make Raine see he meant her no ill. The two of them must find some common ground and begin a new life.

Setting the untouched food aside and rising in one quick motion, Benedict strode toward the tent. He pulled up the flap and stepped inside. Immediately his gaze found Raine.

His wife.

She sat on a low stool while the maid, Aida, brushed her hair. His gaze took in the rippling curtain of auburn, which had so captured his attention that morning.

Sensing her own attention upon him, Benedict met his wife's eyes. He saw what might have been a flicker of anxiety in those golden depths, but it was gone so quickly that he knew he must have been mistaken. The glance she cast him was clearly annoyed and disdainful.

Benedict felt a stiffening in his own body in reaction. Firmly and determinedly he resolved to stay calm. Reason and patience were his way. He would not be drawn into behaving like an untried lad as he had this morn. Marrying Raine was his last hasty act.

Yet her unreasonable displeasure rankled. He could not prevent the frown that marred his brow as she turned and spoke to the maid. "Please leave us, Aida."

The maid looked at him with uncertainty. Raine spoke again. "Please."

When the obviously reluctant woman had gone, Raine rose. The pale pink velvet robe she wore molded itself to the length of her slender form. He found his gaze tracing the enticing curves of her rounded breasts, her narrow waist and gently flaring hips as she slowly came toward him. She stopped a mere handful of steps away, and Benedict noted the way the end of one bright curl caught in the plush fabric that covered the curve of her hip. Only when she spoke, saying, "My lord," did he raise his attention to her coolly assessing visage.

Benedict nodded, attempting to retain his equanimity in the face of her unwelcoming stance. "My lady wife."

She forestalled him with a raised hand. "Pray, allow me to speak, my lord."

In spite of the fact that he very much doubted he would be pleased by what she was about to say, Benedict could not help feeling a trace of admiration as she quickly and brazenly came to the point. "My lord Ainsworth, your coming here has made it apparent that I must converse with you on an unpleasant matter." She paused for a long moment, and it was clear from the flush that accompanied her words as she went on that she did not find this easy. "I would have you know, my lord, that though we are wed and I am indeed forced against my own will to obey your command and accompany you to your lands...I do not intend to be your wife in any other sense.'' Her gaze fell, as if finishing had cost her all the boldness she possessed.

Benedict's brows rose in shock. There was no mistaking that she had come right out and denied him her bed. Affront raced through him in a murky flood. She had no right to deny him. It was her duty before God and man to act as a fitting wife. And that was aside from the fact that it was she who had chosen him.

Despite a determination to keep her from seeing how greatly she had perturbed him, Benedict knew his incredulity was apparent in his tone. ''You seek to send me from you?''

She bit her lip with uncertainty as she faced him, but there was sheer defiance in her eyes. ''I do.''

He shook his head in disbelief. ''You have no right to do so. I am your husband.''

She stepped backward, then quickly squared her shoulders. ''You will not be so in flesh unless you force me, my lord.''

He moved toward her, his anger a tight ball in his belly as he bent over her. She held her ground, a fact that only further infuriated him as he spoke through tight lips. ''I ask you this, madam. What makes you think I would force you if I had come here to claim my right as your husband?''

Her gaze widened as she craned to look up at him. ''I—I simply assumed you would take what you...''

''You assumed wrongly then.'' He heard genuine indignation enter his voice as he added, ''I have never forced myself upon any woman—have never had to.'' His gaze raked her meaningfully.

She flushed, clearly understanding his meaning, and sputtered, "I…then forgive my—"

"Enough!"

Raine went on, not heeding his command, her reluctance obvious as she said, "Again I find myself in the position of offering you thanks. I do not believe I could have… For you are a stranger to me, my lord."

This last remark stretched his control to the breaking point. He swept her with a scorching gaze. "Aye, as you are a stranger to me, Wife. You have done much to beg pardon for on this day, my lady, and yet you continue to rattle on about your own concerns. You have attempted to trick me into marriage, have treated me coldly because I expected you to come home with me, and denied me your bed without compunction. You do dare much, Raine. Yet do not mistake that I could have loved you and well. There would have been no forcing."

An expression of utter fury colored her features a deep peach, yet Benedict was of no mind to listen to her for another moment. He forestalled her by reaching out and pulling her to him, molding the length of her squirming body to his as he pressed his mouth to hers. He told himself that she deserved this, had driven him mad with her accusations and assumptions.

Yet as he kissed her he became aware of the softening of her lips. She went limp, the mounds of her breasts pressing against his chest, the fragile but womanly shape of her easing into his arms.

His body reacted to her response with an intensity that shocked him, and he felt himself become hard and ready in an instant. His intent changed. His own lips softened, entreated, cajoled. Her hands crept up to rest against his chest and he slanted his head, his tongue flicking out to trace her mouth. When she opened her lips beneath his he deepened the kiss and she tilted her head back, leaning into him.

Emboldened by her reaction, he traced the length of her back, his hands coming to rest on her hips. Yet as he held her firmly to the hardness of his manhood, feeling it pulse against the flat line of her belly, she stiffened suddenly, pulling away with a gasp.

She backed away from him, putting her hand up to cover her mouth, which was pink and swollen from his kiss. "How dare you! You said you would not force me."

Benedict felt a fresh wave of anger at the horror in her gaze, this new accusation. He heard the bitter sarcasm in his own tone as he said, "Aye, I did say that, Raine. And have not done so. Mark me well now, woman, you have gained a delay and no more. I will bed you and know that 'twill not be by force."

The confusion and agony he saw on her face brought a rush of sympathy that he could not explain. Disgusted with himself for reacting to that sign of vulnerability, he turned and left.

He did not go back to the fire and the others. He was too agitated to sit and talk, to pretend to ignore the glances of speculation that would surely come his way.

As he strode across the meadow and into the enveloping closeness of the forest he realized that there was something about Raine, a softness beneath that abrasive veneer, that moved him each time he glimpsed it.

It was surely that softness that made him desire her even now as he recalled the feel of her in his arms, the cool taste of her mouth on his, her clearly unwilling, but equally powerful, response to him.

Yet he would control his reactions to those momentary glimpses of vulnerability. He could not allow her to get around him, could not forget just what she was capable of by way of manipulation and deceit.

Chapter Five

Raine rose and dressed as soon as she heard the first hints of stirring in the camp. She had slept for no more than sporadic moments the whole of the night.

Aida, who had shared the tent with her, seemed to have slept little more, for Raine had heard her tossing restlessly upon her blankets. The worried glances she kept casting Raine's way as she helped her ready herself for the day were somewhat disconcerting.

Raine had no words of comfort this morn.

The way she had responded to Benedict Ainsworth's kiss would not be forgotten. Each and every thought of that kiss brought a repeat of the shocking heat and longing she had known as his firm lips touched hers, a memory of the feelings that had turned her resistance to acquiescence.

The fact that it was the first kiss she had ever shared with a man might very well explain why she had not expected such a reaction in herself. But somewhere deep inside her Raine knew that there was more to it than that. She could not, no matter how she tried, make herself believe the touch of just any man would bring such a response. Benedict's face was the only one she could even bring to mind. That the face in her mind was arrogant with the knowledge of how she had reacted to him was utterly mortifying.

Even as shame heated her cheeks anew she heard the sound of a commotion from outside, the sound of raised voices. The anger in those voices told her that something was amiss.

Quickly she stepped out into the crisp spring morning.

The sight that met her eyes made her take in a deep breath of anger and impatience. At the edge of the camp, mounted atop a huge brown stallion, was none other than Denley Trent. At the moment he was shouting down at one of Benedict's men, while the rest of the soldiers were moving toward the two from their various locations about the camp.

There was no sign of Benedict, nor of William, who had insisted upon sleeping around fire with the other men. Even as she wondered where her husband and brother might be, Denley shouted her name.

She looked up to see him bearing down upon her, ignoring the fact that he narrowly missed riding over the men who had moved to halt him. The rage on his face was clear to see.

In spite of the fact that he looked like a madman racing toward her with that mask of fury upon his face, Raine felt no real fear of him. She was under Benedict's protection now, though the knowledge did not rest quite as easily as she had once thought it might. As Denley neared, she had no time to think on that dilemma. She took a deep breath and prepared to meet her nemesis.

Denley's full lips pursed with disapproval and outrage as he jerked his mount to a halt mere feet from her and growled, "What is going on, Raine? I spent the night at an inn last night...your stubbornness left me with a desire for softer compan—'' He broke off with a flush, then blubbered on. ''You know that the court is so crowded...and I thought to give you some time to...''

She had the distinct feeling that he had been looking for comfort of a carnal sort at that inn. She ignored this. ''What do you do here, Denley?''

His color seemed to fluctuate as he went on in a tone of abject betrayal. ''Why am I here? When I returned to court yesterday afternoon I heard that you had left. But not only had you departed, they were all on about how you had married Ainsworth and gone off to Brackenmoore. Married? I said to myself. 'Twas surely impossible, and yet here you are.''

She put her hands to her hips. ''And what concern would that be of yours?''

Utter rage and horror turned her cousin's face a bright purple when she did not deny his words, and he sputtered, ''But how can it be? You refuse my every proposal and then marry a man you have only just met. What are you about, Raine? Has he importuned you in some way?''

She felt a strange urge to laugh, for it had been quite the opposite. Instead she said, ''Nay, Denley, he did not. I have wed him of my own will.''

His round eyes and slack jaw gave away his complete incredulity. ''But why? You could have had me.''

This time she could not completely withhold a gasp of laughter, which she quickly covered with a choking cough. Denley was totally oblivious to how very ridiculous he was. But she knew he would not understand her if she told him this. And now that she had a husband, one whom she knew would not allow anyone to touch her, she felt not one twinge of anxiety in connection to this man. For she was quite aware of the fact that Benedict's men had gathered closely around her as she and her cousin conversed.

She wanted to tell them there was no need for concern, but she spoke only to Denley, wanting him to understand that he must leave. She wished to end this confrontation with no harm done on either side. She could afford her cousin a bit of compassion now that she need have no fear of him. "I appreciate the honor you tried to do me. But rest assured I have no regret in my choice of husband."

This was not true in the least, but she would not have him know that. Even as she thought this she felt an odd prickling along her nape. Turning, she saw that her husband and her brother were just emerging from the edge of the trees. Both of them had damp hair and garments. Clearly they had found some body of water in which to bathe.

In spite of the turmoil of the moment, Raine could not help noting the way Benedict's wet hair, which he had combed straight back, made his jaw look even more strong and lean. Nor could she help seeing the way his damp tunic clung to his shoulders, drawing attention to their powerful breadth.

His gaze, dark and compelling with an emotion she could not name, met hers for one long, infinite moment. Raine felt an odd tension within herself, a strange breathlessness. She looked down, telling herself it was the absolute mastery of Benedict's expression as he assessed the situation that caused her agitation. It had nothing to do with vivid memory of the taste of his lips on hers.

When she raised her gaze to his once more his black

brows arched high with cool amusement. Surprised at his expression, she wondered if he had overheard her assurances that she was well pleased with her marriage. That would certainly explain his amusement.

Deliberately she ignored him. Yet as she squared her shoulders, she remained infinitely aware of Benedict as he moved with quick easy strides across the space that separated them. Not bothering to address her, he faced the other man with disdain. "Why have you come, man?"

Denley looked at him with renewed rage. "You have dared to steal away with the woman I intended to wed."

Obviously Benedict was less reticent about offending the madman than she, for he spoke with contempt. "I informed you before that you would mind your ways with Raine, and you will certainly do so now. You are no longer talking to a woman you may hope to coerce, Trent. You are now addressing my wife, Lady Ainsworth."

If possible, Denley's flush darkened further and she almost felt sympathy for him. Almost. Even the fact that Benedict was far too domineering could not make her forget how recklessly her cousin had attempted to force her into a marriage with him.

When Denley swung around to glare at her rather than face Benedict any longer, she shrugged. His gaze swept the camp, the gathered soldiers, William's set face. Clearly he found no support there.

Benedict spoke again, this time his voice, however calm in tone, holding a clear warning. "You will go now, or know the consequences of trespassing upon what is mine."

Raine felt herself stiffen at his choice of words.

Denley cast one more desperate glance about him.

He was outnumbered. Raine took a step toward him. Her voice filled with entreaty and pity as she experienced a sense of rebellion at Benedict's proprietary manner toward herself. "You must go, Denley. There is nothing for you here."

With a cry of both frustration and fury, he spun his mount about and rode away. Raine made no attempt to call after him. If he would only understand that things were simply not the way he envisioned them, he would not be in such a ludicrous position.

Raine did not look at her husband, remaining uneasy with Benedict's proprietary declaration to her cousin. Yet had she not wanted this? Had she not hoped and prayed that a man would come along who could protect her from the likes of her cousin?

Aye, it was what she had wanted. But she had wanted only his name and did not appreciate being treated like a possession, which was just the way she felt at listening to her husband speak of her.

How could she not, after the way he had treated her last night? He had pressed himself upon her as if her wish to the contrary meant nothing, as if she were indeed his possession to do with as he chose. And she, silly cow that she was, had responded to him as if...well, she had no words to describe the very depth of her reaction. It was especially galling after he had informed her quite deliberately that he would take her when he wished.

To make matters worse, Raine knew that she herself had brought about this dreadful state of affairs. She had married him simply because of the fact that he obviously loved and protected his own family. She'd had no knowledge of how demanding he might be of them in return.

The sudden sound of his voice at her side nearly made her start. "Are you well?" She had not realized her husband had come so near.

Without looking at him, Raine nodded. She could think of no reply. Considering her thoughts, she had no wish to discuss this episode with Denley, or anything else for that matter.

She knew she should show some sign of gratitude to Benedict even though he was concerned only because he thought of her as another one of his possessions. She could not find it in her to do so.

She refused to look at him as she spoke in a voice that she knew only he would hear. "Please, my lord, has enough not been said this day? I would have this behind us. And I am sure that you wish to be on our way." At last she looked at him, unable to completely hide the resentment in her voice and eyes. "Is that not what you desire? To get us all to Brackenmoore?"

Benedict stood there looking into those bitter golden eyes in disbelief. It appeared as if the wench was angry with him. How she could be thus was completely unfathomable. He had only done what she had, in fact, said she wished of him in sending her utterly lack-witted cousin on his way. "Aye, that is exactly what I desire."

He spun on his heel and motioned to those who had gathered about. "'Tis done. Get on with breaking camp. We have many miles ahead of us this day." He was not happy to hear the impatience in his tone.

His men moved in unison to do as he bade, though he knew there must be some muttering about his own obvious and unexpected ill temper. It was quite unlike him to be so abrupt with them.

Benedict could also feel William's weighty gaze upon him, but he did not make eye contact with the boy. Although he was already becoming attached to the lad, Benedict was not willing to let him know how ably his sister managed to agitate him.

Nor did he wish for her to know.

Determinedly he kept his back to Raine, saying not another word to her, afraid that if he did he might give in to the overwhelming desire to throttle her. He simply walked away and went on about his own preparations to leave, doing his utmost to behave normally even though his anger at Raine continued to burn in his chest.

As they broke camp, he continued to seethe, keeping her ever at the edge of his vision, seeing the way she went about with that pretty nose of hers tilted skyward. His preoccupation and impatience only served to gain him several more speculative glances from his men. He only hoped that his aggravation had been attributed to the scene with Denley Trent. For some reason he had no desire for his men to know that he had become so overset by a woman, even if that woman was his wife.

It would not do at all for them to think that his marriage would change anything at Brackenmoore. He stood for more than himself and must certainly learn to control this unwanted reaction to her every insulting word.

The outrage that continued to burn in his chest throughout the day thwarted his resolve to remain indifferent to her opinion of him. Only the fact that he had never failed in anything he set out to accomplish gave Benedict solace as he determinedly stayed well away from his wife and her maid, who were riding in the middle of the party.

He instead tried to concentrate his attention upon the

boy, who rode near Benedict the whole of the day. The lad was obviously eager for the company of other males, though Benedict was not blind to the fact that he kept a worried and protective eye on his sister.

Although he wished to avoid any mention of his wife, Benedict could not prevent himself from nudging even closer to the boy's horse and asking, "What troubles you?"

William glanced at him with a suddenly leery expression. "Nothing really." Yet Benedict saw the way his gaze flicked to Raine.

Benedict gave him a disbelieving glance and William said, "I can tell that you and Raine have had words already. I could see that she was angry with you when we left court, however she tried to hide it. I love her and would not have her unhappy, though I do see your position. It was mad of her to think you would not expect us to go home with you."

Benedict grimaced. "That is betwixt the two of us, William." He then added more gently, "You have no need to worry over her. She will be fine."

William turned to him with a shake of his head, his eyes wise beyond his years. "You do not know her. She will always put me first no matter what." Those green eyes went back to his sister. "She has ever been watchful over me, making sure that I was taken care of and happy, even when Father was alive." His shrug held a hint of uncertainty. "She seems always to be protecting me, as if she were afraid for me to become frightened or worried."

Benedict nodded. He could well believe this and knew that her being overprotective would not help the boy. He himself was determined to be a proper guardian to the lad, which would mean allowing him the room to grow into a man.

Yet he knew he must proceed gently with his wife on the matter of her brother. Though Benedict was angry with Raine concerning other things, he would force himself to concentrate on the devotion that she showed to William. He could not disregard the courage that had led her to make the desperate choice of marrying a stranger to protect the one she loved.

He sensed that Raine did not give of her love lightly, and once bestowed, it would be given without limit. That he would never fall in the category of being loved by her would not vex him. He neither required nor wanted her love, only her compliance.

Through the growing gloom of night, Raine viewed the enormous and imposing edifice of Brackenmoore with haughtily raised brows. As her gaze swept the high, thick, black stone walls, she realized that there was a strange salty quality to the air she had been only peripherally aware of until now. Even as she pondered at this phenomenon she thought how very like an ancestor of Benedict Ainsworth's to build his castle of such a deliberately imposing stone. As they rode up the incline toward the keep, Raine determinedly avoided looking at her husband, who rode just ahead of her. The resentment she felt toward him had not cooled in the days they had spent traveling. It had only seemed to grow hotter.

This was certainly aided by the fact that Benedict seemed completely unmoved by all that he had done, including the fact that he had kissed her. He seemed, in fact, to be almost disinterested in her since the jibe she had directed at him on the morning when Denley had intruded upon them.

Benedict addressed her without even a hint of reproach or discourtesy, just cool indifference. He certainly did not seem to make any effort to avoid her, as she did him. He went about as if nothing of any import had occurred.

His faultless demeanor only served to make her own anger all the more difficult to defend. Yet she had remained angry and told herself for the hundredth time that she had every reason to behave thusly. It was he who was acting strangely. Anyone with half a mind would have been disturbed by what had passed between them.

Deliberately she looked at William, who was gazing about with great interest. His eyes met hers and immediately his expression turned to a frown.

Raine felt her own lips turn down. Why had he looked at her that way? He had spent much time with Benedict and his men on the journey. Raine had been too occupied with her outrage to pay her usual careful attention to her brother, yet she had noted that Will appeared to enjoy the company of the men. And she had also noted that they had treated him with friendly acceptance, especially Benedict.

Surely it was her preoccupation that troubled him. She must certainly have a talk with him, try to explain herself without giving away too much of her situation with her husband. Again Raine's gaze was drawn back to the seemingly imperturbable Benedict, who rode with his wide shoulders thrown back, his head high as if he was master of all of England, rather than only of this deliberately imposing pile of stones before them. Strangely enough, she was both perturbed and reluctantly compelled by that attitude of complete self-assurance.

Raine sighed. Oh, how she wished she were not so foolish as to find the blackguard so very attractive. Her only relief was that Benedict was not aware of this. Casting another glance at her brother, she felt renewed agitation at the very thought of having to explain any of this to him.

As if sensing her rider's distress, the mare began to dance restively and Raine was forced to concentrate on getting her through the raised gateway. She felt a certain sympathy for the mare. She, too, was reluctant to enter these walls, walls that would now confine her and bind her to a life she did not want.

At that moment she felt a strange tingling along her neck. Glancing up, she saw that Benedict, who was now following her much more closely that she had known, was watching her with an expression she could not even begin to read.

She tilted her nose and looked away, telling herself that she did not care to know what he thought at any rate.

As soon as they were through the gate and had entered a wide courtyard dotted with well-tended buildings of both stone and wood construction, Benedict moved up beside her. There was a warning in his blue gaze as she turned her face to his with resentful inquiry. He said simply, "We are home. You will behave as befits the bride of Brackenmoore."

In spite of her resentment at his obvious censure of her, Raine could not help hearing the pride and pleasure in his voice. A scowl creased her brow. Was that all he cared for? Brackenmoore?

As she looked at him, she saw the displeasure in his

expression and knew that matters concerning Brackenmoore seemed to be the only thing that perturbed him. She was very fortunate indeed not to have set her sights on this man for any romantic reasons, which she assured herself she had not in spite of the sudden ache in her chest.

His first and last love was and clearly would continue to be his lands and heritage. And this she did understand on some level. Abbernathy and her brother, William, were all that mattered to her. She would not forsake the trust that her father had placed in her. No matter what the cost.

She met Benedict's gaze with an expression of hauteur. "You need have no worries on that score. I will not shame you or your household before your folk."

The relief on his countenance could not be mistaken. A tiny flame of resentment flickered in her chest. What did he take her for that he thought she would not understand the honor of his position?

She pushed her indignation down. Damn Benedict Ainsworth and his opinion of her. And damn her for reacting to it.

As they brought their horses to a halt at the foot of the steps that led to the wide oak door of the hall, Raine felt a momentary and unexpected twinge of regret. She was a bride entering her home for the first time. Yet unlike the visions she had always conjured of this event as a girl, she had no belongings of her own to lend her new abode an air of familiarity—no sense of hope for the future.

She had nothing but the chests of gowns she'd had made before they went to court, along with her jewels and a few personal items. All here belonged to Benedict and would be a constant reminder that this was not her home, but his.

The door above them opened and a woman came out to stand upon the step. She was a portly dame with rosy cheeks, which gave her a homey look, but her dark eyes were perceptive as she looked at them.

Benedict spoke deliberately. "That is Maeve. She is the head woman here at Brackenmoore." Raine had suspected as much from her manner.

Benedict went on, addressing the other woman now, and Raine was quite aware of the reluctance in his voice as he said, "Maeve, this is my wife, the lady Raine."

The woman's mouth dropped open. "Your wife, Lord Benedict?" Her amazement was more than obvious as she repeated, "Your wife?"

Raine heard equally well the weariness in her husband's tone as he replied, "Aye, my wife."

Anger prickled anew and she cast him a narrowed glance. All the while her assurances that she would not shame him were uppermost in her mind. He would see that she did not go back on her word.

Feeling the great weight of his gaze, Raine raised her head high and went forward. The head woman came down the steps, saying, "My lady, you do not know how welcome this news is to me and will be to all here. We have long felt that Lord Benedict should take a wife, though none would have expected him to be capable of accomplishing such a feat during a journey of less than two weeks. Lord Benedict has never made such a decision in haste, and I am given to think he must have taken quite a fancy to you."

This servant was not one to mince words. Though she was not correct in her assessment that Benedict had taken a fancy to her, Maeve's freedom of speaking told that she held a position of some honor at Brackenmoore. Raine was also beginning to realize that Benedict's marrying her was very much out of character for him. What that might mean to her, she was not yet certain. What she did know was that Maeve's approval or disapproval could mean much until she was able to return home to Abbernathy.

Yet Raine was not prepared to be deliberately tactful. It was not her way. She nodded to the woman, being equally direct. "I have no doubt of your surprise. I was somewhat taken aback myself at the speed of our conjoining, though I was not sorry for it. I was most eager to wed your master with all haste." That much Raine could say with honesty. That she had changed her mind directly afterward she would keep to her own council. She watched as the servant's brows rose when she added, "Beyond that I will say nothing. Should you wish to know more of the situation you must ask my husband."

Raine was in no small measure surprised when the woman's lips curved into a wide grin. "It looks as though haste does not necessarily make for poor judgment. If I may say so, my lady, your honesty does you credit. Now we'll see if this boy has met his match."

Raine could say nothing in response to this overfamiliar statement. She did not even dare glance at Benedict to see what he had made of it. The fact that anyone would call the commanding man behind her a boy was utterly remarkable to Raine. That any servant, no matter how familiar, would go so far as to speak so humorously of the arrogant Benedict Ainsworth's having met his match was completely incomprehensible to her.

Well, how Benedict chose to reply was Maeve's own concern, as she had said. The head woman clearly held the blackguard in fond esteem. Raine did not. Benedict Ainsworth might indeed have met his match, but not in any romantic sense that had been implied by the servant's words. He simply had found a woman who would not readily dance to his tune, as he seemed to think she should.

Glancing at him, Raine saw that Benedict was no more pleased by this conversation than she, for he said, "That will be enough, Maeve. Shall we go inside? My wife and her brother are surely tired and we must see them settled in."

Maeve's unconcerned gaze swept the courtyard behind them, coming to rest upon William with surprising accuracy. The uncertainty in her brother's gaze as he peered about made Raine's heart ache for him. She had not thought he would be so nervous on arriving after his ease on the journey. Seeing his reaction, she was resolved anew to get them both home to Abbernathy as soon as she could.

Maeve had also seen William's reticence and acted from what was obviously a compassionate heart. "Welcome, lad." When he hesitated, she went on. "We've always had young men in this house and gladly so." Raine felt gratitude, for the woman's kindness warmed her instantly.

She blinked to clear the sheen of tears that stung her eyes. She did love William so and wanted his happiness and safety above all. Else why would she even be here, wed to a man she barely knew?

A light touch along her back made her start, for the tingling of awareness that accompanied it told her very clearly that it was Benedict. She swung to face him, leaning away as she saw the sympathy in his gaze. She did not require his comfort, and it was her reaction to that rather than his touch that disturbed her so.

Clearly Benedict saw her startled response and did not care for it, if the scowl that passed over his darkly handsome face was any indication. Yet he overcame his consternation quickly, for he shrugged and turned away, untroubled once more. Raine refused to consider why his doing so left her feeling suddenly and unexpectedly bereft.

She followed as her husband led the way into the keep without another word. His easy dismissal showed that he was quite indifferent to her. That moment of compassion could have been only for the benefit of Maeve or anyone who might have been watching them. He did not wish others to know that their marriage was simply a charade.

Raine meant to make it clear that touching her would not be a part of their truce.

Behind them she could hear Maeve talking softly to William for another moment, before she came forward to say something to Benedict, who was now at the top of the steps and motioned them to follow. As they stepped into the hall with its high stone ceiling, Raine halted and waited for her brother. Better to concentrate on him than the maddening devil she had wed.

William seemed much more at ease as she took his arm. "We are arrived," Raine said, leaning close to him.

He squeezed her hand as if offering comfort to her rather than taking it as she had intended. He whispered softly, "You will see all will be well, Raine. Benedict is a kind man and the others here seem so, too."

Raine realized suddenly that his nervousness had been for her sake. She could not help a quick glance in her husband's direction. His kindness was not in question. What troubled her was that he was obviously too accustomed to others doing his bidding. He seemed blind to the fact that he did not have the right to command her.

She was grateful when Benedict addressed Maeve. "Have you a room for William?"

Maeve replied quickly. "Aye, my lord, if the lad does not mind sharing a chamber with your brother."

William looked to Benedict, his eyes bright with both excitement and anxiety as he asked, "Will Kendran mind?" Raine realized that, for Will's nervous anticipation to be warranted, Benedict must have told the boy a great deal more about his youngest brother than the mention he had made of how he loved to hunt and eat.

Benedict smiled. "He will not mind."

Maeve added, "That one is off on business of his own this evening, and he'll be more than sorry that he was not here to welcome you and your sister. I have a feeling he will be glad that he's no longer the youngest lordling about the keep."

William's pleasure at her words was very obvious. Raine felt slightly uncomfortable with his reaction, but had no opportunity to ask herself why this was so. Her own accommodations had not been settled. She was quite aware of the anxiousness of her tone as she spoke, but could not disguise it. "I will require a chamber as well."

Maeve looked to Benedict. "I had assumed—"

He interrupted coolly, "My wife will require her own chamber."

Maeve scowled, studying them both closely, seeming disconcerted by this revelation. Yet all she said was, "With Lord Tristan, Lady Lily, Sabina and Lady Genevieve away at Molson, their rooms are vacant at the moment and clean. I believe Lady Genevieve's would likely be the most comfortable for your lady wife, as Sabina's chamber is quite cluttered even with her gone.''

Benedict nodded and shrugged, clearly glad to have this problem out of the way. ''Fine, then.''

Raine could not even look at him, for she was more irritated by the lack of feeling in his tone than she cared to admit. Conversely, she did not want him to thwart her in this. Sharing a chamber with him was unthinkable. She focused on the head woman. ''Would you mind if we went up now? I am very tired. It has been a long journey.'' Raine was aware of the exhaustion in her own voice.

Maeve nodded with concern and respect, clearly knowing her place when it was required. ''Yes, my lady. If you would please follow me.''

Relieved, Raine started after her, but they were halted by Benedict's voice. ''I will tell one of the other servants to begin heating water and have the copper bathing tub brought up to Genevieve's room.''

Raine felt surprise and appreciation at his unexpected thoughtfulness. Yet she was reluctant to acknowledge the gesture, for her gratitude made her feel even more exposed and unsettled at being at Brackenmoore where he was lord and master of all. Yet she must try. She turned and smiled with forced brilliance. ''I thank you, my lord. It is most gracious of you to think of me.'' Quickly she swung away, hiding her uncertainty behind a proudly tilted head.

Chapter Six

With a frown of consternation, Benedict watched his wife go to the far end of the hall. Every muscle in his body ached from keeping himself in check. What a time he'd had holding back just now when she'd insisted upon having her own room. But when he'd heard the exhaustion in her voice, he'd felt moved to offer some solace, however slight. The bath had come to mind.

She had said thank you prettily enough, but there was no genuine warmth in that flashing white smile. And that arrogant stance! How dare she respond to his gesture thusly? There was no giving in with Raine.

Damn her. And to think he had even felt somewhat guilty for having informed her she must behave properly after she had conducted herself so well. That was until she had made their estrangement known to all, which was what she had surely done by requesting her own room.

What had he done to himself in marrying this woman? She was as contrary as any female could be and still be so pleasing to the eye. And there was no denying she was. Even when she was glaring at him in resentment, which was most of the time, her golden eyes held the power to bewitch him.

Suppressed frustration and anger ate at his belly. He wanted to think on anything save Raine, and must surely find something else to occupy his mind. Yet he first did as he had told her he would and ordered that hot water and the tub be taken to Genevieve's chamber. As he did so he felt a stab of regret that Genevieve and Lily were gone. The other women's company might have helped his wife to settle in.

Genevieve had gone with Tristan and Lily. She'd said she was doing so because she did not wish to be away from Sabina for three months, but Benedict was suspicious that her need to be away had more to do with Marcel's departure on the *Briar Wind* some weeks ago. Benedict would respect her desire to remain silent on the subject.

He now had his own share of misfortune and torment in the shape of one Raine Blanchett. An undeniably pleasing shape though it might be, it was no less troublesome.

He went to see if his steward had left anything of immediate import for his attention in the library. The worthy fellow need not be summoned until morning.

Benedict was aware of the fact that he had pushed too hard this day. He had done so only because he did not wish to spend another night on the road with Raine. He had not been unaware of the lingering and speculative gazes of his men as he'd bedded down around the fire with them, while his new wife shared the tent with her maid.

Unfortunately, it seemed he would fare little better here at Brackenmoore. Comfortable though his bed might be, it would likely offer no surcease from the thoughts of Raine that had kept him awake each night. Well, she may have demanded her own chamber, but he would not let that stop him when the time came to bed her.

Benedict was not pleased to see that nothing awaited his attention in the library. The table was, in fact, exactly as he had left it, the books and ledgers piled in the particular order he preferred.

He sat in the heavy carved chair behind the worktable and sighed. It had been his father's chair, and in it he felt some link to that beloved man's wisdom, drew on it to make the best decisions for Brackenmoore. Yet today he felt nothing but turmoil in spite of the fact that nothing pressing awaited his attention. He should be glad that all had gone smoothly in his absence, not a common occurrence to say the least. Surely he should simply offer up a prayer of thanks and seek his rest.

But something would not let him. He could not stop thinking about his wife, the vixen, and the fact that she had let it be known to Maeve that she did not mean to be a true wife to him. What manner of woman was she to deny him before a member of his own household? 'Twas bad enough that she would do so in private. The more he thought on the matter, the more disturbed Benedict became.

He could allow his wife to know him better before consummating their union, though he had to admit he would have preferred otherwise. He was, after all, a man. And Raine was without question a beautiful woman. He could not help recalling with disturbing clarity what had happened in her tent. It had been all he could do to reign in his astonishingly potent desire.

Quickly he suppressed this thought. He had controlled it. He was not obligated to control or suppress his pride and dignity. Raine could not shame him before his folk, so haughtily deny him his God-given right as her husband. He was not just himself, Benedict. He was Brackenmoore, and as such was due consideration and respect. To allow anyone to treat him otherwise was to dishonor his own birthright.

And by the true cross, he would not allow it.

He stood and strode across the library, pulled open the heavy oak door. With grim determination he made his way to Genevieve's chamber. All the frustration of the past days boiled up inside him as he grasped the handle and jerked the portal open. The sight that met his eyes when he swung the door wide made him pause as a rush of heat that had nothing to do with anger rose up in his lower belly.

His gaze seemed riveted on Raine, who stood beside the huge copper tub in a heavy green velvet robe, one long, creamy leg draped over the side so that her toes were touching the water. For some reason completely unknown to him, Benedict's gaze focused on those delicate toes, which were small and pleasingly formed. He felt a strange and startling sense of intimacy and an intensification of the heat inside him. He wondered what it would be like to kiss the toes, to run his tongue along them, then on across the bottom of her foot. His stomach tightened again.

Never would he have imagined that he would react so strongly to the sight of any woman's toes. That he would even think of caressing them. What had she done to him, this strange mixture of siren and woman?

With a great force of will he closed his eyes. When he opened them there she was still there, and in no measure less lovely to his sight. Benedict swallowed past the tightness in his throat. So much for thinking he had his responses to her completely under control.

Taking a deep breath he realized that all of this had passed through his mind in the blink of an eye. Before he could make a move to apologize, or leave, or do anything else, for that matter, Raine swung around. With a gasp she pulled her leg back, wrapping the robe closely about her so that not a hint of that creamy skin was exposed. She rounded on him, her golden eyes dark with fury. "Why have you come here, my lord?"

Benedict felt a rising ire within himself. He welcomed it for it covered some of the desire he was feeling. He walked toward her. "And why should I not come here, Wife?"

Her gaze widened and he saw a flicker of anxiety in her gaze before she quickly masked it. She answered him coldly. "I felt I had made myself clear on that, my lord."

He pushed his anger down, replying with a forced calm. "You have indeed, madam. *I* have not made myself clear."

Raine raised her chin, half turning away, and he found himself mesmerized by the sweet curve of her jaw and cheek, the long line of her neck, all of which lay exposed to his hungry gaze, as the wild tangle of her fiery hair had been piled atop her head. Her words brought him back. "And what more can there be to say?"

He moved toward her again and once more glimpsed her otherwise well-disguised uncertainty in the quivering of her delicate nostrils. Benedict hesitated.

On some level he knew it was wrong to plague her so. He was unaccustomed to deliberately baiting women, but she had pushed him further than anyone else had ever dared.

He took a deliberate step toward her. "I will not allow you to insult me. Perhaps I have been lax in making my position as your husband clear."

Her wide gaze focused on his with horror. "What do you imply, my lord, after I have said I will not have you?"

He ran an assessing eye over her, realizing just what she had taken him to mean. God, but the very thought of what she intimated made his blood heat anew. She was his wife. He could not stop the words that came from his mouth, heard the huskiness in his own voice. "Just what do you imagine me to imply?"

Their gazes locked and held for one long moment in which Benedict knew that the desire he felt for her lay bared and vulnerable. Finally Raine took a deep breath and looked away, her breasts rising and falling with a sudden quickening of her breathing. When she looked at him, her anxiety had been replaced by an expression that he was reluctant to name—reluctant because he feared his own desire was what made him see it.

Even as he watched, Raine's tongue flicked out to trace her lips. The gesture made him think of what it would be like to touch the tip of his own tongue to them. His body responded in kind. Her gaze darkened as if in reaction to his growing desire. Her breath seemed to come more quickly.

Benedict felt a strange sense of unreality. Though he was sure of his ability to make her want him should he try, especially after what had occurred in her tent, he had not touched her now. Surely he was mistaken in his interpretation of her reactions.

He grimaced, not certain what was real and what was

not. Benedict now wished that he had not come here, that he had not felt this need to explain his position to his wife, for he was no longer as clear on what exactly it might be himself. He spoke more harshly than he had intended. "You are not the only one who can make demands, Raine."

His words and manner brought a response of bravado. Raine's gaze narrowed as her hands went to her gently rounded hips. "What could you possibly say to me that has any merit in this situation?"

Benedict's brows rose with irritation. The woman, no matter how beautiful and desirable, was contrary and obstinate beyond reason. He would not have her know how greatly she affected him. "I would say that you have no right to make demands upon my dignity. It is you who wanted this marriage. It is you who have taken it upon yourself to decide it will be no true marriage because of your own childish whim. You will never again before my folk make a request that countermands my position as not only lord of Brackenmoore but also as your husband."

She sputtered, her robe parting to expose the length of one long slender leg as she took a step toward him. "I did no such—"

He interrupted her, keeping his tone as cool as possible, for he had no wish to allow her to see that she had riled him, that she had made him want her still in spite of his anger. For that was exactly what she had done, bringing him to an achingly painful point of desire and frustration. "You did so when you told Maeve that you would have need of your own chamber. 'Tis an odd request for a newly wed bride."

She had the grace to blush, but did not waver as she

replied, "You know I will not share a chamber with you."

He shrugged and spoke with forced calm, although the words made his frustration even more acute. "It was my place to tell Maeve that. Not yours."

She moved toward him again, her slender form stiff with outrage. "And would you have done so?"

Benedict drew in a quick breath. In an instant she had gotten to the heart of it. For from the way he was feeling now he was not at all sure of what his actions would have been.

Would he indeed have requested separate chambers had she not forced his hand? His unwitting gaze found the neck of her robe where it had fallen open to expose the curve of her breasts.

Would he indeed?

Realizing the path of her husband's gaze, Raine looked down and gasped. Hurriedly she reached to cover herself, turning her back to him, realizing as she did so that her heartbeat had quickened. She felt him come up behind her, heard his answer with a sense of unreality. "Perhaps I would not have instructed her to give you your own chamber, Raine." His hand touched her shoulder and she found herself turning to face him without realizing she was going to do so. "And perhaps you do not wish for me to do so as much as you would have me believe."

His deep blue gaze was scorching and caused an unexpected feeling of heat within her, just as she had felt only minutes before when he looked at her. It had been with great relief that Raine heard him accuse her of making demands. It had helped her to draw the shattered edges of her composure around herself, to control the confusing and unsettling feelings that had awakened inside her.

Yet now, with his breath hot on her exposed nape, she found herself again falling into that swirling pool of unfamiliar emotion. She wanted to deny what he said, while some other less known part of her held that denial at bay.

Since that night in her tent she had been fighting these feelings, trying to convince herself that they did not exist. But now, with his dark gaze upon her and her own blood beginning to pulse in her veins, she knew she had only been attempting to fool herself. The reactions she felt toward Benedict Ainsworth were more real than anything she had ever experienced in her life.

When he bent his head to kiss her she had no wish nor will to stop him. As his mouth closed on hers, his lips firm and warm, her hands rose to clasp his nape. His lips seemed to become fuller, more pliant, urging a response from her that she was unable to deny. When his warm tongue prodded she opened to him instantly, found herself melting, her blood turned to warmed wine as it flicked over her own.

Hesitantly she ran her own tongue over his, gasping with surprise and pleasure when he suckled it gently. A warm heaviness grew in her belly and she pressed herself more fully against him.

Benedict groaned and held her even more tightly, his hands tracing the curve of her back. They stopped at her hips, pulling that most intimate part of herself into close contact with the startling but compelling hardness of him.

Her own instantaneous reaction to that hardness and all it implied only served to pull her further down into the morass of sensation. Her stomach quivered and her knees felt as if they would not hold her. Benedict seemed to sense this for he lifted her against him, supporting her with one arm while he placed his other hand on the back of her head, holding her there as he kissed her. His tongue urged hers in a hot dance with his, and she complied, kissing him back until her head spun and she gasped for breath.

He drew back slightly, his gaze meeting hers, hot and questioning. She could not look away, knowing what he asked. She could not speak, only closed her eyes and leaned against him.

He groaned, lifting her face to his. His lips slanted across hers as his hand found the opening of her robe, and her heart nearly stopped as that large warm hand found the upper curve of her breast. When it dipped lower to cup the intimate weight that no man had ever even seen, let alone touched, Raine felt as if she could not breathe. She gasped, her heart pounding as her body called out for something she could not name. "Benedict, I want…oh, I know not…"

He traced the line of her body, leaving a trail of heat where his fingers touched her flesh. His compelling blue eyes were dark with longing. "Yes, Raine, let go. Let me take care of you."

She stopped still, her head spinning from his caresses as she tried to recover her equilibrium. She leaned her forehead against the hardness of his chest, trying desperately to slow her breathing, put order to her thoughts. Was that why he was kissing her, touching her—because he wanted to take care of her?

Folding her hands over her chest protectively, Raine took a deep breath and leaned back in the circle of his arms. "Nay, I do not want you to take care of me. Please, stop this." She had tried to tell him why she did not need or want that. She could not rely on anyone so much.

Desperately she shook her head, as his questioning and passion-glazed eyes met hers. "Why, Raine?"

"I cannot allow you to take care of me. I must rely upon myself. There is no other way to avoid being disappointed." His arms loosened and she stepped out of them, wiping her hair from her face with unsteady hands.

He reached for her again, but she evaded him, though she was unable to look away from those blue eyes as he said with utter certainty, "I can be depended upon."

Raine could not doubt his confidence. But she did not wish to depend upon him. As a child, she had depended upon her father, and he had failed her when she needed him most. Her father had depended upon and loved her mother with all his heart and she had died, though from no fault of her own. Raine put her hand over her breast. "You say that, but you do not know. When there is love or need one becomes vulnerable. I cannot allow myself such a weakness."

His face registered surprise and displeasure. "Do not think of such things as weakness, Raine. You are a woman and need not expect so much of yourself. I can be trusted to care for you and William."

She felt his words stab into her. He felt that love and need were fine for her, fine because she was a woman. It was equally clear that he did not feel that he, as a man, could afford such softer emotions.

For reasons she dared not try to explain to him, this knowledge hurt. She realized she could not allow him to make love to her when he felt this way.

"You must go." She was not unaware of the fearful quaver in her voice.

He looked at her for a very long moment, his expression unreadable, then spoke with utter conviction. "I will leave you now, but know this. The time is coming when I will have what is mine. And you will not wish to stop me." He turned on his heel and left her.

Raine did not sleep until the first rays of day were beginning to light the chamber, though the huge, richly hung bed could not be described as anything but comfortable. All she could think about was what they had done, she and Benedict, the things they had said. The way she had felt as he held her in his arms and kissed her, touched her.

Even the angry exchange that had followed failed to wash it from her mind. When she woke her first thought was of Benedict and what he must think of her. A hot flush raced through her from head to toe. Her previous assertions that she did not want him seemed very foolish now.

His parting words rang in her mind like a dirge. The fact that they were likely true only made things worse.

God rot him! Each time he touched her it became more difficult to convince herself that she did not want him.

With a groan of frustration she threw back the coverlet. Raine would not allow herself to languish here the whole day thinking of that insufferable man. He might be able to command her physical presence. He could not control her thoughts or her feelings.

She opened one of the trunks that had been brought to her chambers the previous night. She paused then as a soft and hesitant knocking sounded at the door. Could Benedict have decided to pay her another unannounced visit? Her stomach churned with both anxiety and an anticipation that made her want to thrash herself. Her brows knitting even as her heart thudded, Raine swung around and watched as the portal opened slowly.

An audible sigh of relief escaped her when she saw Aida peek around at her. Immediately Raine knew she had been foolish to wonder if it were her husband. He would never be so hesitant.

The maid's gaze quickly scanned the room, then came back to Raine. "You are alone, my lady?"

Raine replied with a trace of impatience, "Of course. Where is William?"

"He has eaten and gone off with your husband, my lady. Lord Benedict told us not to disturb you."

Had he now? Being of no mind to even discuss the matter, she beckoned. "Please come and help me dress."

The maid was just arranging her hair into two coiled braids when they were interrupted by a scraping at the door. This time Raine did not even consider that it might be Benedict. Well, not for more than the briefest moment as she called out, "Come."

The head woman, Maeve, entered with a large tray. She bowed respectfully. "My lady."

Raine nodded politely. "Good morrow."

The woman's gaze was assessing as she said, "One of the servants told me they heard movement from inside your chamber. I was but awaiting your rising to bring you this." She set down the laden tray, then went on. "After you have broken your fast, my lord Benedict has requested that I show you about the keep."

Raine was surprised at the stab of displeasure she felt at this. The blackguard could not even bother with his own newly wed wife. Immediately she reminded herself that she had not led him to believe he would be welcomed by her. It served neither of them for her to be unjust.

Squaring her shoulders, Raine faced the too perceptive maid with a fixed and purposely amiable smile. She would not allow anyone to know how very much that insufferable man was able to vex her. The fact that he could do so without even trying only made matters worse. She nodded to the head woman. "I would appreciate your showing me about and am nearly ready. I would not keep you, though, if you have other duties."

Maeve bowed. "I would gladly await you, my lady."

There was nothing Raine could say but, "As you will."

Maeve glanced about the chamber. "You have found these accommodations comfortable?"

Raine nodded, hoping that the servant did not intend to question her about requiring her own chambers. "Quite so."

The head woman only smiled. "I thought they would be more to your liking than Sabina's, which are not as large."

Suddenly Raine was curious about Benedict's family. She knew of Lily and Tristan after overhearing Benedict's conversation with King Edward. The others remained a mystery. "Tell me of my husband's family."

Maeve's smile widened. "My lord Benedict has three brothers, Tristan, Marcel..." a brief shadow passed over her face, but Raine had little opportunity to wonder about it "...and Kendran, who was most surprised and pleased to learn of Benedict's marriage when he went to his chamber and found William there."

"He did not mind taking him in?" Raine interjected.

A hearty laugh escaped the older woman. "Nay, he did not. Benedict and the boy were both waiting there for him when he came back from, well..." She frowned with both disapproval and indulgence. "That one has far too fine a face, along with too heavy a measure of charm. But we shall not discuss that. In any event, when they told Kendran the news, Lord Benedict said he lifted the boy up in the air and hugged him, shouting that he was no longer the youngest Ainsworth male."

Raine heard the references to Kendran's charm with a grimace. Someone in the family should definitely possess such a quality. But as the woman finished she stiffened briefly. William was not an Ainsworth. But she said nothing. She must be grateful that William would be treated well until they were able to go home. Which Raine could only hope would be soon, for the sake of her autonomy.

She decided to change the subject. "Your lady Genevieve, will she be away for some time?"

If Maeve felt this abruptness odd, she made no sign. "Aye, Lady Genevieve has gone with Lord Tristan and Lady Lily to his lodge, Molson. They will visit her family, who live nearby. Lady Genevieve did not wish to be without the child and went with them. Since Lord Marcel went away she has been..." She fell silent.

Raine realized that there were things going on here that she did not understand.

Aida, who had been listening along with Raine, kept casting anxious glances at the head woman. Maeve finally looked over at her and smiled. "Have you eaten yet?"

Aida shook her head and Maeve smiled again. "Go down to the kitchen when you have a moment. Cook is baking some lovely pasties."

Again such kindness. Raine did not know how she felt about this. She was no less determined to go home, but was at the same time grateful that their stay here, however unwilling, would not be complete torment. And she was determined to go home. She would not fall beneath the control of Benedict Ainsworth no matter how his kisses made her feel.

As soon as Aida finished the last touches to her hair, Raine patted her hand and said, "Go on now and eat."

As the maid left the chamber, Raine moved to the table. She would eat some of the food Maeve had brought to her in spite of the unrest that rolled in her belly. She would go on as if all was well. Yet the food tasted as she imagined sawdust might. Raine was not unaware of the head woman's attention as she dropped the fresh bread back onto the tray after taking only a few small bites.

She turned to Maeve with a regally raised head. Devil take them all. "I am ready to go now."

Maeve made no comment, preceding her to the door and holding it open with polite deference.

As they moved down the long corridor, Maeve pointed out the doors along the hall and their usual occupants. Because she had no personal knowledge of who was being spoken of Raine could not have recalled which door lead to whose chamber until they came to the last in the row and she heard her husband's name. Raine could not help looking at that portal with some misgiving. She was again conscious of the woman's attention, but ignored it.

All the time they spent in the keep Raine was infinitely conscious of the fact that this was Benedict's environment. He was lord here, and every man, woman and child owed their complete allegiance to him. If their contented expressions were any indication, they gave it gladly. She was also aware of the curiosity that was directed toward herself as the head woman bowed and indicated that she was the new lady of the keep. Judging by their faces, none seemed astonished by the pronouncement. Raine was not surprised, knowing how quickly such news as this circulates a keep. Yet she wondered if they found it odd that Benedict was not the one to introduce her.

It was not until they were outside the keep and exploring the grounds that she was finally able to relax somewhat. Benedict might indeed possess every brick and chair inside the keep. He did not own the air, nor the bright spring sunshine that streamed down from a cloudless blue sky. Nor did he own the song of the white gulls that circled overhead.

The two women toured the kitchens, the buttery, the storerooms, the laundry. Raine could not help seeing that all was in perfect order, that the inhabitants applied themselves diligently to their work with happy chatter, which only ceased when she and Maeve came near.

Although she was of no mind to think well of Benedict, she noted that his folk were contented and healthy. Their eyes and skin were clear, their garments clean and in good repair.

The best thing about the time she and Maeve spent exploring the castle and grounds was that they had not once caught even the slightest glimpse of her husband. Perhaps, Raine thought with a sense of hope, he was not even about the keep. When Maeve asked if she was tiring, Raine replied with honesty, "Nay, not in the least. If there is more to see then let us go forth."

Maeve nodded with what appeared to be approval, and for some reason this made Raine feel less uncomfortable. Though the woman was a servant, Raine was not unmoved by her acceptance.

They went on. At last they arrived at the stables, which they moved through slowly. Raine was impressed with the quality of horseflesh she found there. William was a great one for horses. It was an interest she indulged wholeheartedly, as he had inherited that love and his wily ways with the creatures from their father.

As they exited the far end of the stables, Raine realized that they had come out on the edge of a wide, open field. That its purpose was that of arms practice was evidenced by various implements of battle. A list ran along the far end, arrow butts were arranged at the near end and a well-trampled patch in the center told the tale of regular arms practice.

Yet it was not the purpose of the field that gave her pause. There, not more than fifty feet from them, were Benedict and her brother. It was not their presence but what they were about that made her stop and stare in surprise and concern. Benedict was engaged in teaching her brother the use of the sword.

Even as she watched he pointed to the short sword her brother held, saying, "See here, William. Like this." He made a slicing motion in the air with his own weapon.

She watched as her brother imitated him.

Benedict nodded. "Now come for me."

William raised his weapon and moved forward, but only halfheartedly.

Benedict shook his head. "Nay, I mean in earnest. Hold nothing back."

William ran at him again, this time much more fiercely, his sword clanging against Benedict's hastily raised weapon.

Again Benedict halted him. "Nay, William. Forget

that I am your brother. Imagine that I am come to Abbernathy, that I wish to take all that you hold dear."

William looked at him, understanding lighting his face with grave determination.

A deep voice called out with undisguised amusement, "Go on then, Will. You cannot hurt Benedict."

Raine glanced toward the sound to see a tall young man leaning against an arrow butt, his own sword hanging loosely in his hand. By the thatch of raven hair that covered his head she could only surmise that this must be Benedict's brother Kendran.

She had no real interest in him at the moment, as her gaze went back to her brother and her husband. It was not Benedict that she was concerned for, but William. The man was so large, so powerful. One quick thrust of that gleaming sword could easily cleave her brother in twain.

Yet Raine stood rooted to the spot, unable to give voice to the fear that made her stomach tighten and closed off her throat. This all happened so quickly that only as William charged at her husband with what seemed truly murderous intent did she cry out, "No!"

The sound was lost in the clang of sword against sword. She was even further appalled when Benedict stepped back from the charge with a shout of, "Well done!"

She cried out. "William!"

Her brother swung around with a grin of sheer glee on his young face. "Did you see that, Raine? Did you see the way I went after Benedict?"

His grin faded as she replied with displeasure, "I most certainly did." She pointed to the sword he held as if it were a poisonous snake. "Put that thing down and come with me this instant."

Benedict's incredulous voice asked, "What is—"

Raine swung around to face her husband, interrupting before he could finish. "What were you thinking to put him in danger this way?"

His too blue eyes widened. "In danger?"

William ran over to stand before her, his face grown bright pink with embarrassment and annoyance. "What is the matter, Raine? I was in no danger. He is teaching me."

She dismissed this with a wave of her hand. "He had no right to do so without my consent."

William stuck out a stubborn chin. "I asked him myself. Kendran was practicing and I begged him to let me join in. It was Benedict who said I could not and that I must do so with him first so he might see what I knew."

Another male voice interjected, "No harm will be done to William here." She saw that her husband's brother had approached, his blue eyes slightly angry but more surprised as they met hers. "If there was any danger to anyone it was Benedict. He would let the boy run him through before he would land a blow upon him. He was the same with myself and my brothers. He still bears the scar I inflicted upon his chest. I am also sure that Tristan and Marcel have left their share. There is no man who would be more gentle and careful of your brother than your own husband, which I am sure you will see when he is more known to you." Raine felt the weight of Maeve's agreement, though the head woman said nothing.

The reminder that she had indeed jumped so quickly to judge her own husband so harshly was painful. Especially when it appeared that she had done so wrongly.

It was not in Raine's nature to behave thusly. She felt

even more frustrated at realizing she had allowed her own guilty feelings about what had occurred the previous night between herself and Benedict to affect her judgment.

Though she did not look at him, Raine was aware when Benedict came close to her. Every fiber of her being felt him there, just out of reach. Each and every inch of the skin he had touched cried out in longing even as her mind tried to take control, to deny her reactions.

When he spoke, his tone was far too controlled. "Why must you persist in naming me the villain at every turn?"

For far too long she was unable to find her voice, wishing with all her might that she could deny this. She could not. Her frowning gaze met her husband's.

Without another word, Benedict reached out and grasped her arm. Crying out in surprise, Raine was forced to follow him, nearly having to run in order to keep up with his long strides. She was aware of the attention of all they passed, yet no one dared meet her deliberately challenging gaze.

He did not pause until he had reached her chamber. There he dragged her inside and slammed the door before releasing her. He spoke through tight lips. "If you refuse to be polite you may keep yourself in the chamber you were so anxious to call your own."

Raine rounded on him in outrage. "How dare you give such an order? And after dragging me through the keep? I will not be made a laughingstock before your folk."

He came toward her then, his eyes hard as granite as he backed her toward the bed. "*You* will not be made a laughingstock? If I did not understand that your prickly nature was your way of keeping yourself from caring about anyone besides your brother and Abbernathy, and because you do not wish for him to care about anything but you, I would throttle you before the whole keep. After your insult of refusing to sleep in my chamber last eve none would think me overharsh in doing so, either."

She gasped again, not sure which of the things he had said horrified her most. "My insult to you!" Rage flowed through her, even as she knew a deep anguish and longing for her own home, for she knew what he said was true. None here would defend her no matter what he did. Somehow, someway she must get away from him, from this place.

If he wanted her to bed with him, so be it. Perhaps then he would set her free. Desperately she threw herself backward upon the bed, her gaze boring into his. "Take me now and have done with it. But know that with my innocence I buy my freedom."

Benedict stared at her in utter amazement for a long moment, before his gaze narrowed in some expression she could not begin to read. But then her breathing sharpened as he came close, leaning over her.

Before she knew what he was going to do, he reached out and clasped her hands, raising them to hold them securely above her head. His gaze never left hers as he watched her. Then those unreadable blue eyes slid down from her face, grazing the line of her body.

Raine was shocked at the rush of heat she felt, and she closed her eyes to hide it.

His breath was hot on her cheek as he bent over her, nuzzling her. The thrill that coursed through her delayed her full understanding of what he whispered next. "Tempting though the offer may be, my lady wife, I do not care for the terms. I will await a more palatable proposition.''

By the time Raine had fully realized what he had said, he was gone. With a cry of rage, she leapt from the bed, though her anger might well have been caused more by the erratic pounding of her own heart than anything Benedict had said.

Chapter Seven

After asking one of the women who were taking down the trestle tables to bring him something to eat, Benedict took his place at table in the great hall in solitude and silence. He was in no mood to talk. What had happened on the practice field several days gone by and then afterward had made him realize that Raine would do anything to be away from Brackenmoore. That her offer had been far more tempting than he cared to admit would remain his secret. Benedict wanted her, desperately. He did not want her to ever imagine that she had given herself as some sacrifice for her freedom, which he would never agree to.

A painful ache settled in his chest. He told himself that it was because of Brackenmoore, because he now knew that she would never be able to release her past life and accept the new. He had been mad to marry her, though his desire for her seemed to increase with each passing day in spite of her ill temper.

He sighed, wanting nothing so much as to be alone with his thoughts. Which was why he had come down to break his fast long after he thought the others would have gone. The meals he had taken here in the past few days had been fraught with tension, especially since Raine had taken his command to heart and remained in her chamber. Despite her absence, her presence was felt in the multitude of speculative glances that were directed at him, by William, Kendran and servants alike.

Yet it was only a short time later that he glanced up to see Raine enter the hall, looking far lovelier than any woman had a right to. In a pale green gown, with her hair falling over her shoulder in one heavy braid, she seemed as a maiden from tales of old. When her gaze came to rest upon him, she frowned with consternation.

He watched her shoulders square as she came forward. He forced a smile, not wanting her to know how unhappy he was, how little he slept each night with thoughts of her pressing on his mind. When he spoke, he was pleased at how unaffected he sounded. "Raine."

She nodded, her gaze not meeting his. "I am prepared to be polite but no more."

His tone belied his irony. "I suppose I must be grateful for that."

She ignored this, with a regally tilted nose, and he felt an unwilling admiration for her tremendous aplomb. She distracted him by glancing at the platter of food and asking, "May I?"

He nodded, suddenly realizing that she, too, had come at this late hour hoping to avoid a meeting with him. The knowledge prickled, but he said only, "Please do."

Seeming oblivious to Benedict now, she sat down on the opposite side of the table and took some of the bread and cheese. He studied her, while pretending not to.

If only her simple act of nibbling delicately at the cheese did not draw his gaze to those sweet pink lips. If only her lashes did not lie so full and dark against her cheeks as she carefully kept her gaze on her meal. So occupied was he in thinking these thoughts that it was some time before he realized that she was in actuality eating no more than he.

He was taken completely by surprise when she glanced up at him and said, "Kendran is very like you."

He shrugged, glad to have something besides her beauty and the fact that she was so contrary to think upon. "So it is said."

She looked up at him, her brows raised, her expression measuring. "I know very little of your family. I did, of course, know of Tristan, and Maeve has said that Marcel is away."

Benedict frowned, the ache of missing his brother ever fresh in his heart, even as he wondered why she was suddenly interested in his family. "Why do you mention, Raine?"

She shrugged, her glance grazing his briefly. "I grow weary of arguing with you at every turn. I thought we might have some common ground here. I love my brother. You love yours. And you have said that I must be pleasant if I am to leave my chamber. I grow tired of those same four walls. I did hope I might be alone when I came to the hall, but as you are here, I will do my utmost to abide by your wishes."

He was impressed with her honesty, as he had been from the start. "Do you always say what you think?"

She shrugged, her expression now guarded. "Not always. Shall we talk of your brother?" As she finished, Benedict saw out of the corner of his eye that Maeve had come to the doorway of the hall. She cast an approving look at the two of them before motioning for the rest of the servants to keep their distance.

Benedict knew she was aware of all that went on in

the keep, and made it her place to see that all went according to her wishes. Obviously she approved of this interaction with his wife. Not sure how he felt about this, Benedict answered Raine's question. "Aye, Marcel is away. I miss him greatly."

She nodded, her face suddenly bearing a solicitude he had not known in her before. "'Tis understandable. I do not know what I would do if I were separated from William. He is all I have." For some reason her sympathy moved him more than he would ever have thought possible, that and her sincere admission that William was all she had.

Almost without being aware that he would do so he found himself saying, "Marcel is troubled, though I have tried to spare him his discontent. The loss of our parents affected him greatly and he has never gotten over it. If he had his own lands, perhaps, more to occupy his mind…" Benedict sighed. "Marcel has fallen in love with…well, that is his own affair. Suffice it to say that he does not think the woman could care for him in return, as he feels he has nothing to give but himself."

She murmured, "Genevieve."

He looked at her closely. "How did you know?"

Raine shrugged, her gaze defensive. "I was not prying. It was something Maeve said about his leaving and Genevieve not wishing to be here. Why would he imagine that she would not want him?"

Benedict shook his head. "I was not accusing you, Raine." But he was surprised that she had noted anything around her considering her all-consuming desire to return to Abbernathy. Because of this he found himself telling her, "Marcel is a landless knight, Genevieve a great heiress. Holding her in such esteem as he does,

Marcel would offer her more, not believing that the only thing of value is himself. I...wish there were some way to bring them together, to make them see..." He paused. "I can only hope that Genevieve and Marcel's love for one another will help see them through."

On finishing, Benedict felt a strange sense of longing as he wondered what it would be like to be loved that way. Marcel had no notion of how fortunate he was to be free to give his whole self to another. Brackenmoore must ever be first in Benedict's heart and mind. Thus perhaps it was fortunate that he had wed a woman who would expect no more from him than he could give. Unfortunately, she had no wish to share his life.

He was shocked to hear these very words coming from his mouth. "You, who are my wife, desire nothing of what I would share with you—my life, my body."

She stiffened. "You know my feelings on this matter."

He caught and held her gaze. "Your continued refusal to be my wife is an affront. I see the way the castle folk watch. They have taken note of the fact that I never enter your chamber nor you mine, that you have not left your room for these two days. When Genevieve returns and must find other accommodation because her chamber is occupied, it will be even more obvious that you do not wish to be a proper wife to me."

Raine looked far from pleased at this. "At this moment there is more than sufficient room to house both myself and my brother at Abbernathy."

Benedict felt the twitching of the muscle behind his left eye and closed his eyelids. He would not react. Not to this jibe or any other. He opened his eyes and fixed her with an assessing gaze. "Your insistence on spouting such nonsense will change nothing. It is you who wished to be a wife, Raine. Now you do not care for the consequences.'' He paused, then went on, pleased at the indifference in his voice. ''There is more than sufficient space in my own chambers for you and you will end in occupying it.''

Her gaze widened with horror and he could not deny that the very depth of that horror was far from laudatory. ''Your reaction does you no credit, Wife. Your distaste is not so great as you would have me believe.''

A gasp of sheer outrage escaped the lips that had returned his kisses so very willingly. Those golden eyes were filled with both outrage and, yes, he was sure of it, chagrin, which he knew was a result of the accuracy of his statement.

To his disappointment she was saved from having to make a reply by the decidedly excited and cheerful voice of her brother as he raced up beside her. ''Raine, I went to your room but you were gone. I am glad to see that you are feeling better. It must have been quite dreadful to be plagued by headache so soon after your arrival.''

Benedict saw the way she kept her head carefully averted as the boy talked. Obviously she had told him this story to explain her staying in her chamber because she did not want him to know the truth. As ever, Benedict was moved by her protectiveness toward William. She could have attempted to alienate him from Benedict by telling him of their disagreement. She had not done so. As always her solicitude toward him outweighed her own concerns.

But as William went on, Benedict turned his attention back to the boy. ''I was hoping to find you,'' he was saying. ''Kendran has asked me to go riding with him this morn. He says that we might ride along the beach if I like.''

Happy to have something, anything to think on besides the black-hearted knave near her, Raine turned to face her brother. "Along the beach?"

But she continued to be aware of the maddening Benedict where he sat on the other side of the table. How had she actually been deranged enough for even those few brief moments to feel sympathy for him, to think that he was a special man to care so much for his brothers?

She forced herself to pay close attention to William as he nodded, his eyes bright. "Aye, the beach, Raine. Brackenmoore lies close to the sea." He pointed off haphazardly. "You are able to see it from the battlements."

She nodded, realizing that was one of the few places she had not gone on her tour with Maeve. She recalled how salty the air had seemed as they first approached Brackenmoore. Now she understood why.

She cast a glance toward Benedict. He had not told her his home lay so near the sea and she had been too preoccupied with her own unhappiness to take note of the direction they were traveling in. Of course, she had given Benedict no real opportunity to tell her of Brackenmoore, had he felt such a desire. Which she was sure he did not.

Benedict wanted her at Brackenmoore because she was his wife, his possession, as was everything else he held. He cared nothing for her as a woman. Even his desire for her to share his chambers stemmed from his need to keep others from knowing of their estrangement.

Raine did not care for the strange wave of disappointment she felt at this knowledge. All she wanted was to go home. That she had gone so far as to offer her innocence to secure that end was now horrifying to her. But she had felt such desperation in that moment...

She realized that William was speaking again. "Since you are feeling better, why do you not come with us, Raine? You have never seen the sea, either."

It was true she had never been to the sea and felt a certain amount of curiosity about viewing a body of water so vast. She found herself nodding. "Aye, I will accompany you and Kendran."

Will smiled at the older boy, who stood nearby. "You see, I told you she would not tell me nay. Raine does not try to coddle me."

Raine frowned as her gaze went to Kendran. Obviously they had had some discussion concerning this matter. She felt resentful at being talked of thusly, yet after her actions the first day on the practice field she should not be terribly surprised. Kendran knew nothing of her, and if he was anything like his brother would certainly judge her harshly.

Quickly she told herself that it mattered not in the least what he thought of her. She and William would not be staying. Raine looked at Will. He seemed quite full of enthusiasm about her husband's brother already, and she held much respect for William's judgment as far as people were concerned. That being the case, she realized she should try not to hold her resentment of Benedict against Kendran.

Then, to her utter consternation, she watched as William turned to her husband and said, "You must come too, Benedict, if you are not too occupied?"

Raine did not dare look at him as she prayed silently that he would indeed say he was too busy. He did not.

She listened with a sinking heart as he replied, "I will be happy to accompany you."

William's enthusiasm was profoundly moving as he said, "Will that not be grand, Raine? All of us together."

With a desperation that bordered on fear, Raine wanted to say nay. But she did not want to disappoint William, not when that light was shining in his warm green eyes.

Besides that, she did not wish to give Benedict that kind of power over her. If she did so now she would be setting a precedent that pride would not allow her to set.

Yet how could she go with them? How could she pretend all was well, that she had not wed the most domineering, most obstinate, most uncaring of men? That Benedict was not, in short, the worst scoundrel who had ever been born?

Of its own accord her attention centered on her husband. He was watching her with an expression she could not begin to read.

Raine took a deep breath and squared her shoulders. Heretofore nothing had been allowed to get the best of her, not her fear and loneliness after her mother's death, when she had been forced to take up responsibilities that were far beyond her years. She had not succumbed after her father's unexpected death, nor through her own anxiety over finding a suitable husband. Benedict Ainsworth would not quell her determination now. Deliberately she smiled. "I will join you most happily, William."

Raine was pleased that her voice sounded so calm

and unconcerned. No one would imagine that her heart was beating far too fast as her husband continued to watch her in that maddening way of his. She was infinitely aware that both William and Kendran were watching the two of them. And Kendran, she feared, saw far more of the tension that existed between them than she would have wished.

Raine told herself that as soon as she convinced Benedict to allow her to go home, none of it would matter. She felt less encouraged by this than she would have hoped.

She sighed as William reached for a hearty portion of bread and cheese and began to eat eagerly. "You will hurry, won't you, Raine? We must be off soon. As soon as we have eaten." He grinned happily around a mouthful of bread.

Pleased and surprised as she was by her brother's appetite, she preferred that he chew with his mouth closed. Before she could remind him of this, Benedict spoke gently but firmly. "Do not speak with your mouth full, William."

Raine felt herself stiffen. She could not help the rush of resentment that made its way through her. Correcting William was her father's place. And in his stead, her own. She said, "You may be the one to teach my brother the art of arms and battle. You will please leave the schooling of such things as manners to me."

All three of them, William, Kendran and Benedict, looked up at her in surprise.

It was William who answered her. "It is all right, Raine. As I told you yesterday, I want Benedict to teach me things. He is kind to do so, for I must learn to behave as a nobleman. You need not worry that the

responsibility for me rests all upon your shoulders anymore.''

Raine could think of nothing to say to this, for the
three of them sat looking at her as if she was the one
who was not making sense. She rose, casting a resentful
glance toward her husband. ''Your point is well taken,
William. I must ask your pardon now, for I find I have
no more hunger.''

William spoke up. ''You do recall that we are going
riding. You said you would come.''

Raine felt the reminder like a blow. The last thing
she wanted to do was go riding with the three of them
now, but how could she refuse without marking herself
a coward in her own eyes? She answered with forced
calm. ''I will accompany you. I but go to make ready.''
She finished with what she hoped was an indifferent
glance at Benedict.

Coolly he watched her, assessed her. Damn him.
Raine turned on her heel and left the hall.

Quickly she assured herself that the ache of sadness
in her chest was over William, not Benedict. Her
brother's defection was more painful than she could
ever have imagined.

Raine let the others get ahead of her and slid to the
ground. Leading the mare behind her, she walked along
the shore with determination. The less contact she had
with her husband the better.

She looked far ahead to where William was racing
along between Benedict and his brother. He seemed as
carefree as the breeze that fluttered the hem of her
cloak. This marriage had been good for him. That she
could be grateful for, at the very least. Now he could
be a boy again for a time, rather than living with the

constant fear that they might find themselves pressed beneath the thumb of Denley Trent or possibly worse.

Though he had done his best to hide how great his concern was, she had known. And Raine could not help but see the change in him now. That the alteration had come because of Benedict did not please her, because it only served to remind her of his hold over her.

Then slowly, in spite of her anxiety, she began to realize that she was seeing the ocean for the first time and allowing Benedict to ruin that experience. The sea lay there before her, enormous and awesome, the surface silvered by the sunlight. Her steps slowed and she began to be aware of the piercingly sweet blue of the sky overhead, the cry of a gull, the lap of the gentle waves against the shore. The air that filled her lungs smelled of salt, musky sea and a pleasant dampness. Almost against her will she realized the proximity of the huge and unchangeable expanse of water was beginning to soothe her.

Her breathing slowed along with her steps, became deeper. She stopped still and raised her face to the early spring sunshine, which warmed her cheeks gently. There was no denying how very much the landscape affected her, how deeply she found herself responding, the tension in her shoulders and body easing with each breath she took in.

She had heard that the ocean affected many thusly. She had not expected it to be so with herself. And she would definitely have said it would not happen at Brackenmoore.

Far from pleasing her, this reaction of peace made her more confused. She did not wish to find any aspect of this place agreeable. She felt that to do so would be to give in, to accept Benedict Ainsworth's authority as her husband, his right to keep her here.

Yet she quickly told herself that it was foolish to feel thus. It was in no way disloyal to her own home and folk to enjoy this strangely peaceful sight. When she returned to Abbernathy she would love the familiar hills and dales no less because of it.

But when she glanced up a moment later to see that none other than her husband was riding back toward her, her pleasure in her surroundings was completely forgotten. Drat him, why could he not leave her be?

Because he was Benedict Ainsworth, and all things around him must fall into the places he had set for them. Including her, his recalcitrant wife. She could feel the peace draining from her like water from a gutter. It was replaced by irritation as she watched his approach. Though she did not wish to, Raine could not fail to note the sure and capable way he rode the large chestnut stallion.

When he pulled his mount to a halt just a few feet from her, Raine met his gaze with deliberate scorn. For a moment, as he looked down at her, she thought Benedict's expression was disappointed, but that impression was so quickly gone that she knew it had been a trick of the light upon his handsome face. He regarded her with displeasure. "What are you about, madam?"

Archly, she returned his perusal. "I am attempting to enjoy myself, my lord, in spite of your proximity."

His gaze narrowed and his nostrils flared, but there was no hint of ire in his tone as he raked her with an arrogant glance. "I came only because William was concerned that you were hanging back. He loves you greatly and would not have you hurt for any reason, including the preservation of his own feelings."

She sputtered, "I would do nothing to harm William in any way. He means more to me than my own life."

Benedict took a quick deep breath through his nose, then answered with studied reason. "If that is true, that he means all things to you, then try to do what is best for him in this. He is attempting to be a man, to free you of some of the burden of caring for him. His loyalty is in no way affected by the fact that he wishes for me to fulfill the duties of a guardian. I wish William no harm and he is aware of that, even if you are not. And you only make things difficult for him with these childish displays of yours."

Anger surged in her, not only at what he said, but his superior manner of doing so. "Childish!" she cried. But even as she said the word she could not ignore a stab of uncertainty. William himself had spoken in the same vein.

Utter frustration made her answer harshly. "Very well then, you have every answer, go on as you will. I will not attempt to interfere again."

Benedict heard her words of capitulation but was more than aware that Raine's anger and resentment continued to burn. It was there in her golden eyes, which seemed to pierce him to the core. He hardly knew how to answer such an unwarranted outrage. Yet something, the part of him that realized how very much she loved her brother, made him try. "Raine, you must realize that your resentment in this makes not one jot of sense. Would you have me ignore or mistreat the boy?"

She threw up her hands in exasperation. "It is so like you to twist my words."

Benedict rubbed a hand over his face as he fought his own rising resentment. He did not twist her words, nor anyone else's. Why must she be so very contrary at every turn? He really had no time, nor if he were honest, energy, to continue this confrontation with his volatile wife. Yet for some reason it was important to him that she agree to this out of a true understanding that it was for the good and not because he wished to rob her in any way. He spoke carefully and with more patience than he had even known he possessed. "I am not twisting your words, Raine. I simply wish to understand exactly what it is you want from me. Let us put William's feelings aside for one moment. Do *you* wish for me to care for the boy?"

She bit her lip. "Of course I want you to care for him and teach him. But..."

Benedict felt an unexpected wave of sympathy when he saw the uncertainty and loneliness in her eyes.

He realized that Raine, confident and determined though she was, needed her brother, even more than she thought he needed her. Benedict saw that she felt she was losing her brother, and he did not want that, felt an unexpected desire to preserve her from hurt.

He shook his head slowly. "Raine, you need not worry. You are not going to lose William. He loves you too much for that in spite of the friendships he is forming here at Brackenmoore."

She did not reply, but he could see that he had hit the mark by the deepening pain in her gaze. He added, "Can you not do as William has done and see being here as an opportunity, not to give up anything but to gain? We, my family and I, would be a family to you now, Raine. You are my wife, will be the mother of my children."

As he said the last, he was instantly aware of the stiffening of her body. At that moment he realized

Raine would never fully accept him until she had come to accept her new life. She had lost her father, her home, her existence as she had known it, and felt that to welcome the new would be a betrayal of the old.

She affirmed his thoughts by saying, "I cannot rest, knowing that I am needed at Abbernathy."

Thinking to appease her on that score, he said, "You may rest well on that score. I sent a man to oversee your brother's property the morning after we arrived here."

She gasped, "How dare you do so without allowing me to speak with him myself? There are so many things he will not know, that the common grounds must be distributed differently this year, that less barley must be planted and more wheat. We were expecting the delivery of a number of sheep and must be careful to pay no more than the correct amount or..." She threw up her hands. "He simply cannot know..."

Benedict took a deep breath, surprised at the import of her concerns. He had thought...well, she was a young girl. He'd had no notion that she might actually be worried about specific details of running the property. He'd believed her incessant wish to return was based upon a girlish whim. Now he found himself speaking with more deference than before. "Forgive me, Raine, I did not understand that you were so involved in the work of running the keep. I simply assumed that things had been in turmoil since your father's death."

There was no mistaking the resentment in her golden eyes. "What do you think I have been trying to tell you?"

He could feel the chagrin on his own face as he said, "I...pray forgive me. If I had understood I would have allowed you to speak with Sir Max, whom I assure you is more than qualified after having looked to many of my own keeps for years.'' Benedict saw that she was not assured by this and found himself adding, "If you have instruction for him and would care to put such on paper, I would have it taken to Abbernathy immediately.''

An expression of surprise came into those eyes and she said, "You would do that?''

He nodded. "Aye, I would.'' He looked away from her, not caring for the way it made him feel to realize that there was more to this woman than he had thought. He also wondered why her father had expected so very much of her. Yet he knew Raine would never talk of such a thing to him. She saw him as the enemy. Even now, when she was so obviously heartened to know he would allow her to make sure that all was well at Abbernathy, her resentment was still present in the stiff line of her shoulders.

Raine was afraid that any dependence on him, even a physical one, would imply defeat, that she would relinquish control of her life. He clearly recalled what William had told him about his sister the first time they'd met. The lad was very bright and possibly too observant for his age. He had seen that Raine was pressing forward in order to keep from losing her courage. Her seemingly irrational impulsiveness was simply a way of making sure that she did so.

Even her physical reactions must be kept under tight control, though they had proved too powerful for her to completely overcome them. He did not allow himself to be confused that the depth of her responses was a sign of any feelings for himself, though he did feel a certain unexplained regret at this knowledge. She was simply a healthy and passionate young woman.

What he did allow himself to hope was that they could begin to have some peace in their lives if she would only accept being here, come to care about Brackenmoore as she did Abbernathy.

If there were someone at Brackenmoore, someone who, like William, she loved and thought of as her own and who also belonged here, then she might begin to change her mind. If she had a child...Benedict felt a growing pleasure at the thought. Surely Raine would feel a similar gladness at having her own babe. Surely if they had a child she would feel differently about him, about living here.

Her role as his wife, as an Ainsworth, would be far more acceptable to her. How he was to convince her of this, Benedict had no notion. He was not a man who knew the fine art of wooing a woman. He had spent his days in looking after his lands and people, with only the vaguest of thoughts about such frivolous things. His past relations had been those of mutual understanding between two adults.

He knew that Raine was not indifferent to him no matter how distasteful this was to her. If she could only set aside her reticence for long enough to conceive a child, her feelings about him and Brackenmoore would surely change.

As his gaze rested upon her bent head, and he saw the loneliness in the dejected set of her jaw, Benedict found himself wishing that he did know more about romance. He could not help feeling that Raine was more than deserving of a man who could woo her, make her understand how beautiful and desirable she was. He was not such a man and would simply have to do his best.

But he was not ready to talk to her of this now. It was neither the time nor the place. With a gentleness that surprised him, Benedict said, "I am sorry for your losses in this, Raine, sorry that you feel you have abandoned Abbernathy. It is not my intention to hurt you in any way."

She looked up at him, her own amazement obvious. "I want to believe your sincerity. Yet why would you now show such concern for me when any previous attempt I have made to make you see my position has been met with insult and disregard? When you are kind and understanding I do not know how to…"

Benedict felt a genuine sense of regret and yearning at her uncertainty, the vulnerability in the trembling of her chin. His response only served to further shock him. Before he could halt himself he reached out and touched her arm, surprised at the instantaneous thrill of awareness and, yes, tenderness that raced through him.

Quickly he drew his hand back, something telling him that he must go carefully here. He did wish to be kind and gentle to Raine, as he was to all in his care. He did not wish to relinquish himself to her no matter how appealing that thought might be. He could not afford himself the luxury of putting anything before his responsibilities, not even a wife.

Chapter Eight

"My lord."

As his steward spoke, Benedict looked up from the figures and immediately focused on Alister Harcourt's distinctive seal. He took the role of parchment from his steward with a feeling of misgiving. That seal had become too well known to him in the past weeks.

The fact that this missive had arrived so quickly after his return from court did not bode well. Harcourt could not have debated long on his answer to the king's offer. The fact that Benedict was hearing from him personally was another indication of ill, as it had been King Edward who made the proposal.

He nodded to the tight-lipped messenger who stood in stony silence behind the steward. "You have my thanks. I will form a reply with haste. You may go down to the hall. There refreshment will be given you while you wait." The man bowed with stiff formality and left the library.

Benedict broke the seal and began to read. His expression became grimmer with each word. Finally he sat back, running a hand over his face.

Why did the man insist on personal retribution? Why

could he not accept the king's will? It was mad for him to risk bringing Edward's wrath upon himself by continuing to make demands for Tristan to face him in combat. Which was exactly what he had done in this latest missive.

Benedict knew the answer to his own questions. Alister was Maxim's brother, and was desperate to avenge his death. He did not understand the situation, did not realize the kind of man his brother had been.

Benedict was honest enough to admit that if someone were to murder one of his own brothers they would face his retribution. Yet Alister Harcourt was not in the right in this matter.

Benedict heaved a sigh. If only this were not happening now! If his relationship with Raine was not in such a turmoil he might very well go to Treanly and face the man in person. But he could not do so, not with Tristan and Lily away. In the unlikely event that something untoward were to happen to him, Kendran would be left in charge, and he was but sixteen. Benedict could not call Tristan home, either, especially as he still did not wish for him to know of the man's threats.

Benedict attempted to convince himself his reluctance to go to Treanly had nothing to do with Raine. Yet he knew it was not true. He was sure that if he left her alone, Raine would be off to Abbernathy ere he could return.

He assured himself that he did not care because of any romantic feeling for her. He knew that in spite of her pain and vulnerability as far as her brother was concerned, she was as contrary and unpredictable as a woman could be. He needed more time, time to put his plan of their having a child into effect. In the last week he had racked his mind for a way to broach the subject, to no avail.

Since that day on the beach, they had seemed to come to some silently acknowledged truce. He was reluctant to do anything that might jeopardize the peace, as he was more than aware of how precarious it was. He knew that his wife avoided his company whenever possible. He was also conscious of the fact that she watched him with an expression of wariness whenever he wasn't looking.

Benedict sighed heavily, looking down at the letter. Thinking this way did not get the matter of Alister Harcourt's threats settled. Benedict hit his fist against the table in agitation. He had promised himself that marriage to her would not interfere in his duty.

He looked down at the missive again. He had in the past avoided any personal contact with Harcourt. Mayhap if he was to send a letter of apology for the other's pain and explain his own feeling that there would be nothing gained in more death, perhaps then the man could begin to let the matter go.

Thus thinking, Benedict reached for a quill and parchment. Yet even as he poised his hand to write, another image of Raine came into his mind, Raine as she had been each time he had touched her, her lids heavy with desire, her mouth plump from his kisses. The vision brought a wave of passion and anticipation that was shocking in its intensity. Benedict took a deep breath to calm himself, knowing there was no use trying to deny his reaction. He wanted Raine, had wanted her from the first moment he saw her.

Yet it was the fact that their coming together would surely bring about a child, and thus a real peace between them, that he must focus on. He would not let this desire he felt overcome him.

Looking down he realized with a trace of impatience that the parchment still lay bare before him. Benedict knew that he could no longer delay his efforts to bring about a peace between himself and his wife. Too many other matters demanded his full attention, and though he wished it were otherwise he could not fully attend them while there was so much animosity between them.

Raine knew the hour was late, had sent Aida to her bed long ago. Yet she was unable to find her own rest. She sat before the fire, aware of its warmth on her face, but feeling apart from that warmth and the rest of her surroundings.

She could not drag her troubled thoughts away from Benedict. He had been so gentle that day by the shore, making her almost forget how angry she was with him for the way he pressed her to accept him as her husband. He had made her realize that he was right about one thing: she was holding too closely to William. Benedict meant him no harm. His devotion to his own family, his ward, had been clear to her the night he had spoken of them. She had no doubt that Will would be safe in his care, until she and her brother were able to return to Abbernathy, at any rate.

What had begun to disturb her greatly was her growing preoccupation with her husband, which had not been eased by her efforts to avoid him. In the past days she and Aida had spent long hours embroidering gowns that did not require embroidery and going over seams that were not parting.

All to no avail. Whenever Benedict was near she found herself watching him, measuring the breadth of his shoulders with her eyes, listening for the sound of his deep voice, studying the movements of his supple fingers.

For his part he seemed completely unaware of her interest. She knew she should be glad that he was blind to her obsession. He might take it as invitation to press his suit, a matter he seemed to have fallen silent on. Yet she was not glad. Some wayward part of her wanted him to pay equally close attention to her, but he did not.

She was not such a fool that she was blind to his passion when he kissed her. Yet even the times that he had kissed her, touched her, made her body come alive, had clearly failed to leave the same mark upon him. He was able to walk away without experiencing the emotional turmoil that he left upon her.

This fact did nothing to ease Raine's mind in the least. She continued to think about him night and day.

Perhaps, she thought in helpless desperation, she would be able to set this all behind her if she was ever to experience the things her body desired. Perhaps if he made love to her she could finally put to rest her own confusion and ambiguity as far as he was concerned. For surely it was only a physical desire for him that had left her so very fixed upon Benedict.

There was nothing else about her husband to draw her attention so constantly. Certainly his kindness was a very compelling quality, yet his penchant for domination far outweighed it.

He had in no way made her change her mind about going home. Yet she barely thought on how she was going to make that happen. She was too consumed with her feelings for Benedict. If only she could ease this strange ache, perhaps she could concentrate on more important matters.

Yet was the thought of doing the deed not mad? She could not simply go to Benedict and tell him of her desire to make love with him. Raine put her hands to her heated cheeks, unable to still the swirling morass of her thoughts.

When the door to her chamber opened some time later Raine did not immediately turn to see who had come. The sounds it made, as everything else around her, weighed lightly against her own preoccupation and sense of unrest.

But when she heard Benedict's voice say her name in an oddly hesitant and husky tone, she swung around to face him. The fact that he was wearing a long, black velvet dressing gown was not lost upon her, nor the fact that he looked far too masculine and compelling in it for her peace of mind. His strongly handsome face had a just washed looked, as did his raven hair, as if he had carefully groomed himself before coming.

It was that fact, along with the unreadable darkness of his blue eyes, that made her own breath quicken. For somewhere deep inside herself Raine knew why he had come, that it was her own need that had drawn him to her. Quickly she told herself that she must not leap to conclusions, that he could be here for any reason.

Even if he had come to her in that way, she could not simply acquiesce. It was one thing to contemplate a thing and completely another to do it.

He spoke softly, hoarsely, betraying a trace of yearning. "I have been thinking about us, about our relationship."

In that moment she realized it was true. Benedict wanted her, too. He had come to her tonight because he was beset by the very feelings that coursed through her body.

That knowledge brought another wave of longing that left her knees weak, her stomach aflutter. She rose on shaking limbs. "Benedict." Even she could hear the badly restrained desire in her tone. Worse, she knew that she could have done nothing to hide it had she attempted to.

Their eyes met and held as the rest of the room, the world, seemed to melt away in a smoky haze. There were only the two of them—Raine and Benedict and the full knowledge that they had waited long enough. The inevitable had arrived. When Benedict moved toward her in that surprisingly quick and graceful way of his, she could do nothing but hold out her arms. His eagerness was not only gratifying, it dissolved the very last shreds of her self-control. Even as he took her in his arms, she raised her willing mouth for his kiss.

He did not disappoint her. Those firm yet pliable lips met hers in a hot, wet kiss that made her bones turn to butter, her blood to sweet, warm honey.

He drew back to look down at her and she peered up at him from under heavy lids, dizzied by kisses, seeing the hunger in his gaze with a thrill. His tone was husky with disbelief and yes, even passion. "Raine, I know not what to say. I had not expected…"

Raine put her arms around his neck and rose up on tiptoe, telling him with her body that she was ready for this moment. There was no need for him to say anything at all, only to assuage the feelings driving them both.

Benedict did not know what had brought about this amazing change in Raine's reactions to him. He had pondered long and hard over how to broach the subject of their joining, finally deciding that there was no way but to do it. He had never imagined that she would welcome him as she was, but he was not of a mind to question her now.

All thought of what he had meant to tell her of his wish for them to have a child and thus create a bond of peace was wiped from his mind. The depth of her response had brought home the power of his ill-fought attraction.

In this moment Benedict could not hide the truth from himself. He desired this woman more than he had ever thought he could. That and that alone had finally ended his indecision and driven him from his restless and lonely bed. Only in her embrace could he find surcease from the torment of his unappeasable passion.

His lips found hers once more.

Raine's body strained toward his, and she reveled in the hardness of his chest against her own swelling breasts. When he reached down to trace a hand up her side, Raine realized that her robe must have parted in the fierceness of their embrace, for she could feel the heat of that hand through the light fabric of her night rail. She held her breath as that hand moved up to cup the outer side of her breast for a long infinite moment, then gasped aloud as it closed over that oh so tender flesh. As his thumb found the turgid tip she leaned back to allow him better access.

Benedict felt her nipple harden at his plying and was aware of his own body responding in kind. Groaning, he reached down and lifted her up against him, pressing her belly to his growing need.

He bent to kiss her again, all the cravings he had tried so hard to suppress rising up inside him, expanding out in joyous freedom like a river broken free of its banks. Heat and desire poured from his every nerve ending, leaving him weak with the force of his reactions to this woman.

Raine felt his hardness against her belly and knew a strange clenching inside her, an urging for something she could not name. As the other time when they had only just begun the journey down this road of pleasure, Raine knew that Benedict understood how to end this exquisite torment.

This time she would allow nothing to come between them, not even herself. She no longer wished to deny her own passion. When Benedict lifted her and moved toward the bed, she sighed with relief and undeniable anticipation.

Benedict reveled in the pliant weight of her in his arms as he carried Raine to the bed, then gently laid her back upon the pillows. He looked down at her, saw the passion in her heavy-lidded eyes, with a renewed wave of need heard her murmur, "Yes."

He reached to remove her velvet bed robe, drawing it slowly off her shoulders as she rose to aid him, her gaze never leaving his. Tossing it to the floor, he returned to her, his gaze now taking in the sheerness of her gown, the sweet curves that were only barely disguised by the fabric.

Yet scant as it was, this garment, too, must go. He would see that soft skin, touch it, kiss it till she begged for surcease. Benedict was determined to make this moment last, to hold himself in check until he had enjoyed every bit of her.

Again Raine rose up to help him, seeming as overcome by her own passion as he. Benedict was not prepared for the strength of his body's reaction as she lay back upon the pillows, her eyes bearing a trace of shyness, yes, but also gladness. He opened his own robe and dropped it, wondering if she would be as eager when she saw that he was ready, more so than he had ever been in his life.

Watching her closely, Benedict was aware of the rise of color in her cheeks as she looked at him. She did not turn away, but caught her breath sharply as she took in the sight of his manhood.

That catch in her breath broke the tight hold he had on himself and he took her in his arms, his own desire making his body tremble with longing. Her soft flesh scorched each part of him it touched.

But Benedict wasn't ready to give in completely just yet. He would please this woman who had brought him to such a sharp point of desire, no matter what the cost in self-restraint.

His lips met hers and he kissed her long and hard, pleased at her eager response. He pulled back then, his gaze taking in the perfection of her rounded breasts, so creamy with their deep peach tips. Reverently he lowered his head to take one turgid nipple into his mouth. As he suckled her she cried out, her fingers tangling in his hair.

"Benedict. Benedict."

He laughed huskily, deep in his throat, and moved to ply the other breast. Only when she was squirming beneath him did he slip down to trail hot kisses over her stomach, before nuzzling the soft down curls at the joining of her thighs. When she gasped, he smiled, moving lower, exploring her warmth.

Raine sobbed aloud as she felt Benedict's velvet mouth on that most secret part of herself. She was aflame, burning with a fire that rose up from that place to radiate out through her body in all-consuming need. She could not breathe, could not think as her head rolled from side to side and her fingers tangled in his thick black hair.

Her breath came faster and faster as the sensations built to a fever pitch of wanting. Every nerve screamed for some unknown release. And then at last it came, delight flooding through her as shudder after shudder took her.

Benedict wrapped his arms around her, holding her as she stilled, her breathing slowing. His own need was like a coiled snake inside him, rigid and barely restrained. Thus when she pushed away from him to whisper, "Show me what more there is to this loving," he knew he could no longer wait.

He rose above her, positioning himself over her, his breath catching as she opened herself to receive him. But Benedict bit back the urge to dive without restraint into that beckoning warmth.

Although he had prepared the way, she was still a virgin. And he had no desire to hurt her.

Gently he probed the entrance to her body, holding back, keeping himself in check.

Raine reached out to him. "Please, Benedict."

He leaned his forehead against hers, swallowing hard. "I don't wish to hurt you."

She pushed back, looking him directly in the eyes. "You will not hurt me." And with that she raised herself up, sheathing him in the velvet glove of her womanhood.

Benedict's will completely vanquished, he began to move inside her, closing his eyes as her body fell into an exquisite rhythm with his. He threw his head back, gasping as undulating waves of pleasure spread through him in a dizzying rhythm that matched that of their two bodies.

And then he was falling, tumbling into a bright, hot blaze of ecstasy, all sense of self lost in the oneness of the two of them, their coupled flesh.

He gasped her name, "Raine," feeling the sweetness of it on his lips as he slumped above her. Only when the waves of pleasure had subsided was he able to find the strength to roll to his side, pulling her with him.

He held her in his arms, tracing a hand over the curve of her hip as he felt his breath return to normal. Normal! The word seemed strange. He did not know if anything in his life would ever seem normal again after this wild, abandoned, passionate experience.

He smiled as he nuzzled her tousled red hair. "You don't know how I worried over approaching you, telling you that I wanted us to be together."

She sighed, pushing back to gaze up at him, her golden eyes still dark with passion. "Did you, Benedict?"

He drew her back down beside him. "I admit that I did. I never imagined that you would be so ready to accept me when I came here to end the war between us, to tell you that it was now time for you to take up your place as the lady of Brackenmoore, the future mother of its heir."

Instantly she stiffened, and Benedict frowned at the coolness that had entered her voice as she said, "That is what you came to me for—to tell me that I must accept my place as lady of Brackenmoore and the mother of your heirs?"

He felt a sinking sensation inside himself, but tried to ignore it. He spoke earnestly. "Of course, I hoped that you would see that your doing so would be best for all concerned."

Her voice was distant and bleak as a winter sky. "Best for all concerned."

He answered hesitantly, "Yes. For all of us."

Raine slipped from his arms, and stood, pulling the coverlet with her. Benedict watched with growing unease as she wrapped it tightly around herself before turning to face him. The coldness of her gaze pierced him as she said, "I want you to leave now."

"But Raine..." He sat up, reaching for her.

Raine took a step backward, shaking her head. "Do not touch me. I cannot think whatever could have come over me to allow you to seduce me, when all you wanted was to make things easier for yourself. To put me in my place so that you could go on about the business of looking after your precious Brackenmoore."

Benedict said not a word, but rose from the bed to take up his robe from the floor. His movements were jerky and hurried, but she had far too much time to view the body that had only moments before brought her so much pleasure.

Raine forced her gaze away, looked at the lushly carpeted floor, the bed hangings, the gray stone ceiling, anything but her husband as he made his way to the door. But he was not to leave without a parting shot, the very disdain in his tone making her cringe. "You may tell yourself that you have been wronged, that I somehow harmed you in my reasons for wishing to set things right between us." He paused and his eyes bored into hers. "But I will not allow you to say that I seduced you. You welcomed me, my lady wife, and with open arms."

The sound of her outraged cry was lost in the slamming of the door.

Even as she stamped her foot in frustration, Raine

knew that she had no cause for such righteous indignation. What he'd said was all too true. She had no one to blame for what had just occurred but herself.

It was a fact that only made her circumstances all the more difficult to accept.

After lying awake the whole night, Raine had come to one conclusion. She could no longer remain at Brackenmoore. The fact that Benedict had made love to her in order to secure his dominion over her seemed to have left a jagged and aching hole in her chest. Devil take the man who called himself her husband.

That he had taken her so easily was galling, to say the least. It did not help to know that her own desire for him had made his conquest all the easier. It had been impossible to deny herself when he came to her.

What had she been thinking? Had it really seemed plausible that she would be able to better withstand him if she was to salve the aching need she felt for him?

She had been fooling no one but herself. For now, in spite of his callous reasons for making love to her, she only wanted Benedict Ainsworth more than ever. She had not been prepared for the feelings that he had awakened in her body. Nor had she been prepared for the fact that, having been awakened, they would only clamor all the more insistently inside her.

Even now her body tightened at the memory of how he'd touched her—brought her to aching life, made her yearn for more. She could not face him again, knowing what a tremulous hold she had on her autonomy.

There was only one thing she could do. That would be to leave Brackenmoore, now, before she could give herself any time to reconsider.

That she might be caught by Benedict and kept here,

she knew. If that were to happen there would be very little chance of escape in the future, for he would surely make her even more a prisoner than she was. Yet she must try.

The first thing Raine would do would be to inform William of her decision. That he might not wish to accompany her passed through her mind for the briefest of moments.

Horrified at her own thought, Raine quickly dismissed it.

Of course William would come. He was her brother, Abbernathy his home, his heritage. His loyalties could not have changed so much no matter how attached he had become to her husband and his brother.

Yet even after telling herself this she did not go directly to find William. Raine busied herself instead with readying the few belongings she needed for the journey. The rest of her things she could manage without. Getting away from Brackenmoore and the overshadowing presence of her husband far outweighed the loss of a few personal items.

She would tell Aida, as well. The maid could not be left behind. She was like family to Raine. But the maid would not be told before Raine was ready to make her move. Aida was so very rattled at the best of times. She could not be placed in the position of inadvertently giving them away.

Unfortunately, Aida came in just as Raine finished tying up the small bundle. Raine was saved from having to explain her intent, for the maid knew the moment their gazes met.

Aida put her hands to her lips, whispering, "We are leaving."

Raine nodded. "We are. And now that you know, it must be immediately."

The words produced a sigh of anxiety. "Do you think that this is wise, my lady?"

Raine refused to be drawn into any discussion of the matter. "We will leave on the morrow. You must take only what you can carry with you."

"But how are we to do this?"

Raine spoke with confidence. "You, William and I will ride out from here and meet at the shoreline in the morning after the meal. We will go on to Abbernathy from there."

"My lord Benedict will not allow us to just leave."

Raine shook her head. "He will never suspect that we have gone until it is far too late. He would not imagine that I would leave without William's men."

Aida's eyes rounded with horror. "And we should not. 'Tis far too dangerous for two women and one young lad upon the road."

Raine replied evenly, "That is why we must certainly have a care. Should you choose to stay here at Brackenmoore you may do so."

Aida wrung her hands. "You know I could not let you and William set off on such a journey without me."

Raine nodded. "Very well then. Be at the ready. I will speak to William as soon as possible."

Raine would have been hard-pressed to keep her agitation to herself that evening, and was more than relieved when her husband did not appear at table. If Kendran noted her preoccupation he made no remark on it and seemed to eat quite heartily. As did William.

Though Kendran did make a point of saying that Benedict had certainly been busy during mealtimes of late. Raine, feeling his gaze on her as he spoke, met his blue eyes with what she hoped was a guileless expression. He watched her for another long moment, grinned that oh so dazzling grin of his and promptly went on with his meal. The exchange left Raine feeling as if he knew far more about what was going on around him that he appeared to.

Feeling slightly unnerved, Raine waited until the meal was finished and William was leaving the table to ask him to come to her chamber for a moment. He waved the still smiling Kendran on and turned to follow her.

She knew it would be difficult for him to leave the older boy without saying goodbye. But that was what they must do.

Her informing him of her plan at the last moment had been deliberate. She did not wish to try his powers of deception by expecting him to act normally before the Ainsworth brothers. It was too much to expect from him, especially as he had become so attached to the two. She tried not to appear to hurry as she took him to her chamber and firmly closed the portal behind them.

William frowned darkly as Raine told him what she had decided. Clearly shocked, he studied her for a long moment, then said, "You want me to take a ride alone in the morning. I am to go down to the edge of the sea. And you intend to meet me there, with the plan of you and Aida and me escaping to Abbernathy alone?"

She nodded. "I do."

He took a quick breath. "Do you think that we should attempt such a thing? What will we do, the three of us, unescorted on such a journey? What will Benedict think?"

She did not care for the dejectedness in his voice, but

having some sympathy for his feelings, tried to answer evenly. "William, I told you when we came here that we would not be staying. You know what my husband will say. It was only under duress from him that we came. As far as being unescorted is concerned, I cannot possibly take the chance of alerting your men. We will simply travel by night and hide in the forests during the daylight hours." Raine could hear her own growing desperation as she went on.

Clearly he sensed her dismay, for he said, "I can see that you have thought it all out. And yes, Raine, I do know that Benedict forced your hand in coming here. But why now?" He looked at her closely. "I had thought that you might...that perhaps you might be coming to... It seemed that being Benedict's wife was not as displeasing to you as it had been in the beginning."

She could feel the heat in her own cheeks. "What do you mean?"

He blushed in turn. "I...well, I saw Benedict leaving your chambers last eve."

Raine felt herself flush all the way to the tips of her toes. It would be impossible for her to make him understand that Benedict was not completely abhorrent to her in every way. It was indeed the fact that he was not that forced this decision.

Her gaze met her brother's. His confused and questioning green eyes did not leave her own in spite of his obvious embarrassment over speaking of such a thing.

Again she told herself that William simply could not understand the very real need she felt to keep herself from falling beneath Benedict's complete control, as all others here at Brackenmoore seemed content to do. Raine could hear the strain in her own voice as she said,

"William, I cannot explain all of this to you." She raised her chin. "Please, simply try to understand that we must leave. And also try to understand that I believe it is best not only for myself but for you."

He took a deep breath and let it out in a rush. "As you will. I shall do what you ask."

Raine felt such a rush of relief that for a moment she found it difficult to speak. Again she looked away, not wanting her brother to see the tears that stung her eyes. Only now did she realize how very much she had feared that he would not be willing to follow her lead as he had before her marriage to Ainsworth. She could not hide the huskiness of her voice as she answered, "Thank you, William, for your loyalty."

She felt a hand on her shoulder and realized that he had seen far more than she wished to reveal. She was determined to keep herself from breaking down, from making him fearful that she might do so. As always, she must stay firm, must never allow William to experience the terror and loneliness she had known when her father had fallen into despair.

He spoke softly. "My first loyalty is and will always be to you, Raine. We share the same blood. No matter what occurs I pray that you will never question that."

This time she did look at him, uncaring that he might see too much. She was overwhelmed by a sweet rise of warm emotion in her chest. "I love you, William."

"And I you," he replied with a blush, suddenly seeming embarrassed by this display of emotion. "Now tell me again exactly what you mean to do and how."

Raine felt another rise of affection for her brother. For all his sensitivity he was still just a boy. Taking her cue from him, Raine began to describe her plan.

Despite her happiness and relief that William had indeed made clear his devotion to her, Raine could not completely disregard a nagging sense of regret. She had felt it when she made the decision to leave, had thought it was because of her anxiety over what William might say.

Yet now that he had agreed to her plan and with such a clear declaration of his support of her, she was not so certain. Somehow she suspected that it was connected to her leaving Brackenmoore. She told herself her feelings had nothing to do with Benedict. Nor did they have anything to do with the fact that she had resolved to never again allow herself the pleasure she had found in his embrace.

Chapter Nine

It had been a journey of sheer determination. Nothing else could have kept her going through those two long miserable days when she had lain awake praying that no one would discover their hiding place beneath the trees. Nor had the nights been any better as they had ridden on, unable to do more than trust the horses to find their way over the uneven roads.

When they had at last arrived the previous night, Raine had been unable to summon even a hint of joy. She'd no energy for anything beyond the relief that they would sleep in their own beds, no longer uncertain and fearful.

So tired had she been that she was incapable of answering any of the questions posed to her by the servants, who were clearly overjoyed to have them home again. Raine was sure that Aida would be happy to satisfy their curiosity come morning.

But when the sun coming though the tall windows prodded her lids open the next day, Raine was instantly and eagerly awake. Sitting up in the bed she had slept in since she was a child, she looked about her bedchamber and waited for that expected feeling of contentment and security to swell within her. It did not come. Her gaze ran over the chamber with bewilderment. What was wrong?

The ivory hangings were pulled back, as she had not bothered to close them in her exhaustion the previous night, and the whole of the room was exposed to her view. All was exactly as it should be. The spring sun slanted through the window, casting a warm glow upon the table that stood beneath it. The lovely tapestries her grandmother had stitched before she was even born hung upon the walls. The silver mirror and comb her father had given to her one special Christmas sat atop the chest at the foot of the high oak bed. A fire had been laid in the hearth at some hour and flickered cheerily.

All was as it should be. And yet it was not. For reasons she could not explain, Raine had an uncomfortable feeling that something was missing. What it might be she dared not even allow herself to imagine. For deep inside her there gleamed a trace of anxiety that this feeling might be connected to one Benedict Ainsworth.

As soon as the thought entered her mind, Raine leapt from the bed, took up her bed robe and strode to the door. She would not sit here and allow herself to think such impossible thoughts. She did not care one jot about that too controlling and domineering man.

She went to William's chamber. He was just combing his deep auburn hair as a final measure to dressing. He swung around as she entered, obviously eager to see her. "Raine."

The depth of the pleasure in his gaze told her all too clearly that he, too, might have been feeling lost. His words as he continued confirmed her suspicions. "It is very quiet here this morning. At Brackenmoore Kendran and I woke early and went straight down to break our fast together.''

Raine bit her lip at the yearning in his voice. She knew that he had become attached to the older boy. Never having had a brother, he found it a new experience to share such things. Even she could not deny that Kendran had been quite kind to the younger boy.

Slowly she moved to sit on the end of the bed near where he stood at the washstand. "Aye, it is quiet here, Will, but that is not only because we have grown somewhat used to life at Brackenmoore. We must realize that it will feel strange and lonely here until we become more accustomed to—" her voice broke but she forced herself to go on "—to Father's being gone."

He looked at her closely. "I suppose you are right, Raine. His being gone was not so hard when I was able to play chess with Kendran of an evening, ride with him or Benedict during the day." His shoulders slumped. She saw that the manly pose he had adopted when Kendran was present had lapsed here alone with her.

Damn Benedict for making them go to Brackenmoore! If it had not been for him, William would have been growing more accustomed to their loss, as would she. Yet in the face of William's confidences, Raine did not wish to give voice to the resentment she felt toward her husband.

It was through no fault of William's that Benedict had failed to treat her with any consideration. She put her arm around her brother's slight shoulders. "I know how difficult this is for you, Will. But we managed before going to court and meeting Benedict, and we shall again. This is our home and father would wish for us to remember that."

William nodded. "No doubt that is true." The words were spoken calmly enough, but she could not mistake the lingering loneliness in his tone. Not long ago her own company had been all that William required to make him happy. Yet even as she told herself this, she wondered at the truth of it. William had spent much of his time buried in a book, or with the horses. Even when her father was alive it had been thus.

Being with Kendran and Benedict seemed to have made her brother realize that there were other, less solitary pursuits to occupy his time. And even Benedict, for all that he had estates of his own to run, had made an effort to spend time with the boy.

Well, all she wanted now was for herself and William to be as they once had been—relying upon no one but each other. She was not a boy of sixteen, but she would do her utmost to be a good companion.

She was also determined that William would be enough for her. The fact that she had relived each and every moment of the night she and Benedict had been together over and over again did not rest easy in her mind. Yet she would put that from her. There was naught else to do.

Benedict rode on, pushing himself, his men and their mounts beyond the point of common sense. He knew that his animal was exhausted, just as he could feel every mile of the journey along the dusty road in his own aching body. Yet he could not stop—not until he reached Abbernathy.

Anger surged in him as he again recalled the moment he'd realized Raine had gone. He had looked at Maeve, standing in the doorway of the library at Brackenmoore, and been unable to comprehend her words until she repeated them. The head woman's tone was incredulous. "My lord, they are gone—your lady wife, her brother and the maid."

"Gone?" He stood, shaking his head. "What mean you?"

Maeve took a deep breath, her gaze filled with regret as she faced him. "I know not where they have gone, my lord, only that they have. No one has seen them since they went out riding this very morning."

Benedict threw up his hands, causing Maeve to stare at him in surprise. "I gave orders that I was to be informed should they attempt to leave together for any reason."

"They did not leave together, and no one thought—"

"Her men, are they missing as well?"

"No, my lord. They seem to have no notion of where their lady might be."

Benedict felt a twitching behind his left eye. He could question the men, but his instincts told him that Raine had not confided in them. If she had they would not have allowed her to go off unprotected. Benedict knew he could have the castle grounds searched and the area all 'round, but would not find them. He knew whence they had gone and why.

He paused only long enough to order his men and William's to their mounts. The latter would be able to guide them directly to the Abbernathy keep.

Benedict's fingers tightened on the reins and he urged his mount to an even faster pace. Raine would soon learn that she was not a law unto herself. She could not simply leave without warning, taking her eleven-year-old brother off across the countryside without any guard to keep them from harm, worrying not only Benedict, but everyone else at Brackenmoore. He could not even allow himself to think that she had not managed to reach Abbernathy. The depth of anxiety he felt at considering the alternative was numbing.

Surely the reason could only be his own feelings of responsibility toward her. He was married to Raine, had joined their lives by that act. It would be completely mad of him to have any personal care for what she did. The fact that the night he had spent with her had been the most physically satisfying of his life did not enter into it.

She had run away simply because he had tried to make her see that they two must set aside their differences for the good of his heritage, provide an heir. It was another sign of her own irresponsibility and selfish need to have her own way at all costs. It would please him in no small amount to arrive at Abbernathy before her, to welcome his wayward wife as she deserved. It was doubtful that Raine, an eleven-year-old boy, and the maid had been able to make such good time as he and the men.

He had no idea how much more time had passed when the castle wall came into sight. Benedict rode straight to the gate and called out, "Open."

A man came out to peer down at him in the darkness. His immediate appearance pleased Benedict, for it meant he had not been sleeping upon his watch. It indicated that Sir Max, whom he had sent to Abbernathy, was seeing to his duties properly. Then Benedict had no more time to think on this as the fellow answered in a tone of authority, "And who demands entrance?"

Again he was glad for the attention to security, but he had no patience for any discussion. "'Tis I, Benedict Ainsworth, husband to your lady Raine."

There was a long silence while the man obviously

pondered this news. Then, with more hesitancy than before, he said, "You are my lady's husband?"

Benedict replied with calm but unwavering demand. "I am and I will brook no further delays in this. If you do not open the gate, I will take this wall down stone by stone. Mark me well, by then I may be angry."

The man spoke hurriedly, the pleading in his tone obvious. "Please, my lord, but wait while I summon someone to come and allow me to do your bidding. I cannot act without first doing that no matter how you might threaten me. I will summon Sir Max or the lady Raine. If you are telling the truth my lady will certainly wish for you to enter."

She was here. Benedict refused to acknowledge the depth of his relief, holding tightly to his anger.

He answered as evenly as he could, understanding that it was not this fellow's fault that he was angry with Raine. "I will wait for the count of one hundred, and hear me, not a moment longer."

The man disappeared without further discussion. Benedict did not count off the time. He knew that the guard would be doing so. It was not long before the sentry, his breathing labored, called down, "You may enter, my lord, and I beg your forgiveness of the delay."

Benedict did not reply, but moved closer to the gate, hearing the wheel squeak as it was raised.

Having been warned that he had come would not give Raine any advantage. For Benedict did not require surprise to accomplish his purpose. He would take her home to Brackenmoore no matter what she might say or do.

In the courtyard a silent and wide-eyed crowd had already begun to gather. Benedict ignored them. He motioned for his men to dismount, then told them to take their horses as well as his to the stables, even as he noted that the grounds were in good order.

Inside the keep the castle folk stood at the far end of the hall near the tall, wide hearth. They watched him with open curiosity. News that he had come had obviously spread throughout the keep. Benedict was not of a mood to explain himself. He moved toward the far end of the room, where a wide set of stone steps led upward. He could only assume the family's rooms would be up those steps.

He met Raine before he even reached the top.

Seeing him, she halted in her own headlong rush down the stairs, her hands going to her hips. "Well, you do have a most charming way about you, Benedict Ainsworth. Did you have to attempt to intimidate the guard at the gate?"

He glared at her, even as he took in the pallor of her creamy skin, the faint dark shadows beneath her lovely golden eyes. Against his will he felt a stab of sympathy, realizing the journey must have been very difficult. He brushed it aside as he answered, "I was not making an attempt to intimidate. I but made my wishes clear, which as your husband I may do." His blue eyes examined her. "It would appear that you are far more perturbed than was he. It troubles my mind not in the least to have given you some measure of displeasure. I have spent the last two days in the saddle."

"By your own stubborn will," she replied with heat. "No one forced you to come after me."

Benedict clamped his mouth shut on the angry words that clamored to issue forth. He would not argue with her. He raised dark brows. "Prepare yourself to return to Brackenmoore immediately."

Her mouth dropped open. "Are you mad?"

What a gall she had, to ask that of him. He fought down his own anger and frustration. Not wanting her to see how very disturbed he was, Benedict simply stared at her.

With a gasp of outrage, Raine cried, "You cannot force me. I will never consent to go with you." She swung around and raced away from him.

Benedict followed, not hurrying to keep her in sight, as his strides were so much longer. He was not pleased at the way his gaze centered upon the sway of her hips. He had no desire to think of anything besides making Raine understand that he would not put up with any more recalcitrant behavior on her part. She was the lady of Brackenmoore and would conduct herself accordingly.

At the far end of the long corridor, she opened a narrow oak door and disappeared inside. He heard the bolt slide home as he came to a halt before it.

Without hesitation he stepped back and threw his weight against the door. It swung open with a loud crash.

Raine was standing in the middle of the room, her hands over her mouth. It was with some satisfaction that he saw the expression of horror and shock on his wife's face as she cried, "What are you doing?"

He folded his arms over his chest. All he could think of was that she was his wife and that he would no longer tolerate this insurrection. The calmness of his tone surprised even him as he said, "As I told you, make ready to return to Brackenmoore."

She seemed completely taken aback at this, then her golden eyes narrowed with rage. "How dare you, you black-hearted knave. You cannot break down my door, then order me about in that cold way of yours. I will not have it."

"You will not have it?"

She glared in hatred. "Do you have any idea how humiliating it is that you do not even show any anger when you order me about? Why, you might be telling me that you did not care for dinner." She tapped her chest with her open palm. "I and my feelings are of more significance than that and you will not dismiss me so summarily."

Benedict could not prevent his eyes from widening in incredulity. She was enraged with him for being calm! Through tight lips he asked, "Would you prefer then that I turn you over my knee and lesson you as you deserve?"

Raine gaped at him, wrapping her arms about her, but quickly recovered enough to shout, "You would not dare."

He took a step toward her. "Would I not—"

A voice interrupted from behind them. "Please, Benedict, do not."

Grimacing, Benedict swung around to face an extremely agitated William. He wished the boy to know he did not mean to carry through with his threat, but would not admit as much before Raine. He chose instead to change the subject. "You are to make ready. We will be leaving forthwith."

Raine broke in. "We will not."

Benedict closed his eyes as frustration made his temple throb. Raine had accused him of being too calm. If only she knew what the effort cost him. He took a deep breath and looked at the boy, who shrugged and said, "I beg pardon, Benedict, for any worry we caused you."

Benedict shook his head. "I thank you for that, but you are not to feel responsible for what has gone on here. It is Raine who should bear the guilt of this."

William sputtered, "But Raine did not—"

Gently, but firmly, Benedict interrupted him. "You will please leave us now, Will. I must speak with your sister." When he hesitated, Benedict ruefully added, "Go on, you know I will not harm her."

The boy nodded, seeming relieved, though his gaze remained troubled. The moment he was gone, Raine cried out in anger. "I have no reason for guilt."

Benedict rounded on her, his eyes narrowed. "Am I to take it then that coming here, with no escort to protect you, was William's notion—or possibly Aida's? It is only by God's own grace that the three of you arrived safely. Any one of hundreds of disastrous events could have occurred."

At his words she blanched, but raised her chin in defiance. "Nothing did."

In spite of her bravado, he could see that his words had struck a vein. The journey must have been more difficult than she had expected. Even as he told himself that he was glad, as it might keep her from behaving so rashly in the future, he felt a stab of protectiveness.

Surprised at his own reaction, Benedict pushed it away. It would in no way benefit Raine for him to give way to such feelings now. She must see the error of her ways.

He leaned close to her, realizing even as he spoke that his voice was now too controlled, too tight, betraying his agitation. "If you have any sense at all in that beautiful head of yours you will cease baiting me and make ready for the journey."

She shook her head, flushing. "Not after the way you used me."

He sighed heavily. "I did not use you. You are my wife. My hope to have a child with you, that you will come to accept your place as my wife, is far from unreasonable."

For a long moment she bit her lower lip, then to his surprise Raine reached out and clasped his hand. "Come."

So shocked was he that Benedict followed as she led him out her door and down the corridor. What she could be doing and why was a complete mystery.

She opened a door at the far end of the corridor, pulling him inside. His gaze scanned the chamber, which was a large, richly appointed room with a wide curtained bed, a thick carpet and other fine appointments. Obviously the chamber was not in use, judging from the heavy layer of dust and the air of emptiness.

Raine released his hand. Something, a fierce tenseness in her body and face as she slowly stepped close to the bed, told him that he must go gently here in spite of his confusion over what she was doing. Thus it was very quietly that he spoke. "What are we doing here, Raine?"

She looked at him and he saw the sheen of tears that she so clearly did not wish to shed. Quickly she turned away. "This was my father's chamber. It was here he died."

Benedict was not surprised. But why had she brought him here? Without being asked, she went on. "It was in this room that I made the promise to care for William and his lands until he was able to do so."

"And that you have done. Most admirably."

She turned to him. "Have I, Benedict? Have I looked

after them when you tell me that I no longer belong here?''

He nodded without wavering. "Aye, you have, Raine. No one could have done better. William and his lands will be safe until he is able to rule them for himself.''

Her shoulders slumped. "I have tried...wanted...to keep myself from faltering, to do what was right above all things.'' She moved to stare out the window, her voice taking on a distant tone as she told him, "It was a terrible time after my mother died.''

He heard the gentleness in his own voice. "Tell me.''

She went on. "I was so small, not more than eight when mother walked into this room and never walked out. Father himself did not leave for many, many days after her death, and when he did emerge, it was in a drunken stupor.'' She took a deep breath as if this next admission was difficult to make. "I was so frightened....''

Her words made Benedict recall the pain of losing his parents, the uncertainty he had felt at realizing he and he alone must hold the family together. But he had been a young man of eighteen. Raine had been a young child. He found himself saying, "It must have been terrible for you, especially as you had just lost your mother.''

She shook her head, not looking at him. "The baby, William, he cried and cried. Donalda, the head woman here at Abbernathy, found Aida to nurse him, but he would not stop crying. He seemed to somehow understand that Mother...she was gone. I soon found that if I stayed by him, touched him, he was better, did not cry so endlessly. I knew then that he was mine, that I must always care for and love him no matter what happened, that I would never leave him alone and frightened…as Father had me. For even when he was better, more himself, he needed me to help him with things, to be strong.''

Benedict moved to stand behind her, finally understanding some of why she was so determined to look after Will and his lands. He wanted to reach out, to comfort her, but did not believe his gesture would be welcome. Raine felt he had interfered in her duty by insisting they live at Brackenmoore. It was doubtful that anything he could say now would change that, yet he tried. ''I, too, had to take charge when my parents died. I knew I must honor the trust my father had in me. You need not take this upon yourself, Raine. You need not fear making your father's mistakes. You are a woman, your obligations different from a man's.''

She rounded on him. ''Are they? Perhaps I do not wish for them to be. Perhaps I am proud to be strong and dependable as you are. Should I be content with simply being the bearer of the Brackenmoore heir, to put aside my own thoughts? Perhaps I do not wish to settle back and allow another to choose my life for me!''

He felt an overwhelming rush of sorrow and immediately covered it with a mask of arrogance as he held her angry golden gaze. ''There is no shame nor degradation in being the mother to the heir of Brackenmoore. My own mother was proud to hold that position.''

''I am not your—''

''Raine?''

Benedict swung around to see that William was standing in the open doorway. His face was troubled, making Benedict wonder how much of the conversation he had overheard.

Before she could reply, William spoke again. "Your pardon, Benedict. Would you leave me to speak to my sister for a moment?"

Looking to his wife, Benedict saw that she had crossed her arms over her bosom. Meeting his glance, she glared in resentment, her stubbornly set chin an open challenge to his authority.

He wanted to refuse William's request, to force her to see reason. But looking at the boy Benedict saw that he was completely in earnest, his green eyes pleading. Benedict nodded. "Aye, you may." He then flicked another cool glance at his wife. "But be assured it will not change the fact that she will do as I say."

Raine felt the tightness of anger in her chest as she watched her husband leave the chamber. As always, Benedict thought he could simply command and have his will become fact. And all without ever raising his voice.

Although her outrage burned, for he made no apology for believing she should be more than content to have no purpose besides that of bearing his offspring, there was another part of herself that was surprised and confused that he had come here after her. He had admitted that he had ridden for two straight days in order to do so, and he seemed somewhat ruffled. She knew a faint sense of pleasure at this. She quickly suppressed it. His state of mind was no concern of hers. And she was certainly not returning to Brackenmoore with him.

She swung around to face her brother. "You need not fear him, William. He cannot force us to accompany him."

William looked at her with regret and sadness. "I am not afraid of Benedict, Raine. You cannot blame him for wanting his own wife to be home with him. He is not the one who is wrong in this. You...we brought this upon ourselves. He is only acting as any husband would.''

Raine felt the shock of his statement with a sense of resistance and betrayal. ''William, how can you say that?''

He sighed. ''Raine, do you believe I wish to say this to you? I love you best of all people on this earth, but it was wrong of us to return here. Somewhere inside you know it as clearly as I. Before God, you are Benedict's wife.''

She wanted, needed, to deny him, to preserve her freedom and autonomy. But looking into his green eyes, so sincere, so certain, she could find no words to refute him.

Finally she turned away, not wanting to see that he was right, that she was indeed bound by honor and her own word before God to return to Brackenmoore, to live there with her husband.

Without another comment, Raine turned and went from the room, her heart heavy. Though she realized that William was right, telling her husband she would accompany him would not be easy. She wished there were some way of doing so without allowing Benedict to believe he had bested her.

Unfortunately, she could think of no way to accomplish this. Trying to hide her dejected state of mind, Raine went to the stairs. She could only assume that Benedict would have gone to the hall.

It was as she rounded the last bend in the stair that she heard the sound of raised voices. What, she wondered, was Benedict doing now? Biting her lip in consternation, she hurried forward. What met her gaze as she came to the opening to the great hall made her stop dead in surprise.

For there, waving his arms about like a madman, was her cousin Denley. Even as she watched, he shouted, "Where is she? Don't try to hide the fact that Raine has come here, and without you, my lord Ainsworth. I have been told the truth." There was no mistaking the anger and disdain in his voice as he looked at Benedict, who was seated at one of the trestle tables, calmly eating. "I can only assume that you arrived after my messenger left the keep last eve."

"Spy, more like," Benedict remarked placidly.

Raine was aghast, running forward without thinking. "You set a spy in my own keep? Who is it? Never will they set foot in Abbernathy again."

Denley rounded on her, holding out his arms. "You have come to your senses and returned to me."

Raine stopped short, her anger over having had a spy among her own folk forgotten for the moment. "Returned to you! You are without a doubt the most despicable and insensitive man in all of England."

She heard the quick intake of her husband's breath and cast him a quelling glance. Even in that instant she knew that he was surprised that she would admit to finding anyone more despicable and insensitive than him.

Then Denley was talking again and she was beset anew at his lack of judgment. "Raine, do not try to hide your regret over having made the mistake of marrying this man." He moved to take her arm. "We will get an annulment."

An annulment, she thought, shaking her head. "I cannot get an annulment."

"Then perhaps—" he put his hand on the hilt of the

sword she had not noted until that very gesture "—I will simply end our dilemma by making a widow of you."

Raine felt herself pulled away from her cousin and pushed behind the solid wall of Benedict's body before she could so much as take a breath. She rose up on tiptoe, attempting to see over his shoulder as he said, "I have warned you once too often, Trent. Now you will pay the price of your threats."

Even as he reached to take his own sword from his belt, Denley ran at him, his face a mask of rage. Raine gasped, but she need not have worried, for Benedict met that charge with his blade.

The sound of the contact reverberated through the hall, even as it did her mind. "Dear God," she whispered to herself, watching Benedict move forward, now on the ready. She gasped as Denley charged anew, his madness and desperation lending weight and force to his assault even though he lacked the finesse and grace that were so much a part of Benedict's actions. Her cousin swung wildly, forcefully, cleaving a table with one blow.

Benedict did not seem perturbed by the sheer insanity of her cousin's actions. He simply fought on, seemingly nonchalant in the face of the other's wild attacks. He met each thrust with calm indifference.

Then slowly, as the fight raged on, Raine realized that Benedict was not nearly as indifferent to the other man as he appeared. She began to see that there was a deliberate purpose in his method. Where Denley was now panting and sweating profusely, Benedict appeared fresh, his breathing barely changed.

Raine watched as with each furious stroke Denley's arm became slower and slower.

She saw the grim determination on Benedict's face as he, too, noted the other man's growing exhaustion. For a brief moment she felt sympathy for her cousin. He was, beneath all his bravado, a mere simpleton. Yet he had brought this ill upon himself. If Benedict killed him now, it would be no worse than he had asked for.

When Denley finally staggered backward, his sword falling to the floor, she caught her breath, her gaze going to Benedict's face. There was no way of gauging his intent, as his handsome features were set in that unreadable mask she had come to know too well. He held his sword out before him, taking two steps toward the other man.

Seeing this, Denley raised his own weapon once more, but there was no mistaking the fact that he was weary. In spite of this, he called out tauntingly, "Come and take me then, you bastard. You've stolen all else that matters to me."

If the situation were any less serious Raine would have rolled her eyes. Never had she belonged to him, nor had she even truly mattered to him as anything beyond a means to gain Abbernathy for his own.

But her attention was fully fixed on Benedict, who said nothing. His eyes continued to hold his opponent with that same cold emptiness.

This only seemed to make Denley all the more desperate, for he called out again. "Well, then, come at me, Ainsworth. What are you waiting for?"

Again the silence stretched to the breaking point. Not only Denley, but all who had gathered around them now waited to see what Benedict would do next.

Finally, with a glance of sheer disdain, her husband replied, "You are not worthy to bloody my blade. Get you from this place and never return."

His tone dismissed the other man as if he were nothing. Denley's bulbous eyes grew even rounder as the insult of this statement finally struck home. Then his renewed rage seemed to give him strength. Raising his sword high, and with a shout of frustration, he ran at Benedict.

Raine's heart leapt in her throat as a cry of warning issued forth from the depths of her being.

But she need not have worried, for Benedict swung around so quickly that his sword was a blur as he brought it up to ward off the downward stroke. All would have been well if Denley, in his fury, had not thrown himself against his opponent. When he did so, Benedict's blade twisted, sliding downward and into Denley's chest.

Raine cried out again, this time with horror as her cousin looked down with shock at the edge of the blade in his chest. Immediately Benedict pulled back. But the damage had been done and Denley sagged to his knees, his sword falling to the rush-strewn floor with a clatter.

Before Raine could even think to do anything, Benedict had turned to the crowd of onlookers. "Bring water and bandages." When they simply stood there, staring in horror, he shouted, "Now!"

This seemed to break the shock and confusion that held them all immobile, including Raine. She rushed forward even as the servants hurried to do as he had bidden.

She knelt beside the fallen Denley, seeing the blood that stained the front of his bright green houppelande. He looked up at her with eyes as confused as a truant child's. "He's done me in."

She shook her head firmly even as she pulled his garments aside to see the wound. "He has not." She viewed the gash with relief. Barring infection, her cousin would recover. She met his gaze with a stern one. "Hear me now and never speak on this matter again. You have brought this upon yourself. You must go home and thank fortune that Benedict has not killed you this day." She took a deep breath, then went on, realizing that she must say something that might keep him from ever acting so foolishly in the future. "My coming here to Abbernathy was not a sign of my displeasure with my marriage. You must understand that I am content. I do not want you to rescue me from my husband."

Denley looked up over her head, his expression a mix of pain, frustration and hatred, and she knew that Benedict was standing behind her. He had heard every word she said. She would not let that worry her. Her wish to squelch this madness in Denley before it ended his life and brought further pain to her was all that mattered.

Her cousin looked back into her eyes. "Raine."

She shook her head. "Nay. No more will be said." Rising, she turned to Donalda, her head woman. "Please, see that the wound is cleaned and bandaged, then have my cousin taken home."

Wide-eyed, the serving woman nodded. Raine was more than certain of the woman's ability to perform this task properly. Raine felt that to have any more personal contact with her cousin might only cause more conflict. He was so very adept at seeing things the way he wished to, and for her to tend his wound might cause all manner of impossible fantasies to grow in his mind.

Without looking at anyone, she mounted the stairs to the upper floor of the keep. She went directly to her room and moved to stand before the window. She gazed out upon the view that she had seen each spring of her life, without truly seeing the cloud-dotted blue of the morning sky, or budding trees in the garden that lay beneath her window, or the young shoots that pushed their way through the rich earth.

She now knew that she had been a fool to come home. Things could never be as they had been.

William had been right. Her life, however lonely, was now with Benedict. But even as this melancholy thought passed through her mind, she felt a strange thrill of awareness. Quickly she brushed it aside. She was not interested in the meager comfort Benedict was willing to provide her with his body.

Chapter Ten

When the door opened behind her, Raine knew who was there even before she turned to face him. Every room that Benedict entered took on a palpable feeling of barely leashed energy.

"Raine."

Slowly she swung around, her eyes meeting his blue ones. Instantly she wanted to look away, for those eyes had the power to move her, to make her recall how it had felt to see them dark with passion. She resisted, giving him measure for measure, as she asked, "Is my cousin away now?"

He nodded. "He is and the woman, Donalda, has confirmed your opinion that all will be well for him."

She sighed. "I am glad of that. Though he be a madman, I would not have his death on my hands."

Benedict shrugged. "'Twould be myself who must claim that ill, should he perish."

She shook her head, again catching his gaze. "Nay, it was my own rash thinking that brought this about. I should have realized that he would come once I had returned here."

"He is the very thickest of men."

She took a deep breath and let it out in a rush, knowing as she spoke that she was putting her freedom and autonomy behind her. "Please, Benedict, allow me to finish what I have to say before you speak. I have realized that I have been wrong about many things, including the fact that you have treated me ill in expecting me to abide at Brackenmoore. I should not have expected to marry a man, receive his protection and give nothing in return." She paused to take another deep breath and said, "I will return to Brackenmoore without resistance. I give my word not to run away again." Then she quickly added, "But there will be no more orders."

To her surprise she did not see the gloating expression she had expected, only a trace of surprise and another odd emotion she could only think of as remorse. But that made no sense. He could be nothing but gladdened by the news that she would accompany him without defiance.

But there was no recrimination, only a decided softness in his voice as he answered, "I thank you for this, Raine, and tell you that what has been behind us will remain behind us. We will depart at your leisure."

At her leisure? From whence had come such a concession? Rather than reminding her that none of this would have occurred had she remained where she belonged, which she had fully expected him to do, he was behaving with more civility than she would have thought possible.

This new and softer side of Benedict was strangely appealing. Her gaze slid over his powerful frame and she found herself pausing at his hands, hands that had brought her so much pleasure. She felt herself flush with both heat and chagrin. Benedict had hurt her by making love to her for the sole purpose of creating an heir.

Yet a part of her knew he did not know how to be any different. Brackenmoore was and would always be first with him. Even before his own happiness. Though that pained her, she also realized there was good in him. Even as the stinging certainty that he would never love her, could not love her, settled over her, she wondered if they could have some life together.

Benedict must learn to show her some measure of respect. The fact that he had not refuted her demand that there would be no more orders gave her some encouragement.

Raine replied, "If it meets with your approval, my lord, I would remain here one day for the purpose of making sure all is well and informing the servants of what is going on. When we left we had expected to return...." She gulped past the lump in her throat. "I would say goodbye."

Benedict watched her for a long moment. Finally he nodded. "That would serve me well enough. I have driven the men hard and will send them to their rest."

The morning they left Abbernathy it was with grave ceremony. The castle folk came out to wave them off, but there was a feeling of heaviness in the air. Clearly Raine and William would be greatly missed. Benedict had seen her with her folk in the past day, had watched her genuine care and concern for those here, for the proper running of the estate. That her manner was completely in opposition to that at Brackenmoore he could not help seeing, and only hoped that might change with time.

Although Benedict was still surprised and pleased at

the fact that Raine had decided to accompany him without resistance, that she had, astounding as it was, conceded that he had not wronged her in asking her to go to Brackenmoore with him, he felt strangely deflated. Perhaps it was because he had finally understood why she behaved as she did. Her father's heavy reliance on her had greatly affected her, understandably so, but there was no longer any need for her to worry. She would always have Benedict to see to her well-being now.

He felt an overwhelming sense of protectiveness and compassion, but knew she must accept the truth before there would be any relief inside her. Benedict glanced back over his shoulder to where she rode, silent and pale, beside her maid. As if feeling his gaze upon her, she looked up, her golden eyes widening as they met his, her lips turning up in a hesitant smile, a smile he had never expected to see directed toward him. His heart thudded in his chest and Benedict found himself smiling in return. A deep flush stained those creamy cheeks, before she looked down at her hands on the reins of her chestnut mare.

Surprised and uncertain of what this might mean, Benedict nevertheless found that his body reacted as it always did to Raine. He felt a tightening in his lower belly that told him how very susceptible he was to her, to a mere smile from those lovely lips.

The sky remained overcast and gray for the whole of the morning as they traveled. When the moisture in the air became so thick that it misted about them in damp pockets, Benedict decided that he would stop for the night. Although he knew that Raine would be perturbed at his halting their progress for her sake, Benedict could not allow her to go on for so long in poor weather. It had only been a short time since she made the journey to Abbernathy. Her strength was not boundless in spite of her wishes to the contrary.

He did not allow himself to believe that he felt any hint of anticipation at what might lay behind his wife's smile. Yet as he held up his hand to call the party to a halt, he found his gaze straying to her again.

Without thinking, he dismounted and went to stand beside her. She flushed as he held out his hand. "Let me help you. The ground here is slippery from the rain."

Her searching eyes held his for a moment, before she reached out to place her hand in his. He was well aware of the collective gazes that watched them, but refused to acknowledge them. She was his wife.

He held her closely as he helped her to the ground, felt that now familiar tightening in his lower body. Looking down into her wide golden eyes, he wondered if she, too, had felt something in that contact.

Quickly Benedict told himself he must not think that way. Raine had made her wishes clear. He pushed his desire to the darkest core of himself. "I will see that your tent is erected immediately. You should get in out of the rain."

She glanced down at her folded hands. "I...thank you, Benedict."

He felt suddenly awkward as a young lad, glancing about them restlessly. His gaze came to rest upon a grinning William.

Immediately he stepped back from her. He did not wish to give the boy any false hopes. He knew that Raine would not thank him for that. When he said, "Well, I must be about setting up camp," she made no demur.

Benedict made no effort to approach his wife as a meal was prepared. He busied himself with tending the fire and horses once the tents had been erected. But he remained infinitely aware of her where she sat with Aida on the log William had rolled close to the fire. It surprised him that though she wore her hood pulled up close to block the moisture that hovered about them, she did not seek shelter. What could be made of this Benedict dared not imagine.

He instead concentrated on William, who for his part seemed quite cheery since Benedict had helped Raine from her mare. He had joined the men on the opposite side of the fire, laughing as they teased and talked with him. William was well liked already.

But Benedict did not for one moment lose consciousness of every gesture Raine made as she talked to her maid, every bite she took from the roasted fowl he had taken earlier that morning. Her every breath held a fascination for him.

Just as the sun was setting Raine stood and made her way to the edge of the forest. Believing he knew whence she was going, Benedict did not interfere or call attention to her as she ducked into the thicket.

Yet as the minutes passed and she did not return, Benedict began to grow somewhat troubled. He knew that it was all too easy for one to take a wrong turn or step into a hole and twist an ankle.

As if reading his mind, William looked up at him from across the fire. "Raine has been gone for a long time."

Casually Benedict nodded. "Aye. Methinks I will go and see what is keeping her." Deliberately he kept his tone light. He knew how protective the boy was of his sister. He was sure there was no need for concern.

Benedict rose and followed the path she had taken into the forest. When he had gone only a short distance into the dense wood, Benedict stopped in consternation. Here the trail branched into two equally well defined pathways.

He looked right and shook his head, then with a nod of decision, turned and took the path to the left. If he knew anything at all about Raine it was that she was apt to take the least likely course. Well, he conceded with a trace of amusement, the one least likely to himself. He continued on. He wanted to call out to her when he did not see any sign of her after a few more moments, yet he knew Raine would not appreciate his acting overconcerned. He was still fairly certain that there was naught amiss.

As he walked he began to be aware that the weather was worsening. The rain, which had been drizzling from the low gray sky for the last hours, began to fall in earnest.

Luckily the temperature was unseasonably warm in spite of the moisture, and he felt no real cold or discomfort. Still he moved on through the forest with added determination. It would be best to find Raine before she got soaked.

Striding on, he came to a particularly dense part of the woods. Here even the path was nearly overgrown. He wondered if he could have taken the wrong way, but something told him that he had not. He pressed on.

In spite of feeling that he was indeed going in the right direction, Benedict was nearly ready to give up and go back the way he had come when he reached the edge of a clearing. His gaze searched the area, and came to rest upon her where she stood near a row of trees, her face turned to the sky, her eyes closed as if she was in silent prayer.

Raine had needed some time to herself, time to think, to consider why she was reacting to Benedict so very strongly. Perhaps it was because he was at long last showing her some of the gentleness she had sensed in him that first day at court. Could it be that he might at last be coming to see how very difficult all of this—the conflict with Denley, her fears over doing what was right for William, over leaving her home—had been for her?

Perhaps those were not the reasons. Perhaps it was because he now felt that her capitulation was complete. The thought was a painful one, but one she must consider, no matter how difficult it might be.

Raine shook her head, finding herself no closer to making sense of it all. She told herself that it was simply because he was too near. The mere brush of his body against hers as he helped her to dismount was enough to set her blood singing. Having him close by had proved tumultuous for her emotions from the very beginning.

Yet when she had come here to the wood, she had found herself no closer to a resolution. It was as if her emotions, her feelings were set alight, as if some strange flicker of awareness had entered her and would not be snuffed. She was beset by images of the night they had spent together, the way he had touched her, kissed her.

Her face, her neck, all of her felt flushed and hot in a way she could not quite describe. Raine had walked on, unheeding of where she went, until she came to this quiet glade. Deep inside herself she had sensed the peace of this place and hoped it would ease the turbulence inside her.

From her pocket she took the tiny clear stone she had found on her last walk with her mother. They had gone to the forest together, as they often did. Her auburn-haired mother had been laughing and beautiful in spite of the fact that her belly was growing so round. They had gathered roots, then sat beneath a large tree to eat freshly baked bread and talk of the birds and the sky and how much joy the babe would bring.

Sitting here, Raine realized that those memories did not reside at Abbernathy, but in her heart. Yet leaving was so very hard. For the first time since her mother's death her tears fell freely. When the rain began to fall, she wanted nothing so much as to ease the heat inside herself in its coolness. Somehow she felt the rain would wash away some of her sorrow, that she would be renewed by the sweetness of it on her face.

Slowly a feeling of peace came over her. She knew a sense of oneness with her long dead mother; her weak but loving father; the forest, which stood in silent worship. Knew suddenly that all was in constant movement, that change was a part of life. She was revived and fed by the life-giving moisture of the rain. But then something, some indefinable stirring in the hairs at the base of her nape, made her look up. She was not surprised to find Benedict standing there, his eyes dark with an emotion she dared not name, for it answered one that blazed within herself.

She met that gaze and held it. It was as if in some way her being here this way had empowered her, had freed her from the anxiety that had been so much a part of her thinking of late. She spoke from her heart. ''I am sorry for many of the things I have said and done, Benedict. For a very long time all I could see was my own need to return to Abbernathy, to love and care for those who needed me, as I had for my whole life. The peace we knew then disappeared with my father's death, for there are too many who do not respect nor understand the role I have played, being but a woman. I was a fool to believe your name alone would protect us from Denley and his ilk. I have owed you a debt of gratitude rather than antagonism and anger, for I think you have at least attempted to see my position. Have done all that you could.'' He moved to speak but she forestalled him for a moment longer. ''I also wish to thank you for allowing me to see that all was well before we left and for giving me the opportunity to say goodbye.''

He came toward her, obviously moved by her words, for his voice was husky as he replied, ''I require no thanks, Raine. It was not too much to ask once I understood what you had been, all that you had taken upon yourself.''

She shook her head, her gaze unable to break contact with those blue eyes. ''Nonetheless I am grateful.'' She could hear the breathlessness in her own voice.

He took a deep breath and another step toward her, ''Raine, I...'' Then he hesitated.

It seemed only a natural part of the moment for her to hold out her hand, whisper, ''Come to me, my husband.''

When he continued to hesitate, she acted on the impulse that shot through her and drew her wet clothes from her body in a mere moment. Then, standing unashamedly before him, she spoke more urgently, reaching out her other hand. ''There is no need for hesitation. Let us make love together in the spring rain, take part in the renewal of life.''

Benedict stared at those two slender white hands, then his gaze moved down her body, every lovely inch of her bared to the falling rain. The raindrops glistened upon her creamy breasts, making him want to lick them away, feel the softness of her flesh beneath his tongue. That one experience with her had shown him that her skin was velvety and smooth, the kind of skin that beckoned a man's touch, made him forget all else in the caressing of it. His gaze dipped lower to the curves of her hips, her legs so long and lovely. Those legs had gripped him so tightly, made him want to slip into the warmth of her flesh.

And more than that was the depth of warmth and welcome he saw in those golden eyes. It was a welcome he had never thought to see. His mind was awhirl, his blood like a river of fire pounding through his heart.

From whence had she come, this creature of life and nature? Benedict did not know. All he did know was that he could not deny her—or himself.

He raised his own hand, moving toward her without conscious thought. When her cool fingers closed around his, he drew in a sharp breath at the degree of desire that shot through him. Such a light touch, so delicate, but so arousing. Benedict groaned at the rush of sensations that raced through him.

All his attention, his entire being was centered on Raine as she came closer, her golden eyes focused on his. Without a word she reached for the hem of his tunic. His knees weakened as she began to lift.

He moved to help her, trying desperately to give himself something to do, something to think on save his own body's overwhelming reaction to her touch. But his actions gave him little aid, for as soon as the garment had passed over his head, Raine spread those cool hands of hers across his chest. Benedict shuddered at the sensations that pulsed through him.

Raine felt him shudder and smiled. She did not know what had happened to her, nor where her brazen courage had come from. The fact that Benedict had come upon her here like this was surely a sign from the heavens above that she should be with him.

It was as if the wildness of the forest throbbed within her. Or perhaps it was the pounding of her own need for this man?

Whichever was the case, Raine was past caring. It had been too hard to fight her own needs and desires. Her eyes met his, which had darkened to indigo with the passion he could not disguise. She felt a rush of elation. She, Raine, had brought about this reaction in him.

Feeling an answering thrill within herself, she lifted her mouth, inviting his kiss.

Benedict could not ignore the invitation of her mouth. He dipped his head and claimed her lips as his arms closed around her. When her soft tongue prodded at his mouth, he opened to her, his head whirling afresh. Determinedly he pulled himself back from that precipice of pleasure as his tongue met hers, sliding along that tender length with deliberate intent. For he did not mean to allow her all the advances. He, too, meant to give delight, to see her react to his own caresses with passion.

His hands traced the curve of her back, sliding lower to grip her hips for a long moment, before molding the luscious curves of her bottom. He pulled her more closely against him, reveling in the fact that she gasped and held his shoulders tightly as he did so.

Obviously Raine, too, felt this deep and overwhelming need. He kissed her again, sucking at her bottom lip and chuckling softly in the back of his throat when she moaned with pleasure.

Raine was on fire. With each kiss and caress the ache in her lower belly grew thicker, more delicious, more compelling. She pressed herself more closely to him and gasped as he reached down to grasp her bare hips, pulling her against his burgeoning desire. She reveled not only in the feel of those strong, sure hands on her flesh but also in the fact that in his hardness lay the end to her torment, the culmination of all her desire.

Her fingers twined in the top of his hose, tugging urgently, and Benedict knew what she wanted. Just the thought of her eagerness made his manhood react. Benedict had to close his eyes for a moment, take a deep breath to gain mastery of himself. But in some part of himself he knew that what was happening was beyond his control. He had become a creature of pleasure, taking and giving without conscious thought.

And he, too, wanted to be bare—exposed to not only the woman in his arms but the wildness of the forest and the rain.

Quickly he drew away, but only far and long enough to jerk off the hose. The moment he tossed them aside he moved to take her back in his arms, but Raine resisted him, stepping away so that she could see him. Benedict held his breath.

In the last dying rays of the day, he was so powerful and unbelievably beautiful in his nakedness that she caught her own breath. Her gaze found his without shame, telling him openly how moved she was.

Strangely humbled by her regard, Benedict pulled her back into his arms. He kissed her—kissed her so thoroughly and so deeply that the world tilted and her blood sang with wanting.

When his now free manhood pulsed against her belly, Raine felt an answering reaction in her own core, was aware of the swollen need of her own womanhood. She clasped her hands to his buttocks, holding him tightly to her as he had done to her only moments ago.

He gasped in reaction and she smiled a secret breathless smile of satisfaction and undeniable hunger.

When they had made love at Brackenmoore, it had been because he'd wanted to have a child, that he wished for the conflict between them to be over. He had imagined that he could make things right between them simply by going on as if it were so. Now she wanted him to make love to her because he could not do otherwise.

Though she knew it was not love they shared in this wild joining, she wanted Benedict to feel the way she felt. She wanted him to lose control of himself and his reactions as she had.

It was as if this would, in some small way, make her feel less alone, less mad for not being able to control her own attraction to him.

She was determined that this time it would be she and not Benedict who took command of what they did. With this thought in mind, she stepped back from him once more, catching and holding his gaze as, with deliberate intent, she reached up to slowly trace a hand over the hard muscles of his chest. She paused, teasingly stroking the tips of his nipples.

Raine smiled when he gasped, his mouth opening as his breath quickened. How good it was to know that she could evoke this reaction in him.

When he reached out for her she shook her head, her

voice an unrecognizable utterance of both passion and assurance as she whispered, "No, not yet."

She moved to place her mouth where her hands had been on his smooth hard chest. Her tongue tasted the rain and salt on his skin and she sighed.

His hoarse murmuring of her name only served to drive her on, to further embolden her. Without pausing to consider, she dipped her head lower, trailing her lips over his abdomen and nuzzling at the base of his belly. She could hear his breathing become more ragged with each movement of her lips. Benedict's reactions drove her on.

She closed her hand gently over the hardness of him. In her mind was a sharp memory of the way he had once pleasured her. She kissed that heated flesh.

Again Benedict moved to halt her, but she would not be thwarted. This moment was hers to command.

She slipped her mouth over him. His gasp of "Raine," was enough to tell her that she was indeed pleasuring him, driving him beyond the steel wall of control he had erected around himself.

Benedict was drowning, his mind and body awhirl with the sensations she was awakening inside him. She, Raine, was the center of the universe, and all things in it were mere worshipers of her radiant warmth and light. Wave after wave of sweet delight rippled through him with her every movement.

Yet even as his pleasure mounted, from some distant place inside came the knowledge that he must find the will to halt her. He would soon be unmanned, and that he did not want. More than anything in his life he wished to pleasure her, to know the rapture of bringing her to culmination.

With a great force of will he pulled away, hearing

the rasping sound of his own voice calling, "No more, Raine, no more."

He drew her up to hold her against his body, taking deep gulps of air as he rested his hot forehead against her wildly tangled hair. When she wriggled against him, her own breathing quick and harsh, he lifted her in his arms and laid her on the soft grass beneath them. And even as he positioned himself over her, Raine opened to him.

And now they danced together, their bodies finding a rhythm as old as time and as irrefutable.

Raine no longer thought of making Benedict lose himself, for she, too, was lost, merging with the delight that drove her on. Merging with Benedict, the feel and touch and taste of him.

The sensations built until she felt as she was poised on the brink of all creation. Yet it was only when she sensed the shudders of completion that rippled through Benedict that she fell over that brink, falling—falling into a place where there was only ecstasy.

Benedict sagged above Raine, his mind and body still pulsing with desire even though his climax had passed. Finally, weakly, he rolled to lie beside her on the dampened earth. And even though he knew that he should now be aware of the grass against his bare skin, the rain on his face, he could concentrate on, was aware of nothing save Raine. He knew each breath she drew in, felt the prickle of the fine hairs on her flesh as she began to experience the coolness of the rain. He was aware of the ripples of sweet fulfillment that pulsed gently in her belly, the pleasing languor that weighted her limbs; all were as vivid as if it were he experiencing them.

So shocked was he by what he was feeling that for a long moment Benedict did not quite understand what was occurring. But when he did realize that somehow what had passed between them had made him a part of Raine, in some mystical way that he could not even begin to understand, he shot to a sitting position.

Only then did the sensations cease. In their wake was left a powerful need to deny them. Yet that he could not do. No matter how unexplainable, what he had felt for those moments had been real. With that realization came the certainty that he could not allow such a thing to ever happen again.

He was Brackenmoore. Never could he let himself be absorbed, bewitched by any woman, however unknowingly. For he did not imagine for even a moment that she had cast some spell over him. He was not so foolish as that.

He must think on what had led up to this moment, to the fact that Raine was clearly beset by guilt at having been so angry with him. For reasons he could not begin to understand he did not want her guilt, not when making love to her had made him lose himself so completely. Without looking at her he rose and began to don his wet clothing.

Raine's voice halted him as he jerked his houppelande over his head. "Benedict?"

When he turned to face her he saw that she was now standing, her gown held before her protectively, her eyes filled with disbelief and confusion.

Sympathy made him say, "Raine, I…" But he halted without finishing, for what was he to tell her—that their lovemaking had so moved him that for however brief a moment he had felt as if he was inside her? As if he, Benedict, had somehow become her?

He could not do so. She would never believe him, and any lesser reason would not suffice to explain why he must now hold himself from her. For that was what he knew he must do. She was recalcitrant enough now, but far too erratic in her behavior. Raine had no true care for him and thus might not continue to hold him in favor. Likely would not do so. He ignored the ache this thought brought to his chest.

A cry of disillusion escaped her as she quickly drew on her own clothes. He kept his gaze averted, only looking at her when she was finished, saying, "We should go back to the camp now."

Angrily she shook her head. "I will not go back with you. Leave me to make my own way."

He frowned, deliberately keeping his voice even. "You know I cannot do that."

The next thing he knew she was shaking a small, furious fist in his face. "Do you know how very much I hate it when you do that?"

He took a step backward in surprise at this unexpected attack. "Do what, madam?"

"When you act as though nothing matters, as though you are not affected by anything."

He raised dark brows high, the very accusation bringing a stirring of indignation to his own breast. "I do no such thing. Many things trouble me, especially of late." He cast her a pointed looked. "I merely accept that I cannot afford myself the luxury of losing control, of giving in to my every emotion."

This seemed to only further enrage her, for she sputtered, "You cannot afford yourself the luxury of losing control? That your responsibilities prevent you from being human is all in your own mind. The only reason you keep such a tight hold on yourself, Benedict, is that you are very glad to feel yourself superior to the rest of us. Your need to control everything has nothing to do with doing your duty. It is your way of protecting yourself.''

A blinding wall of outrage rose up to hold him silent for a long moment before he found his tongue, and when he did he had no care for how much anger he betrayed. "How dare you, you shrew. You think that you do not do all in your power to control everyone and everything about you. That is exactly what you do when you rush ahead with every impulsive notion that pops into that pretty head of yours.''

He caught her hand before it could connect with his chin. Trying to jerk away from him, she cried, "I do not."

He held that fist in his own, his eyes boring into hers relentlessly. "You do, madam, you do. Why do you think you rushed into marriage? It was not only to care for William, though I do grant you that played a part. You say that William has not had opportunity to mourn your father. Have you? I tell you that you cannot run from such pains, they find you. I tell you this as well, Raine—you cannot do what is best for yourself or anyone else lest you learn to stop and think what may happen as a result of your running."

She shook her head in utter desperation, her hair flying about her wildly. "Mourn? As usual you are right. That is exactly what I was able to do before you came upon me here. Though what good it has done me when you continue to behave like a knave I do not know."

With that she jerked out of his grasp and raced down the path. Immediately Benedict followed her, but he made no move to catch her. Something told him that he had pushed Raine far enough.

And truth to tell there was another reason for his hanging back. Now that his anger was cooling he was beset by self-doubt. Could there be any truth to her accusations that he was only using his responsibilities as an excuse to remain above and distant from others?

Determinedly he shook his head. It was not true. He only did what he had to. It was Raine who was hiding from her emotions. He could not allow himself to be caught up in worrying over such wild accusations.

He had enough on his mind with trying to master the strange feeling he had experienced after they made love. He must prevent such a thing from ever occurring again. For deep inside he knew that whatever had brought about the sensations had the power to destroy him as he knew himself to be. That was something that he could not allow to happen. Too many people depended on him to see to their happiness, their very existence. She said she had mourned her loss. He was glad for that, but no less concerned about how her life had shaped her. She was as wild and impulsive as in the beginning. Was in fact more so, if what had just occurred between them was any indication.

Losing himself so completely, as he had in Raine for those moments, could jeopardize his ability to do what he must. Which was to put no one being above the others—including a wife. Especially one who had no care for him.

Chapter Eleven

The remaining days upon the road stretched long and unbearably for Raine. Benedict seemed completely unaffected by what had passed between them in that terrible confrontation where he had accused her—her, for the love of all the saints!—of being the one who had to be in control. Since then he had more than proved her echoing words by being as controlled and unemotional as a stone. He was polite and deferential to the point of driving her mad, seeing that she was made comfortable and her every physical need met—save one.

Raine was so confused she did not know where to turn. She certainly could not answer his cool indifference with like behavior. It was completely beyond her to even attempt such a thing, as it would be for any feeling being—a category Benedict obviously did not number among.

Their return to Brackenmoore brought very little relief. To conduct herself with any sense of pride or courage, she knew she could not remain sequestered in her chamber. Yet when she did come out there were many speculative glances cast her way. None of the servants, not even Maeve, made any remark on her running away, taking Benedict's lead and treating her as if she were queen of all England. But she knew that her actions could not have been met with approval.

All she could do was hold her head high and avoid interacting with anyone unless necessary. Meals were the most difficult occasions. There was nothing to be done but appear. Only William's presence kept her seated at these debacles, for each time Benedict asked her a polite question, such as how she had spent her day, or if she would care for more wine, she wanted to scream.

She had taken to preparing herself for these interminable episodes of torture as if she were attending court functions. Fine garments and carefully coiffed hair, in some sense, acted as a sort of armor against Benedict's insufferable coolness. It was as if in her finery she was saying that she, Raine, was more than equal to this place, this man she called husband.

It also gave her something to think about instead of the anguish she had felt looking into Benedict's eyes only moments after he had made love to her, and seeing a remote coldness that had made her blood turn to ice. Whatever had brought about the sudden change she could not begin to fathom. She knew only that her heart would not withstand another such rejection.

She need not worry on that. He made no such overtures.

The hours when she was not in her chambers she spent with William. He sensed her unhappiness, though she did her best to deflect his every query on the subject. She told him she was missing those at Abbernathy and would soon be herself again, though she did not believe it for an instant. She encouraged him to spend time with Kendran, who continued to be kind to her brother. More than once she found herself thinking, with regret, that if Benedict were only able to shed that air of reserve and autocracy, he might be very like Kendran. Yet it was clear he would never do so.

Thus it was with head held high that Raine entered the hall one night after her sixth week back at Brackenmoore. Seeing that Benedict was alone at the high table, Raine hesitated, but when he glanced up and nodded briefly, she had no choice but to move forward and take her place.

She felt his eyes sweep over her, but refused to meet them. The cloth-of-gold gown and royal-blue overdress were, by her own admission, too fine for this occasion, but she did not let that concern her in the least. In this she must please no one but herself. She certainly had no interest in pleasing a husband who had no interest in her.

She was gladly distracted from such thoughts by the arrival of William and Kendran. They were laughing, and as she looked at William, Raine saw the happiness in his green eyes, the healthy glow in his cheeks. It was such a marked change from his demeanor before she had wed Benedict. This, she told herself firmly, made any unhappiness she was experiencing in this marriage bearable. Did it not?

She tried to answer her brother's happy chatter in kind, but had no real concept of what she said in reply.

Raine's wayward gaze spent too long upon her husband. Why did he still look so handsome to her? Why did her heartbeat still quicken every time she thought of the way they had made love in the forest? Why were her dreams filled with images of the two of them…?

With an inward groan she pulled her gaze away. Benedict's lack of attention to herself or the two boys told her that he was too preoccupied with his own concerns to be thinking the wild thoughts that tormented her so.

Quickly she assured herself that she did not care about his lack of interest. Not in the least. Yet she remained very aware of him and his distracted air.

"Raine!" It was with some confusion that she heard her name being said with a trace of impatience. Turning, she realized that William was looking at her with an expectant expression.

Raine drew herself up, smiling with forced ease. "I am sorry. I was not attending. What was it you wanted?"

He arched his brows high, watching her closely. "I can see you were not listening, Raine. Is all well with you?"

Quickly she nodded, smiling all the more widely. "I am fine. I was but...it matters not. What is it you need?"

"I wish to go to Wyndam with Kendran on the morrow."

Raine looked at the older boy. He was smiling at her with that compelling charm of his. Once more, Raine could not help feeling that when he was older and that manner of his became subtler he would be irresistible. As it was, she was not swayed in the least.

She found herself thinking that a mature and direct approach would be more appealing. And realized she had turned to face her husband once more.

Horror filled her. Had she gone completely mad? Benedict was not mature and direct, he was cruel and heartless, willing to do or say anything in order to keep command of all around him.

Determinedly Raine looked back toward her brother. She was not at all sure she wished for him to go off with the older boy. She queried, "How far is Wyndam and when will you return? Do you mean to take a troupe to protect you?"

There was a long silence and Raine felt herself blush. She was infinitely aware that they were likely thinking of her rashness in taking William with her to Abbernathy.

Benedict spoke up then. "They will take the proper measures, Raine. The keep is but a four-hour ride away. The two of them will be back by day's end the day after tomorrow."

She frowned. Her chaotic feelings about him made her reply coolly. "I will thank you to allow me to make this one decision for myself."

His gaze swept her with surprise and indifference as he said, "By all means then, do decide."

The sound of a heavy sigh drew her gaze to William's unhappy one. Instantly Raine realized she had made a fool of herself and for no good reason. Only her troubles with Benedict made her react this way. Deliberately she kept herself from looking toward her husband again. She must somehow find a way to relax in his presence, behave civilly. It would be unbearable were she not able to do so.

She took a deep breath, concentrating on William. "You may go with Kendran."

William smiled with pleasure, though she noted there was still a trace of sadness in his gaze as he met hers. He said only, "Thank you, Raine."

She could feel Benedict's attention on her as she rose, but she refrained from looking at him. "Your pardon. I find I am very tired."

Quickly Raine left the hall, realizing that this last statement was indeed true. She had been very tired of late, sleeping far more than she had ever done before. With this realization came a lurking suspicion that made her begin to count the weeks with an expression of amazement and, regretfully, sorrow. For the news was not welcome to her, not as things stood between herself and Benedict.

She rose early the next morning, having slept less than in recent nights. Donning her clothing without aid, she went to the window and opened it, leaning out as she took in deep cooling breaths of the fresh spring air. It did not help ease her understanding that this day stretched before her, as interminable and painful as the rest. The knowledge that burned in her heart only made matters worse.

Though she never went out without William, he was gone, and she could not remain here in her room. It would give her far too much opportunity to dwell on what Benedict would think if he knew her secret.

Taking up her cloak, she left her chamber and made her way through the keep. Many of the castle folk watched her as she passed, a few nodding with grave formality. No one made any effort to speak to or detain her. Raine told herself she was grateful for this. She did not care to make polite conversation with anyone connected to her husband. Even when she exited the castle gate she was allowed to pass unmolested.

This surprised her somewhat. She would have thought that Benedict might have instructed the guards to watch her for fear of her leaving. The only assurance he had that she would not do so was her word. Raine did not allow herself to believe that her word carried any weight with him. The blackguard was just too sure of himself to think she would ever do such a thing a second time.

Pulling her cloak more closely about her as she started down the sloping castle mound, Raine determined to shrug off her irritation. She would not allow Benedict to ruin the remainder of her morning.

Raine turned in the direction of the sea. It had been beautiful there, the feelings of peace she had experienced still alive in some distant part of her memory. Perhaps she could find them again, especially as this time Benedict would not be present to disturb her.

Benedict again! Squaring her shoulders, Raine trudged on, concentrating on the path. So occupied was she in keeping her thoughts from straying to Benedict that she failed to take more than cursory note of the fineness of the blue sky overhead, or the richness of the grass beneath her feet. When she reached the cliffs, she found the circuitous trail that led down to the beach was quite steep, and she paid close attention to where she stepped. Once on the sand she quickly started off to her left. She was aware of the expanse of the sea to one side of her, the height of the cliffs on the other, the weight of the sand beneath her leather shoes, but her agitation remained a constant distraction. Then slowly, the sound of the waves pulling against the sand began to soothe her with their gentle and steady rhythm.

Though she was not completely at rest as she started off once more, Raine was now aware of the blue of the sky and the mournful cries of the gulls overhead.

She had not gone much farther when she looked up to see that she had inadvertently come upon a slender young woman sitting on a rock at the edge of the sea. Feeling that she was intruding upon the solitary figure, she paused in preparation of turning back the way she had come. Then something halted her, something troubling in the lovely profile of the young blond woman who stared so intently into the waves. Raine bit her lip in indecision as an inner voice bade her speak. She knew that the woman would likely resent her intrusion, yet she could not walk away.

Giving in to that seemingly uncontrollable impulse, Raine moved forward, saying, "Good day."

The young woman swung about, her gray eyes registering surprise. Quickly she rose and bowed. "My lady."

Raine nodded in return. Obviously her identity was known to this stranger. This fact should not surprise her. Their overlord's taking a wife would be of great import to all who dwelled in and around Brackenmoore.

She could see that the young woman was nervous by the way her fingers kept pleating the skirt of her blue wool gown. Thinking to put her more at ease, Raine said, "Forgive my intrusion. I simply saw that you, too, were enjoying the view."

She watched closely as the girl looked out over the ocean, then replied, "You are not intruding, my lady. I was but thinking about..." Raine could not help seeing the longing in her gaze as she took in the distant horizon.

Feeling even more certain than before that something was quite amiss, Raine obeyed the impulse to step even closer, her gaze searching out and holding the other woman's. "Is aught amiss?"

The girl gave a visible start. "Why would you think so, my lady?"

Raine was nothing if not direct. "I do not know. But I cannot dismiss the feeling that—"

To her utter amazement the girl put her hands over her face and began to cry, her sobs shaking her slender shoulders. Before she even knew that she was going to do so, Raine found herself wrapping a supporting arm about those shoulders, murmuring soft words of comfort. "There now, tell me what is wrong."

The girl raised tear-filled eyes. "I can tell no one."

Raine looked at her with compassion, but also unwavering conviction. "You can tell me. Nothing can be so very bad as that." She paused as the sobbing began anew, but went on after only a moment. "Why do you not begin simply then, perhaps with your name?"

The tormented maiden gulped, then raised her head once more. "My name is Leandra."

"That is a very pretty name."

Again she put her hands over her face, crying, "That is what he said."

Raine felt a dawning understanding. "I take it that your distress has been brought on by something this 'he' has done?"

In a muffled and tormented voice, she answered, "Aye, my lady."

"The blackguard."

The tears stopped as suddenly as they'd begun. Leandra replied fiercely, "Your forgiveness, my lady, but he is not a blackguard. He is good and kind and—"

"Then what is the trouble?"

A deep flush stained the girl's cheeks. "My lady…I am…" Her hand went to her belly as again her yearning gaze turned to the sea.

Seeing that gesture, Raine knew what had occurred. Quickly she said, "He has abused you. And refused to do what is right by you."

Leandra looked at her bleakly. "Nay, not abused. I was most willing." She flushed even more darkly but did not look away. "We met at the winter festival. He was handsome and strong. We drank too much wine and..."

"Again I ask, what is the trouble then?"

She sighed. "I have not told him of the child."

Raine put her hands on her hips. "Why have you not done so? You must."

The other's lips set in a stubborn line. "I will not. He has not spoken to me since and I do not wish for him to wed me out of duty. I love him and want him to love me."

Ah, love, Raine thought. It was an emotion she could well survive without. It made this unfortunate girl speak of her despoiler as if he had been wronged, and not she who had a child on the way and no man to care for it.

Yet Raine knew her opinion of the fellow would not gain her Leandra's confidence, and that was exactly what she must have if she were to be of any help. The father must be told of the child, thus averting the disastrous remedy the girl was surely contemplating. Raine said, "I believe you do love him and only want to protect him. But I am also most certain that he would wish to know of his child."

Leandra began to cry again, but more quietly. "I do not wish for him to wed me for the child. I want him to choose to come to me for my own sake. He is handsome and strong and brave, and my heart aches for his love."

Raine felt herself flush from the top of her head to the soles of her feet. The very words conjured up an immediate and intense memory of the way she had felt when Benedict kissed her, touched her. And the knowledge of just what had resulted from those embraces.

As if sensing that she had said too much, Leandra put her hand to her mouth. "I beg pardon, my lady."

Raine's voice was far too husky as she replied, "That is quite all right."

The girl stared off dreamily. "Of course you would know of what I speak, being newly wed to a man such as Lord Benedict. R—my love admires his master well."

Raine had no reply to make to that. At least none that she would voice aloud. What she did gather was that this unknown fellow must be in Benedict's retinue. "So this man is in the service of my husband."

Leandra admitted reluctantly, "He is, my lady. And I would not wish for him to lose his place." She closed her lips as if determined to say no more.

Raine realized she would get no further here. She would have no choice in this matter but to go to Benedict, though the very notion made her stomach roll. The only thing that made her certain she must indeed do so was the fear of what Leandra might do if she did not.

When Raine opened the door to the chamber the serving woman had directed her to, Benedict looked up, his gaze registering surprise. Immediately the expression was covered by that accustomed mask of reserve.

Fighting a disappointment she did not want to feel, Raine lost no time in platitudes. "I need converse with you, my lord."

He turned to speak to another man she had not previously noted. The fellow got up from his seat across the table, which was heavily laden with books and ledgers, as Benedict indicated him with a wave. "My steward."

Raine nodded at the man's formal bow.

Benedict then told him, "Please leave us. I will send for you when I am ready to continue."

She felt a momentary sense of gratitude that her husband would put aside his business on her request. Quickly she pushed it aside, telling herself that she should not be surprised by his deference. Treating her with such a civility made him feel that he behaved properly.

As soon as the steward was gone he stood. "What do you wish to speak to me about, Raine?"

She moved toward the table, noting as she did so that she had never seen so many shelves of books in all her life. Though the fact was surprising, she must keep her thoughts on the problem at hand. "It is a matter of the utmost import." Taking a deep breath to calm the anger that rose in her at the very thought of what had been done to Leandra, she went on. "I went for a walk along the shore and there I met a young woman named Leandra."

He nodded. "I know of her."

"That is well," she told him. "I may then get to the point quickly."

He folded his hands before him in an attitude of studied attention, and she felt a twinge of resentment. Why did he have to be so insufferably self-possessed?

Damn him, she thought in frustration. But she would ignore her differences with him long enough to get this said. Quickly and with a cool deliberation of her own she told him the tale of how she had met the young woman. She was pleased at the way Benedict sat up straighter, his expression becoming seriously troubled even before she ended with, "The young lady has told me she is with child and I believe one of your soldiers is responsible."

He spoke harshly. "Who is he?"

Raine shrugged. "That she would not tell me, for she has some silly, romantic notion that he must ask her to wed not for the sake of the child, but for herself. She feels that his learning of the child would force his hand." Raine avoided Benedict's gaze as she spoke of the other woman's child, fearful that he might read her sensitivity to this subject in her eyes. She was not prepared to share this secret with her husband, though she was not sure why.

Benedict came around the side of the table, thankfully oblivious to her dilemma. "That is ridiculous. My men are a decent lot. I am most certain that any one of them would wish to do the right thing by her for her own sake."

Raine raised her brows. "Do you really believe so, Benedict? Simply because they are friends to you does not mean that they are all of such sterling and honorable character. You are not above hurting another." She stopped herself, appalled that the words had come from her mouth.

He frowned at her, chagrined. "We are not talking of you and me, Raine. I tell you I know the hearts of my men."

She shrugged, hiding her surprise at his discomfort. "I will not debate with *you*. What I do wish to know is what you intend to do about her predicament."

Benedict remained silent for a very long time. At last he looked at her and said, "Raine, I do not know that it would be right for me to intervene. I have long since made a vow not to interfere in such matters." He stared down at his hands. "I cost Tristan and Lily much in the way of peace and happiness by intruding in their relationship. Although I did genuinely feel that it would be a mistake for him to wed the daughter of our enemy, I was dreadfully wrong. If it had not been for me, they would not have had to run away in secret, and their babe would not have been born in a carriage in the dead of night. And Lily would not have lost her memory.''

Raine did not understand all of the details of what he was telling her, but she could hear the pain in Benedict's voice, believed him completely sincere in his motives in this. Yet she had to make him see that the two instances were not the same. She glared at him in frustration. ''The situation cannot simply be left as it is.''

''Can you not understand what I am attempting to tell you, Raine? What must be done to rectify this kind of situation may seem perfectly clear, but that does not mean it is. I have learned that it is best to allow others to take care of their own love affairs. Surely time will bring all to the correct order.''

She stamped her foot, her frustration at his inability to fully involve himself in his own marriage making her speak sharply. ''Will you not hear me, Benedict? We cannot simply stand by and hope for the best. This is one moment when you must act in spite of your belief. And it must be done now, without further thinking.''

She paused to glare at him again, and when he made no immediate reply, said, ''Have I not made myself clear on this? I fear for the girl's well-being. When I found her there she was staring out into the sea as if… I fear she means to end her life.''

A dark frown marred his brow as he took her arm in a tight grip. ''Did she say as much?''

Reluctantly Raine shook her head. ''Nay, but I am certain—''

His face relaxing somewhat, he interrupted her. ''Though I do believe you most sincere in your intent here, it is possible that you have misread her purpose. What you have asked of me goes against all I have experienced in such situations. I must think on it, Raine."

Outraged that he would be so very obstinate, Raine threw up her hands. "I quit you then, my lord. I cannot stand by and watch as you consider this matter until it is too late." With that she swung about and stormed out.

Benedict watched her go with a dark scowl. Surely she was overreacting. How many times had he seen her rush headlong into disaster?

Her anger at the way he had turned from her after they made love was more than apparent, in spite of his efforts to treat her with every courtesy due a wife. Though he did regret that, Benedict had, as yet, found no solution to the problem. He could not risk losing himself—his very existence as he knew it—in the unpredictable Raine. That he was capable of doing so was more apparent with each passing day. For far from forgetting the incident in the forest as he had hoped, he had become consumed by it, thought of it incessantly, woke dripping sweat from dreams of it.

As the days had passed he'd attempted to busy himself with the running of the keep, with answering the steady stream of letters that continued to pour from the angry quill of Alister Harcourt. All to little avail. Benedict knew the situation with Harcourt must be concluded. He simply could not focus on a solution, which was more distressing than he would ever admit, even to himself. He had always been able to think, to act, as he must. Until now.

As Benedict moved to call his waiting steward, he

could not quite ignore a nagging feeling that in this matter of Leandra, Raine might be correct. It galled him to admit, in even the smallest way, that her method of jumping into murky waters without thinking could be correct.

Yet her assertion that Leandra might be contemplating a permanent way out of her dilemma was worrying. If Raine was correct, any delay could well end in disaster.

What were the chances that she was correct? Raine was far too impulsive for her own good. She very well might be reading more into the situation than there was, simply because she had not stopped to ponder the matter for a moment.

But what if she is correct? he mused.

It was highly unlikely. Yet again he realized that his hesitating here could end in tragedy. He had made a vow to remain neutral in such matters. But perhaps there were times when... The woman was driving him mad.

With a groan of frustration, Benedict went to the door and called for his steward. "Are you ready to go on then, my lord?" the man asked.

Benedict frowned darkly, his tone far sharper than he intended. "Nay, I am not. I want the maid Leandra found and brought to me here."

The steward's surprise at Benedict's uncharacteristically agitated manner could not be mistaken, as he replied, "As you wish, Lord Benedict."

Benedict pretended not to see this, bringing another assessing glance his way as he began to pace, adding, "And see that she is found immediately. Understand that this is a matter of extreme import. If there is any difficulty in finding her, I wish to be informed without delay."

The steward bowed and hurried away without another word. Benedict continued to pace, running a weary hand over his face. He did not care to be making such a spectacle of himself by behaving like an overworried maiden aunt. He knew how important it was for his people to know that he was in control, that all would be well with his guidance.

He had no reason for such anxiety and told himself that he was simply allowing Raine's own fearfulness to affect him. Yet Benedict could not rid himself of the pressing need to make sure that Leandra was indeed well.

Benedict rubbed his tired eyes. The last hours had been emotionally charged ones. Leandra had been found, and had reluctantly admitted Raine's worst fears were indeed correct. After first assuring her that such a solution was never the answer to anything, Benedict had eventually and with much coaxing been able to gain the name of her babe's father. That young man, who had been away at one of his other keeps these last months, had been sent for, and had agreed to wed her before Benedict could finish telling him of her plight.

Now, relieved though he was that the issue had been settled, Benedict could not rid himself of a sense of regret. Raine had been right and he had treated her like a child. And the reason for that was very likely his own guilt over what he had done to hurt her.

A heavy sigh escaped him.

"My lord?"

He looked up to see Maeve standing just inside the open doorway of the library. With more difficulty than he cared to admit, he dragged that accustomed mask of composure over his features. Despite his troubles with

Raine, he still had this keep to run, his people to care for.

He answered softly, not caring for the slight note of despondency that colored his tone in spite of his resolve to mask it. "Yes, Maeve. Is there aught that needs my attention?" He could only hope that she would not be aware of how troubled he was.

Her words did not encourage him. Nor did her worried and sympathetic expression. "There is nothing amiss, my lord. I but came to thank you for your care of Leandra. She is family to me. The daughter of my cousin."

This did not surprise him. Maeve seemed to have an endless supply of cousins. He nodded. "Your thanks is well met, though Raine was the one who brought this to my attention. I admit that it took some convincing on her part before I was persuaded to do my duty." As he said the last he knew it was true. Again he sighed, thinking of the way they had parted.

Coming a few steps into the room, Maeve said gently, "Is all well with you, my lord?"

Benedict looked away, unable to hold that gaze as he shook his head in denial. Even though Maeve was the closest thing to a mother that he and his brothers had known since their parents' deaths, it was difficult to accept her concern. He was responsible for too much to allow himself to fall apart now, to leave anyone, including Maeve, in any doubt as to his ability to go on, to do what he must no matter what occurred in his private life.

He replied with forced reserve, "All is well. You need not concern yourself about me."

Maeve remained silent for a very long time, though he could still feel the weight of her gaze upon him.

Finally he raised his eyes to hers. The care he saw there made his heart ache all the more. She said, "I know, my lord, that you are a strong and independent man, that you wish to remain ever in control and calm. Yet there are times when even you must have difficulty keeping all inside."

He began to shake his head in denial, but she stopped him with a raised hand. "I know I overstep myself in speaking thus to you, but I love you as if you were my own son, you and your three brothers. You are the children I have never borne. I know you too well to be indifferent to your pain. And I know its cause."

Benedict focused on that raised hand, which was broad and rough from the many hours of work done in his service. He knew there was no point in continuing to try to avoid the truth with this woman. She did indeed know him too well. He sighed. "She will never come to accept her life here."

"Lady Raine will eventually come to do just that. She is only afraid to love us because she thinks it would be a betrayal of her past."

His lips twisted wryly. "She is not capable of loving us—of loving anyone but her brother."

Maeve smiled gently. "There you are wrong, my lord. It is love for her brother that makes me certain she is capable of loving others. No one could give such devotion from a miserly heart. That heart will not forever be denied no matter how she tries. See how she put herself forward for Leandra this very day, a stranger of no consequence to herself."

"Aye, that is true. And mayhap that is why she was able to do so. Helping the girl did not threaten her loyalties in any way."

Maeve sighed, watching him as she said, "You know

my love for you is not in question, thus I tell you this. If you wish for Lady Raine to love you someday, you might show her that she is of some worth to you.''

Benedict spoke in surprise. ''I have shown her every deference. I cannot coddle her, neglect my duties to write poems to the damp gold glory of her eyes.''

He stopped as Maeve's eyes grew sadly knowing. ''Forgive the forwardness of an old woman, my lord.'' She bowed and left him.

Benedict was glad of her exit. It served neither of them to argue this matter. Raine did not intend to love him no matter what he did, had shown very clearly that she did not wish to love anyone but William. He felt a shockingly painful ache of sadness at this. Roughly he brushed it aside. He did not require his wife's love. He was the head of his family and could not afford such self-indulgence.

Surprisingly, his certainty did not bring the same feelings of confidence that it always had in the past. To his utter devastation all he felt was emptiness.

Chapter Twelve

Raine went immediately to her room. The hours passed, but her anger did not abate. Benedict Ainsworth was a knave, accusing her of all manner of infractions whenever he found opportunity to do so, while completely ignoring his own very obvious weaknesses.

It was only a short time later that Raine looked up from the sewing she was attempting to concentrate on as a knock sounded at her door. Her heart thudded even as she called out, "Come."

The portal opened to reveal Maeve. Raine's brows rose in question. The head woman hesitated for a brief moment, then came forward, determination on her face.

Raine had the distinct feeling that she did not wish to have any part of this encounter, yet she found herself saying, "Yes?"

The woman spoke both respectfully and directly. "There is something I believe you should know, my lady."

Raine sighed impatiently. "If Benedict sent you there was no need."

The woman's surprise could not have been feigned. "Lord Benedict would not send me to plead for him."

Immediately Raine realized that she had been foolish to say such a thing.

For the sake of this woman, who had been kind to both her brother and herself, she should have some consideration. She spoke gently. "Pray forgive me, my position as your mistress does not afford me the right to be rude. Please, Maeve, do tell me what you wished to say."

The head woman seemed much mollified by this and looked at her with a long and approving glance as she said, "I came to offer my thanks for your help in the matter of Leandra. She told me of what had occurred this day, of how you went to my lord Benedict with her troubles, which he was, I am glad to say, able to resolve."

Raine could not help interrupting with amazement. "Benedict has resolved her problems?"

Maeve looked as though she was quite surprised by this question. "Of course, Lady Raine, why would he do aught else after you had convinced him there was a need?"

Raine did not know what to say. No one could have told Maeve this but Benedict....

Maeve went on, oblivious to her mistress's thoughts. "Leandra was worried about what you must have thought of her." She shrugged with resignation. "She is the daughter of my cousin and a good if somewhat silly girl and very dear to me. She told me how adamant she had been in her desire that her lover marry her without knowing of the child. Because of you, Lord Benedict was able to gain the father's identity, and the man agreed to marry her—with enough enthusiasm to appease her. She did not realize she had not seen him again because he had been sent to serve at one of Lord

Benedict's other keeps." Maeve paused, blinking back sudden tears. "Leandra also told me that she had been contemplating ending her life when you came upon her. I tell you, my lady, that you will ever be held in gratitude by my folk for the service you have done us this day."

Raine found herself flushing not only with discomfort, but also with unexpected pleasure. She had not been trying to gain anyone's loyalty. She had only acted out of the need of the moment, because she could not do otherwise. She said, "I thank you for your kind words, but I did nothing to gain your gratitude."

Maeve smiled. "Nonetheless you have it."

Raine looked at her for a long moment, seeing how freely her thanks was given. In that moment Raine knew there was something she, too, must say. "If that be the case, then you must also hear me. Your kindness to my brother and me, your coming here today in spite of things I have done that may seem, shall I say, less than loyal toward your master, have been most gratifying."

Maeve nodded gravely, obviously weighing her next words. "I understand that there is much between you and Lord Benedict that I have no right to speak of. But there are things I would have you know. All here at Brackenmoore are a family. Lord Benedict has always treated his folk as such and encouraged all to do the same to one another. He is a very special man, is my lord. Took not only the raising of his brothers to heart when their parents died, but the well-being of all on his lands, and has not once wavered in that trust." She paused for a long moment. "He will care for you in the same dependable manner. Though he may be somewhat preoccupied with many responsibilities at times, he will not waver in his duty to you."

Raine was aware of Benedict's love and care for his family, his dependability, had sensed these qualities that first day when she had listened in on his conversation with the king. What she had not known then was that these were all he could give. Brackenmoore and all it stood for possessed Benedict as surely as he possessed it. She had no wish to be a duty, but a wife. Unfortunately, Benedict did not truly have room in his life for such things as a wife.

His cool indifference to herself was evidence of that. Even anger would have been preferable, in her mind. That Benedict did not afford her enough credit for even that expenditure of emotion was obvious in the way he had treated her in the last weeks, showing her every honor and civility but naught else.

Unexpectedly, Raine felt an odd sense of longing. If only things were different... She halted that thought immediately. She did not require more from Benedict.

Instantly an image of them together, their bodies entwined, so wild and abandoned in the falling rain, came to her. She felt herself flush to the roots of her hair. Perhaps that experience and the memory of it were distorted in her mind. Perhaps he had not wanted her as she had thought. Perhaps he simply had not known what to say at her overt offering of herself, for that was exactly what she had done. Raine could not allow herself to pretend otherwise.

Her face grew even hotter. He had neither touched her since nor given any sign that he had desired what had occurred.

Realizing that she had remained silent for far too long, Raine looked at the expectant face of the head woman. Knowing how she, along with every other soul at Brackenmoore, was bound to Benedict not only by duty but by love, Raine could say nothing of her thoughts, her isolation. "I thank you for your consideration in coming here, Maeve, and for your encouragement." She smiled overbrightly. "I will certainly think on all that you have imparted."

Maeve continued to regard her, but now her expression seemed somewhat sad. "As you will, my lady. I will leave you to your thoughts."

Watching her go, Raine realized that above all things she dreaded being left alone with her thoughts.

The day passed in a strange haze for Raine. Now that she had had time to take it in she could not deny her amazement that Benedict had actually acted on her advice about Leandra. Yet Raine could not allow herself to believe that it actually meant anything, that he was beginning to have some regard for her.

She tried to busy herself with mending the torn hem of one of her gowns, but was twice forced to remove the threads. It was as she was attempting this task for the third time that Raine heard a knock upon her door.

William would never knock. And he was away.

Even as her mind went to Benedict, the portal opened and there he stood in the doorway to her chamber, looking powerful and larger than life as he always did. "May I enter?" The words were said with a surprising hesitancy.

She wanted to send him on his way, tell him that she did not wish to speak to him, in spite of the fact that he had come to his senses and done what was right for Leandra. He had been so rude to her, dismissing her as if she did not matter. Something, perhaps the uncertainty in his blue eyes as he raked a hand through his uncharacteristically unruly raven hair, would not allow her to do that.

She murmured only, "Aye, my lord."

Immediately she reprimanded herself for that gentle tone. No matter what occurred, no matter that Benedict might actually see that he was not treating her as he should, she would not allow herself to display any soft emotions or to be moved by any seeming indications of such on his part.

To do so would bring her nothing but pain, as it had after they had been at Abbernathy. It would be foolish to let her attraction to him, or her own feelings of loneliness, so weaken her that she left herself open to the hurt he was able to inflict without even thinking.

Thankfully, the man before her was aware of none of this. She would not have him know how deeply his rejection had hurt her. Pride was all she had.

To her chagrin, Benedict seemed slightly encouraged by her soft tone, for he came inside and closed the door. "I wished to speak with you. If you will allow it?"

His self-effacing manner beat at the wall she had erected around her feelings. Raine shrugged, not wanting him to know how very much she wished to speak with him, have more than this cold distance that had grown up between them. She wanted even more to tell him of their child, of the sadness she felt at having the joy of this knowledge taken from her by her despondency over their marriage.

Yet she did none of these things.

She watched as Benedict moved into the room and sat in the chair before the hearth. Raine had to restrain a wave of sympathy, and another more troubling emotion, as he ran a tired hand over his face. She was aware of the fact that it must have been a difficult day for him.

She said nothing. Benedict would not welcome her pity, feeling as he did that it was his duty to deal with every issue with forbearance. Raine held her head high. "Would you care to come to the point, my lord?" She put aside her sewing and rose. "I was about to prepare for bed."

He looked at her, his gaze unreadable. "I will be brief." He folded his hands in his lap, staring down in contemplation, then said, "I have come to tell you that you were right this morning and I should not have treated you so rudely. I should have taken your own experience in running a keep into consideration."

Of all the things he could have said, this was not among any she would have named. For a long moment she stood there silent with amazement. At last she found her tongue. "What has brought about this change of heart, Benedict?"

His jaw clenched and his gaze registered an emotion she could only read as chagrin. "I...suffice it to say that I *have* had a change of heart."

She shrugged, putting her hands on her hips. "How very good of you."

He frowned as he looked at her, surprising her even further by saying, "Must you be forever at odds with everything I say, even an apology?"

"I am not..." she began, and closed her lips on the words. For was he not right in what he said? Her resentment of him and the wrongs he had done her colored all her thinking as far as he was concerned.

He went on as if she had not spoken, and he knew she was hard-pressed not to give in to the new rise of resentment that brought. "I have been thinking about what you said and I realized that you may be right about something. Perhaps I am too accustomed to everyone doing as I tell them. Perhaps I do not have the right to expect the same from my wife. But I do not know how to be different. So many depend on my certainty of thought and deed. When you are responsible for so much you cannot rely on others to make your decisions for you."

She shook her head in exasperation. "Benedict, no one, including you, has a right to expect you to always be right. The fact that you nearly always are is irrelevant." Her amazement that he was even here and willing to discuss this with her made her speak bluntly. "It prevents you from ever really unbending."

He frowned. "I am not unbending. You cannot understand my position."

Sighing, she replied, "Can I not? Circumstances beyond my control have forced me to see that it is wrong to hold too closely to what I thought I must never forget—the past. I have had to accept the fact that I could not do all that I expected from myself. In some ways realizing that is almost liberating." She looked at him with brows raised in irony. "I suppose it is yet another thing I have to thank you for—for the understanding that I am a mere mortal. What binds you, Benedict? Your own comprehension of this fact would greatly change your life."

He stared at her with what she could only interpret as disbelief, and she knew that he could not accept her assessment. Benedict would never allow himself to see that he, too, could let go of his image of himself.

He averted his head, sighing with resignation as if he simply could not bring himself to argue the point, as if she were not worth convincing. For some reason this was more painful than she cared to admit.

Raine felt the regret and, unexpectedly, the yearning

as she looked at Benedict's averted head. Yet she could not hide it.

Oh, how she wished things were different between them. That the two of them could have actually begun a life together that day in the woods as she had hoped.

But they had not. Benedict would ever be bound in the prison of his own self-control. To give that up would mean that he was vulnerable to hurt like those around him.

The reality of her own vulnerability was something Raine knew well. For had she not experienced the pain of realizing that she could not make life turn out the way she wished it to be? Had she not been forced to see that her father was gone and her life would never be the same again?

On that Benedict had been correct in his advice to her. She could not bring him or the life they had known back by denying her own future.

Yet she could see no point in further trying to convince Benedict that, in his own way, he was as frightened of letting go as she had been. He would not heed her, and though that was painful to her, knowing as she did that there could be no real marriage for them because of it, she said nothing. His methods had served him well in his position as overlord here at Brackenmoore. Unfortunately, they also made it impossible for him to let go and really love anyone—or to feel another's love.

Raine felt an unexpected and overwhelming rise of sympathy for this man. Without being aware of it she moved to stand behind him, her gaze fixing on his nape, which seemed so vulnerable as he stared down at his hands. How lonely and isolated was Benedict Ainsworth, baron and lord of Brackenmoore, overseer and protector of all who dwelled within. Slowly she reached out and ran a hand over the thick hair at the back of his head.

He turned to look at her, his eyes registering surprise and a trace of another emotion that made her own heart begin to pound. For she knew that emotion was desire. But what he said was, "I came not to quarrel with you, Raine, but to apologize, not only for what I said today but for anything I may have done to hurt you in the past weeks."

The words were shocking, the undisguised passion in his eyes even more so. If he still felt desire for her, why had he turned away from her? She moved to stand directly before him, and her response issued from her mouth before she could stop it. "You want me still. If that is so why did you behave as if making love to me in the forest that night had sickened you?"

He shook his head, the sudden astonishment on his face more than evident. "Sickened me? I assure you, Raine, that is as far from the truth as anything could be."

His words sent a ripple of amazement and—she could not deny it—pleasure through her. It was not only an emotional gratification. There was a strong trace of the sensual in that reaction.

He continued to look at her, and as he did so his gaze darkened to indigo. Suddenly Raine knew that the passion had always been there between them, even when she had mistaken it for anger, irritation or indifference. For some reason, it had been carefully banked, but never wholly suppressed.

He said, "Raine?"

She shook her head, putting her fingers to his lips. "Let us not speak anymore now." He had come here to beg her pardon with unquestionable sincerity. For the moment that was enough.

"Are you certain?"

She nodded. "Yes." Raine did not want to think on all the things that were wrong between them, wanted only to find surcease from her own loneliness and need. That release could only be found in Benedict's embrace.

For now she was willing to accept that no more would be had there. A momentary regret tugged at her heart. Then it was forgotten as he reached out and touched her shoulder. Raine was surprised and awed to feel that his hand was trembling. The knowledge that Benedict was indeed moved by what was happening made her breath come even more quickly.

She placed her own hand over his, then raised it to press her lips against his palm.

Again Benedict whispered, "Raine." The sound of her name was a caress that slid along her skin, made the fine hairs reach for him.

She met his gaze, knowing that she hid nothing, that she could not in this moment, for the knowledge that he had always desired her made her too vulnerable. "Benedict."

Benedict could find no other words to say, did not know what had brought about this change in her. All he knew was that his previous need to keep himself from her seemed mad. Surely he had been exaggerating what had happened that day in the forest. If he were not, it was due more to the fact that they had made love so wildly, so passionately in that undeniably magical place with the rain falling upon their exposed flesh, heightening every sensation.

Here in his own keep, he had no reason to think that

such a thing would occur again. Raine was a woman, like any other, and his duty to produce a child had not gone away because of his foolish and fanciful notions of what he had experienced that day.

The very ridiculousness of his reactions now made him all the more determined to overcome them, to give in to his overwhelming desire to make love to his wife. So beautiful she was, so lush and decidedly woman. Looking into those passion-darkened golden eyes, he realized he had indeed been a fool.

Slowly he leaned toward her, his lips brushing hers, their breath mingling as he prolonged, experienced this moment, his head reeling with the knowledge that she would have him. He flicked his tongue over her upper lip, tasting her, Raine, his woman.

He heard the vulnerability in her voice as she sighed. "I thought you did not want me."

Guilt made his chest ache as she said this again. Benedict ran a gentle hand over her delicate cheek and whispered against her lips, "Aye, Raine, I do want you. Have always wanted you. I will show you through the pleasure I give you now."

The words made her shiver. His mouth left hers to trail a path of hot longing down her neck. Her head fell backward, allowing him better access even as her limbs quivered at a weakening surge of pleasure.

He smoothed his hands down her back, reveling in the beautiful curves of her—his Raine, his wife. From the very beginning he had felt this attraction to her, this overwhelming craving and longing, one he had known with no other woman. Before he had known only the quenching of a physical need.

The fact that Raine seemed unable to fight her own desire for him, in spite of the fact that he had hurt her, battered the precarious boundaries he had erected around himself in the past weeks.

Awe raced through him. He could touch and caress her as he willed and she would welcome him. And that was exactly what he meant to do.

Benedict slipped his hands down her sides, molding the sweet and beguiling curves of her body with his fingers. To his utter gratification she pressed herself more closely to him, moving her lips over his slowly, sensuously.

Her own fingers tangled in his hair, and he slanted his head, deepening his kisses in answer to her gentle pressure. She sighed, throwing her head back, and he nipped at the hollow of her neck. Her fingers clenched convulsively in his hair.

Raine felt the strength of him, the hardness and masculinity of his body. She felt herself quicken, her lower belly becoming heavy as it always did when he touched her.

Benedict reached down and lifted her gown. He was impatient with the barrier between himself and Raine. She brought her own hands up to aid him, and both her dark green samite garment and creamy underdress soon lay in a pool on the floor. In the warmth of the candles he saw that the sheer fabric of her shift was no barrier to his heated gaze. Holding his breath at her beauty, he tenderly traced the lovely mounds of her breasts, feeling the perfect weight of them in his palms. Their deep pink tips hardened beneath the gossamer covering, seeming to beckon him as he watched.

Benedict took a deep breath, trying to calm his now racing pulse even as he took in the erotic shadows of her trim waist and gently flaring hips. They offered a promise of indescribable rapture.

His thumbs found her nipples, circling. At the quick intake of her breath his eyes met hers and he saw that her lids were heavy, those golden orbs molten with heat. She swayed, leaning toward him.

His own body quickened and he reached for her, pulling her supple form against him. Immediately he became aware of a deep frustration when his own clothing hindered his enjoyment of the well-remembered velvet of her skin.

He leaned back to relieve himself of them. His passion was brought to an even greater pitch by the eagerness of her slender fingers as she reached to aid him.

His garments followed hers, and again he reached to pull her close.

Raine held back for one long breathless moment, before sighing again. "You are beautiful, Benedict, as no man has a right to be." And she knew it was true: his legs were long, the muscles strong and well defined, his stomach flat and washboard hard. His golden chest drew her eyes, which examined its powerful breadth with open yearning. But it was the rise of his manhood that held her attention for the longest time, proud and strong as it rested amid a nest of dark curls. Her gaze met his. "So beautiful."

A rush of some emotion that he could not name raced through him, warmed him, humbled him. Never had he thought of his own hard warrior's body as beautiful. That Raine did moved him in a way that he had not thought possible.

It moved him so greatly that he was nearly frightened by his own welling feelings of tenderness and protectiveness. Unwilling and unable to examine them, he drew her back to him, burying his face in the softness of her hair. The memory of how it had felt against his flesh gave a certain urgency to his action as he reached out and pulled it free of its coiled braid.

Raine realized that Benedict was loosening her hair only a moment before it tumbled about her. Her heart thudded in response, for that small act seemed somehow more intimate and familiar than all the things they had done before. It was as if in freeing her hair he was saying that what they were doing, what they were about to do, was more than an act they performed with their bodies. More personal even than the deep intensity of pleasure they had shared.

She felt something soften inside her, someplace where she had not even known she was holding back. Raine knew in that moment that she belonged to Benedict. Would always belong to him. Had always been meant to do so.

Pulling back from him, she reached down and drew off her shift, her gaze never leaving his handsome face. His eyes darkened as they moved over her with hunger, and she shivered.

"Benedict." She spoke softly, holding out her hand. He put his own hand into it.

Slowly she drew him toward the bed, that great lonely bed where she had lain awake thinking of him, only to dream of him—of them together—when she did fall asleep. He followed her.

When they reached the edge of the bed, he bent to kiss her again, his lips hot on hers, before they trailed down her throat to close over the tip of one swollen breast. She gasped, holding his head to her, as her knees buckled and a sweet moistness pooled at the joining of her thighs.

Benedict felt her sag against him, and lifted her in his arms, gently laying her on the bed. His gaze lit upon her slender bare feet and he recalled how moved he had been by the sight of her toes that first night at Brackenmoore. Feeling a strange sense of reverence, he slid his hands down her legs, feeling her shudder as he leaned over and kissed those toes, each one perfect and lovely because it was Raine's. She sighed his name, "Benedict," squirming when he began to slide his tongue over each one in turn. He felt something inside him expanding, growing, and he was moved in a way that was more than just the rush of physical desire, heating his blood to liquid flame.

Raine reached out to him, crying, "Come to me." And he could not resist her or his own need. When she pulled him down to her, her legs opened. Benedict found himself slipping into the velvety-sleek warmth of her body.

Raine threw back her head, a gasp of pleasure escaping her as he entered her, filled her. She followed his rhythm, slipping into a void of unthinking pleasure, knowing that he would take them both to ecstasy.

And inevitably the sensations built, climbing higher and ever higher as she wrapped herself around him, all thought of herself as a separate being forgotten. Where Benedict ended and she began Raine could no longer fathom. She was awash in, drowning in Benedict.

Wave after wave of sensation rose up, then ebbed, then rose again more intensely. Then, finally, the swell of pleasure built until it broke inside her. She dissolved in a shower of ecstasy and light, crying out his name with a gasp of delight.

As he stiffened above her, she sobbed with joy, knowing that Benedict, too, had reached that place of perfection. And when the spasms in his body stilled she held him close, her heart filled with rapture, with love.

And as that last realization entered her mind, she froze. Dear heaven, it was true. She loved this man more than her own life, loved him as she had never thought possible.

But he did not love her, had never made any secret of that fact. He had admitted that he was willing to share this with her—the passion and delight. But he was not willing or even able to see that there was more that he could give—and take—from their joining.

Yet with the understanding that she loved came an unshakable certainty that now anything less would only bring unbearable pain.

She lay completely still, her body stiffening more with each painful thought. Tears stung her eyes, for now his body, however beautiful and pleasurable, would never be enough for her. When he touched her, made her feel all the things he made her feel, she would only long all the more intensely for what she could not have—his love.

Without saying a word she rolled away from him. She felt his gaze upon her, felt the pressing weight of it, but did not meet it, could not do so for fear of his seeing the truth of her love in her eyes.

Rising, she picked up her robe and wrapped it around herself. The act of covering her body did not make her feel any less vulnerable to him.

He sat up in the bed, his expression filled with so many mixed emotions she could not hope to read it. "Raine, what is it now? I…" His face showed the effort he was making to remain calm. His voice emerged full of reasoning entreaty. "How are we ever to be a family if we…"

His obvious referral to the hoped-for child chilled

her. Yet it was not that but his very calmness, his inability to lose himself in her, in them, that frightened her so much. Her voice was more husky than she intended. "You need come to me no more Benedict. Your purpose has been accomplished. I am with child."

Benedict felt the words hit him with the force of a blow. The loneliness in her voice, the strangeness of her withdrawal, which had come so closely upon a moment of such deep connection and wondrous pleasure, deadened him for a moment to the sheer import of her words.

And then, in spite of his confusion and concern, the words penetrated his mind. Raine was with child.

With child. Saints be praised, he was to have an heir, possibly even a son who would carry on the family name.

Pride swelled inside him like a newly ripened apple left out in the warmth of the sun. For a moment he was filled to overflowing with the unlimited joy of that news.

But then it was completely overshadowed by her other words. He need not come to her again. Regret filled him, replaced his ecstatic emotions with indescribable sadness.

Though he had not felt a repeat of that mystifying experience he had known with her in the woods, he had felt a tenderness and care that he had never imagined. And now, she was sending him away.

He did not wish to feel such a close and tender bond with this unpredictable hoyden. Without a word, Benedict rose from the bed. In spite of the warmth of the spring night outside the open window, he felt chilled as he never had before. Quickly he reached down and took up his clothing.

When he looked around again, Raine had moved to

gaze out the window. The rigid line of her back did not invite conversation.

Even as he watched her he was again assaulted by misery. They were to have a child. He wanted to go to her and hold her in his arms, kiss her, cry his joy into the heavy curtain of her hair. Wanted to again experience that moment of complete joining.

He wanted to ask her what had happened, what had made her turn from him this way, but he could not. Not when her rejection had come so completely without warning, or warrant. Unless she had some notion of repaying him for his perceived wrongs against her, in which case he could not allow her to think she could use her whims against him by reacting to this.

She had made her feelings very clear.

So be it. She would have this her way. Spinning on his heel, he left the chamber.

Chapter Thirteen

Restless, Raine paced the stone floor. She could not sleep, could not sit, could not reason. The realization that she was in love with Benedict played over and over again in her mind—the impossible, irrefutable reality of it. As did her horror at this devastating fact. She was ever reminded of just how firmly Benedict was entrenched in his role of lord defender to all at Brackenmoore.

Every dreadful detail of their conversation and lovemaking came again and again, relentlessly—along with Maeve's assurances that Benedict would take care of her as he did everyone else. Raine did not wish to be cared for in that way. She wished to be loved as she loved her husband, with all her heart and soul. If only what he offered could be enough! If only she did not wish so badly, in that deep, secret place inside herself, that Benedict would love her.

Yet it was not enough. Raine did wish he loved her, could not accept any less. Not if she wished to retain any self-respect. How could she accept so little when the yawning ache in her heart told her that she had already given so very much?

Raine groaned, running a hand through her tousled hair. The heavy silence of the keep seemed to close in upon her in the dark here alone. She could not spend another entire night this way. If only she had something besides her troubles to occupy her mind. A sudden and unexpected image entered her mind. The library. Never in her life would Raine have imagined so many books in one place.

Without thinking, she took the lit candle from the table and moved to the door. There she hesitated.

The library was obviously Benedict's sanctuary. Her husband had appeared very much at home in that carved wooden chair. He would not welcome her intrusion there.

Immediately she drew herself up. What cared she for Benedict's opinion? She was his wife and was due some deference. He had repeatedly insisted that Brackenmoore was her home. If he begrudged her entry to his library it was no concern of hers. She jerked open the portal and made her way down the hall.

The castle was so still and dark at this hour. Filled with self-righteousness as she was, Raine was glad she did not have to go through the great hall to get to the library. She would not have wished to try to explain why she was wandering the keep in the dead of night, even though she continued to assure herself that she had the right to do as she pleased.

When she reached the closed library door, Raine paused, wondering if it would be kept locked when not in use. Shrugging, she turned the handle. It swung open on well-oiled hinges, and she told herself that it had been foolish of her to think otherwise. Benedict was far too self-assured to worry about locking anyone out of his room.

Once inside she looked about, seeing how the shelves full of books cast eerie shadows all around her. She realized that her one candle did not shed sufficient light for her purpose. She went to the table, certain that there would be more candles there. Her assumption proved accurate. Quickly she lit the two candles she found.

It was only as she was placing the second down on the table that her gaze came to rest on a sheet of parchment that lay open upon its surface. Before she even realized she was doing so she read the name that was signed with great flourish at the bottom: Alister Harcourt.

Somehow that name seemed familiar, and she searched her mind for the reason. Finally the answer came. It was the name of the man Benedict had spoken to King Edward about the first time she had seen him. Biting her lower lip, she moved closer, curiosity getting the better of her.

Quickly she read the document. A troubled frown knit her brow as she took in the threatening and angry tone. Obviously the king's intercession had been for naught. The man was demanding to be met on the field of honor.

In spite of the fact that Benedict was more than capable of looking after himself, she felt a trace of anxiety. Yet she knew he would not thank her for it, would likely think her a fool. She sighed heavily, regretfully.

As she did so a sound behind her made Raine start. She looked up, into the coolly assessing eyes of her husband.

It was only long after he had gone to his bed that Benedict realized he had left the letter from Alister Harcourt lying open on the table. He did not wish to believe that his sleeplessness had anything to do with the way Raine had sent him away after telling him that they were to have a child. Nor did he want it to have anything to do with the strange longing that gripped him each time he thought of the tenderness he had felt as he made love to her.

Nay, it was only because of the letter. He did not wish for anyone to see it, as he had shared none of the ongoing conflict with anyone but his steward, who had arranged for the letters to be carried back and forth between them.

Benedict did not want others to know because he did not want Tristan to learn of it, even inadvertently.

When he arrived to find the library door open and a light coming from inside, he paused. But when he stepped through the opening and saw his wife standing bent over the very letter that had brought him from his bed in the dead of night, he felt a scowl mar his brow.

Raine, who had no care for him nor anything he stood for, was the last person he would share such a problem with. But then she sighed, a heavy, lonely sigh, and he felt an unexpected sense of regret, his own breath escaping in an answering sigh.

At the sound of it she looked up and met his gaze, giving a start. Putting her hand to her lips, she looked down at the letter, then up at him again as she backed away. "I...excuse my intrusion. I did not mean..." At his continued silence she drew herself up and spoke haughtily. "Your letter was lying there and I... You should not have left it if you did not wish for others to see it." She shrugged off-handedly, making it clear that she considered it entirely his fault that she had read it.

Benedict was not quite prepared to accept this. If there was one thing he did know, it was that Raine had been completely aware that she was trespassing when she read the letter. Her guilty start had been proof enough of that.

Yet he doubted very much that she would ever admit it. He moved forward to take the missive into his own hands, rolling it carefully. "I did not expect anyone to sneak in to read my private correspondence behind my back."

She stiffened, her body as rigid as the steel of her will. "I did not sneak in here behind your back. Would not lower myself to do such a thing." She gestured about them. "I but came for a book, if that is not over-stepping myself too greatly."

Benedict felt his irritation ease slightly. However intentional she had been in reading the missive, she had not come here for the express purpose of doing so. He sighed again. As she'd so helpfully indicated, it had been he who had left it out. Fairness made him say, "Your pardon, Raine. I do believe you. As you said, it is through my own fault that it was lying here. Anyone could have come upon it." He registered her obvious surprise at his words even as he went on. "I ask only that you do not talk with anyone of what you have read."

With a grimace of sudden animosity she said, "And whom would I tell? Aside from William I am alone here."

Now Benedict frowned, starting forward. "You are not alone here. Why do you persist in speaking this way? Why must you declare yourself the outsider at every turn when it is by your own will?"

Her mouth dropped open in obvious shock, even as she took a step toward him. "What say you? That I am alone here by my own will? Pray tell me why I would believe this, when you display to me on each and every day that I am nothing to you?''

He shook his head. "You are making no sense. It is you, Raine, who wishes to keep yourself separate from all here, including me. I have tried to make concessions to you, to our marriage. You know that I have responsibilities, that I cannot simply put aside all that I stand for in order to please you. It is you who wishes to continue a conflict between us. You sent me away from you after speaking of our child, the heir to all I hold dear, as if it were no more than a vexation to you, simply to revenge the slight you felt I had given to you. I understand why you were upset with me…I did not treat you as I should, but I did all I could in begging your forgiveness and hoping to start afresh.''

Her eyes narrowed as he went on, and she folded her arms tightly across her chest. Her reaction gave Benedict a growing sense of unease. When she spoke again he realized that his discomfort had only just begun.

Raine felt the anger that she had been trying to suppress since the previous night rise up inside her in a rushing tide. She could no longer withhold her resentment. "You have made concessions? I am vexed at the fact that I carry your child? You see all as it relates to you and Brackenmoore and nothing else. You care nothing for me. Yes, I was angry with you for the way you treated me. You, who put your hands upon me that night in the forest, made love to me as if the world were soon to end, then walked away from me. But that is not why I cannot rejoice in the coming of my own babe—'' Her voice broke, but she recovered immediately, her gaze hard on his. "Can you expect anything else when you have made it abundantly clear that your one continuing interest in me has been that of getting me with child? It is true, Benedict, that I do owe you much, but I do not owe you all of myself when you have naught to give in return.''

She saw the chagrin that colored his face before he quickly tried to hide it behind that damnable mask of reserve, but the mask slipped again as he replied in a too husky voice, ''That is not what I meant to...''

Raine watched in amazement as, for the first time since she had met him, Benedict seemed to lose the tight hold he had over his emotions. ''Raine, I am...forgive...it was not my intent... Dear God, Raine, please forgive me for the way I treated you.'' He halted, running a hand over his face.

Raine did not know what to say to this. She had thought Benedict indifferent to her, but his reaction to her diatribe made her wonder if he was not completely unaffected by her sorrow.

He buried his face in his hands. ''Forgive me, I did not know what I had done.''

The very depth of his uncharacteristic display told her that this discussion was achingly painful for him. Something was dreadfully wrong for him to become so overset by what she had said, and she could not believe it was because of her. Yet whatever it was ran deep. She sank down in the chair behind her, for her legs felt suddenly as if they would not hold her.

Shock made her forget she did not wish to give away her own hurt and anxiety. Her voice was no more than a whisper as she asked, ''Why, Benedict, why do you treat me thus? I thought...''

He shook his head. ''I cannot explain. Only know that I did not mean to hurt you, had not realized how much my actions had affected you.''

She raised her hands in question. "How could you not see? You just..." She flushed, realizing just how much of her hurt and shame she was giving away, but unable to stop herself as she went on. "I have given myself to you as my husband. And I thought that we might be making a start on more than one occasion. Yet..."

"I have wanted that, too, but things have been..." His face hardened to granite even as she watched. "You would not understand. I have told you repeatedly that I cannot forget who I am, what my responsibilities are."

Raine did not know what he was talking about. She was not asking for him to forget anything, knew that nothing would ever come before Brackenmoore in his mind. She had wanted only a small place in his life, his affections. Yet he denied her that without even being aware of it.

He interrupted her painful thoughts with a roughly voiced query. "What would you have of me, Raine?"

Angrily she answered in kind. "I ask you to give up nothing for me. I accept what must be, which is why I sent you from me. There is no real place in your life for me." Her voice broke as she continued, "You—you say you wish to have a family, an heir, but you have nothing left over to give them." She gestured wildly toward the letter, which he held so tightly, so protectively in his hand. "I believe that it is your own fault. You place yourself as guardian and keeper over all. That is not your responsibility or even your place." She met his gaze directly. "Do you believe your brother would thank you for this? He is a man. A man who has the right to defend himself and his family. As I see it you are guilty of the crimes you made me realize I was committing in the name of protecting William, and he is merely a boy.''

Benedict's blue gaze turned to ice before her very eyes. ''You do not know of what you speak.''

She raised her chin, not willing to give an inch even though something told her that the thick wall Benedict had erected around his emotions was very close to giving way completely, and when it did he might not be able to control his actions. ''I do know more than you imagine. Maeve has told me of your parents' deaths, of the weight you took on your shoulders. Truth to tell I find your actions admirable. But the time to let go has come. Your brothers, with the exception of Kendran, are men. You need not bear all of their troubles. You have a right to your own life.''

Benedict's dismissive gesture cut the air sharply. When he replied, his voice was hard and filled with more rage than she had ever heard him express. ''You understand nothing. The last time I saw my father he spoke of his faith in me, his trust that I would look after my brothers in his stead. Nothing and no one could make me put aside my father's faith in me. Not even a wife.'' He glared at her, his breathing coming quickly from his chest, which seemed to have swelled to twice its normal and not inconsiderable width. His large hands clenched and unclenched around that piece of parchment, and she could not help wondering if it were her own throat he was imagining that he held. Seeing the path of her gaze, he threw the parchment on the floor and pounded his fist against the wall of his chest. ''Do you not think I wanted to lie down the day I learned of my father and mother's deaths and grieve until there was no more grief in me? Do you imagine that I did not wish that it were myself rather than my father who died? He was as near a god to me as has ever walked upon this earth. I did what I knew he would wish for me to do. I went on. He put Brackenmoore first and I can do no less."

Her heart ached at his anguish. But she could not speak of it. Had she ever actually wished for him to lose control, to become angry?

Raine now realized that she had been a fool to hope for such a thing. For he was more than slightly intimidating in his rage. She refused to show her anxiety as she replied, "And my father asked the same of me. It was none other than you, Benedict, and rightly so, who helped me to understand that I have done my duty to my brother by finding someone to care for him and teach him to be a man. Someone who had successfully reared three brothers of his own." She stood, throwing her arms wide. "I conceded then and now. You were right. William was not aided by my coddling. Nor was my father honored by my holding on. I see that life must go forward."

As Benedict continued to glower down at her she faced him with unwavering regard, in spite of the shiver that ran down her spine at his looming size, quickly drawn breaths and black scowl. "You must, for the sake of your child, if not for me, follow the advice of the wise man who told me to let go when it is time. Your fatherly duty to your brothers is done. Letting go will not mean putting aside your other responsibilities. Yet it might help you begin to see that there can be more to your life."

He answered through tight lips, and she could feel the barely controlled heat of him as he leaned even closer. "My duty to them will never be done. You think I have a choice in my life? Do you not imagine that I would not wish to simply be Benedict, that I would not wish to lie with a woman in the spring rain and feel her soul merge with my own? I felt myself become a part of you. But that sort of weakness is something I cannot allow myself. I am not just a man. I am Bracken-moore.''

His admission of what he had felt when they made love made her realize something that she had not fully understood. Benedict was distrustful of his feelings for her. What he described, what should have been a moment of beauty and joining, had only threatened his concept of himself as invulnerable.

Her heart filling with disappointment and frustration, she cried, ''You only love where there is no danger to you, where your heart is safe and secure.''

He thumped his chest with his open palm. ''How can you say such a thing? I love many, and well. I have come to love your own brother, William, as if he were my own.''

The fact that Benedict did not mention her made Raine's stomach tighten with pain, made her go on, speak more frankly than she had ever thought to do. ''Is that what you really believe, Benedict? After what you have just admitted to me? Can you say that you could ever love *me?*'' Once the words were said, Raine wished that she could take them back, for she did not wish to hear his reply. But that was not possible.

He was silent for a long, agonizing moment. Finally he said, ''That is not the same, Raine. You are so unpredictable, so impetuous.''

She looked at him, in that moment uncaring of how much she revealed or did not reveal. ''Love is not given where it is safe to love. It is given because your heart cannot do otherwise.''

And who would know that better than she?

Pity for herself and for him rose up inside her. "I do not wish to be married to Brackenmoore. I wish to be married to a man. How could you expect me to celebrate in bearing you a child if you are not human? A child needs a father who is real, not a figurehead."

His arm snaked out to sweep everything from the desk to the floor. Groaning out loud, he blanched, closing his eyes as he took a quick harsh breath. When he opened them again he was shaking as if taken with palsy. He raised one arm, pointing toward the door. "Out, woman! Get out of here this instant."

Raine did not wish to go. It galled her to run when she was so obviously right. But an inner sense of self-preservation told her Benedict had been pushed far enough.

With a groan of outrage and frustration she took up her candle and stormed from the room.

Yet as she went to her chamber she realized with a sense of unexpected sorrow that though much had been said, nothing had been resolved. The situation had, in fact, gone from dreadful to completely unbearable, for now she knew there was no hope for them.

Benedict did not desire to include her in his life. He was Brackenmoore, and as such needed no one.

Raine was not at all certain why this knowledge hurt so very much, why her heart ached as if it might surely stop beating. It was not as if she had ever expected him to love her.

She wiped a tear from her cheek with the back of her hand.

Benedict slammed his hand on the table, his body shaking with the force of emotions boiling in him like hot tar.

How dare Raine speak to him that way? She understood nothing.

Yet even as he told himself this, a creeping sense of misery began to penetrate his rage. Saints above, she could not be right. He would never deliberately withhold anything—including his love. He could not love Raine because of who she was.

But who is she? asked that familiar voice inside him. She was wild and unpredictable, true. But was she not also loyal, honest, selfless to those whom she loved? Suddenly feeling as if his knees would not hold him, Benedict sank into the chair.

Unconsciously he rubbed his hands over the arms, his mind seeking desperately for something familiar, something that could bring him back from the brink of complete self-doubt. It was a good chair, a solid chair. It had been his father's and in it Benedict had made uncounted decisions concerning the lives of hundreds of people.

Never once in all that time, even as a lad of eighteen, had he ever felt such an overwhelming sense of uncertainty and confusion. That this self-doubt was brought on by the woman who had just thoroughly and forcefully decried all that he stood for made matters all the more distressing.

How dare she accuse him of only being able to love where it was safe? Why, he had loved his family and folk to the utter submergence of himself and his own needs. Why could she not see this, understand him?

Mayhap she understands you all too well. Benedict heard the voice again, wondering from whence it came.

From your heart. It seemed that although he did not

wish to listen to it, the voice inside him would not be stilled.

Because you love her and you are afraid of that love. With that Benedict put his face in his hands, feeling his world crumble around him as he realized that no matter how he wished he could deny the words, they were indeed true.

He did love Raine, had loved her from the first moment he saw her. He had tried to convince himself that he had believed and protected her for numerous other reasons. None of them had been true.

In that first instant when her golden eyes had met his, he had been lost. Then afterward, learning of her courage and love for her brother had only made him care all the more. Benedict realized that they two were more alike than not, both of them driven by their sense of responsibility and care for others. It was their way of accomplishing this that differed.

But surely he was not afraid of loving her, had only denied it in himself because he had not realized that truth. *But what kept you from realizing?*

Groaning, he leaned back in his chair, wishing for that almost forgotten sense of rightness and well-being, yet knowing that feeling was gone for all time to come.

A sound at the entrance to the chamber drew his unintentionally hopeful gaze. It was not Raine, but Kendran. Benedict sighed, feeling slightly chagrined at the reproachful expression on his younger brother's face.

Kendran spoke first. "I was just coming in from...well, that matters not. What matters is that I overheard all you said to Raine. She is right, you know. You cannot keep putting your duties before your wife. Truth to tell, Benedict, many of them are not yours to take on. If there is some trouble that involves Tristan he would not thank you for keeping it from him. He should be informed.''

Benedict scowled at his brother, realizing that he had likely been exercising that undeniable charm of his on some willing maid. He asked, ''And where have you been?''

Kendran shrugged. ''It would not be chivalrous to reveal that. Let us stick to the subject at hand, please.''

Looking into those eyes, which many said were so like his own, Benedict decided to leave the matter of his brother's late return for another time. He replied, ''I seek to save Tristan this trouble. He and Lily have known so many.''

Kendran answered with a directness that gave evidence of the strong man he would soon become. ''And you and Raine have also known troubles. Think on that and what it costs you to protect others who have no need of protecting.''

''I but sought to—''

He was more than a little surprised when his youngest brother interrupted him with open impatience. ''What you intended is not in doubt. Yet it was not, and is not, necessary. Hear this—you are wrong in one thing. Father did not put Brackenmoore first. He put Mother first and then us, his sons.''

Benedict's brows arched. ''How can you know such a thing? You were a small child.''

He shook his head. ''I may have been young but I recall the way it felt to be with them, the warmth of our being a family. Where else do you imagine you learned to care so much for your brothers? And ask yourself this—would a man who put his lands above all else take his wife to Scotland to visit her sister?''

Benedict had no reply. He had been too caught up in doing what he must to consider such a thing.

Kendran went on. "You need concentrate on your own marriage." He paused, holding Benedict's unhappy gaze. "She is a good woman, your Raine, if somewhat bruised about the edges. She does have difficulty in showing her care for anyone other than William, but that is changing. Methinks she need only be given a chance to show her care for you, my brother."

Benedict started, then shook his head fiercely. "Me? Raine has no care for me."

"I never thought to call you a fool, Benedict. As you told her you felt about Father, to me you have been as near to a god here on earth as any man could be. But this day I will call you a fool. Her anguish and the tears she shed as she left this room after hearing you say that you could not love her are proof enough for me. Though you may be right that she has no tender feelings toward you now. After your making such a statement it would certainly be debatable."

"I did not mean—"

Again Kendran interrupted. "What you truly meant matters not at all, lest you are prepared to try to mend the damage you have done." Kendran paused before going on, his voice sounding weary. "I had come to tell you that I will be away from Brackenmoore for two days."

Benedict frowned. "A woman?"

Kendran shrugged. "Perhaps you might mind your own affairs before worrying over mine." He swung around then and left before Benedict could form a reply.

For a long moment Benedict sat there immobile. His mind swirled with the things Kendran had said. He could not deny the truth in his assertion that their father had loved his family best. His actions did, in fact, prove that.

Raine was right. Benedict had been a fool bound to a notion of duty that was not even real.

Never in his life had he shied away from anything difficult. He would not do so now. He must face his feelings for his wife, commit himself to their marriage. Though after what he had said to her, there seemed little hope of her forgiving him. All he knew was that he must try. It was the only possibility of filling the ache of longing he felt whenever he thought of Raine.

But first he must make a place for her in his life. Whether or not she would choose to occupy it was up to her.

He reached for a sheet of parchment and a quill. He would write to Tristan, tell him of the situation with Alister Harcourt, and he would do so now.

Raine walked slowly along the sand. The late spring sunshine was warm upon her head and the sky was a shade of blue that would make angels weep in reverence, but she felt no pleasure in her surroundings. She felt alone and submerged in an aching loneliness.

At last she halted, taking a deep breath and looking out over the vast expanse of the sea. It was awe inspiring and eternal, as nothing in her life had ever been.

First her mother, then her father had died, leaving her to care for William. She had been afraid of giving in to her own despair and fear, the despair at losing her parents, her fear of lacking the courage to go on. Now she must live with the uncertainty of her marriage to Benedict.

Perhaps she could learn from William. He had lost the life he had known as well, yet he had found a place here. But she could not imagine that she would ever be able to accept Brackenmoore the way her brother had, for Benedict did not, could not love her. How could she be content with the meager portion of himself that he was willing to afford her?

The events of the previous night were imprinted on her mind for all time to come. She now realized that she could never leave Brackenmoore. There was no point in being anywhere that Benedict was not. Yet the knowledge that she must indeed live out her life here so near him when he did not love her was devastating.

Heaven help her, why must she care so? Because he was Benedict. His gentleness and kindness had helped her to understand herself. He was the rock Brackenmoore was built on, the one constant in all the heavens that could be counted on. Unfortunately, it was his very dependability and strength that made it impossible for him to love any one woman, even his wife, above any other in his care.

Her hands went to her stomach as she felt the spot where she imagined the child must lie. Yet even in this she found little comfort. For however much she loved her babe, that could not replace the heartache of knowing that she was not loved by its father.

She walked on, oblivious to her surroundings, until suddenly she realized the beach had narrowed greatly. It had in fact narrowed so much that she was now picking her way among the rocks in order to avoid walking in the sea.

Turning, Raine moved to go back the way she had come. It was as she walked between two large boulders that she felt something heavy fall across her head and shoulders. She cried out in surprise even as she felt herself being pulled backward against a sturdy chest.

That her captor was far stronger than she, Raine realized as soon as she began to struggle. Her efforts were further thwarted when her feet were lifted up by a second assailant.

As she was lifted high, she ceased her struggles, aware of the babe inside her. Even if she were able to break free now it would mean a fall, and that might injure the child.

Only a moment later she felt herself being laid across a saddle. One of her captors mounted behind her, keeping one hand on her back at all times.

Trying to breathe evenly, to think, Raine attempted to fathom what was happening, why anyone would do this to her. The answer came in a flash of outrage.

"Denley!" She called out his name, and even though the heavy fabric muffled the word, she knew they must have heard her. There was no reply. The blackguard would not wish to discuss the matter with her. He would want her far from the protective presence of her husband as quickly as possible.

Anger rolled in her. Yet she felt a certain sense of relief in knowing that it was her half-witted cousin who had abducted her. She realized that he meant her no good, but did not believe that Denley would actually do her physical harm. The best course open to her would surely be to bide her time until they reached their destination.

Chapter Fourteen

The ride was uncomfortable and long, but not as long as Raine had anticipated. She had thought Denley would wish to be many hours, perhaps even days from Benedict's intimidating reach before he halted his flight.

While her captors lifted her off the horse, Raine prepared herself for dealing with her cousin. She was determined to present a reasoning attitude in spite of her anger. She knew how very obstinate he could be and wished to convince him to simply take her home with no more harm done. Whether or not she would be able to accomplish this remained to be seen. She had never thought that Denley would have the courage to kidnap her.

She was aware of the fact that they entered a building when she heard the sounds of their booted feet on a hard wooden floor, then she felt herself being carried up a flight of steps that seemed to go on forever. When at last they reached the top, a door opened. The next thing she knew, she had been deposited quite abruptly onto the floor.

Even as she reached to remove the covering from over her head, she heard the door closing. Hurriedly she pulled her head free, searching the small, dimly lit chamber for her cousin.

Disappointment made her stomach clench as she realized that she was alone. Raine called out in desperation, "Denley! Denley! How dare you do this? Coward! I insist you speak to me this instant!"

Silence was the only reply.

She slapped her hand against the rush-strewn floor in frustration. How was she ever to make him see reason if he would not talk to her? He had to let her go before Benedict realized what had happened.

For the sake of his woman and children she wished to see Denley come out of this unscathed. Only God in his heaven knew how furious Benedict would be when he learned that her cousin had taken her.

Benedict found that no matter how hard he tried he could not concentrate. He kept getting up to look out the window of his library, seeing the blue sky overhead, the castle folk working about the grounds, the goats that nibbled at the grass. Yet it was not the fineness of the spring day that drew his attention, for in truth he saw little of what was laid out before him.

His thoughts were of Raine. Raine and their babe.

He, Benedict, was to have a child. Perhaps the babe would be a son, an heir to his lands and heritage. It was joyous news indeed. Yet he felt an inescapable sense of melancholy.

Frustration swept through him. How was he supposed to feel? The mother of his child could not abide being in the same room with him. It was his own fault that this was so.

He recalled again Kendran's certainty that Raine cared for him—had cared for him. If it had ever been true, which was very difficult for Benedict to believe, it could not be now after the way he had treated her.

What woman would wish to be wanted only for the purpose of producing an heir? Which was precisely what he had led her to believe, had in fact led himself to believe. What a fool he had been.

He could not even use the defense that his feelings for her had changed in recent days, for they had not. They had never been what he wished them to be.

He had always wanted Raine for herself, for her honesty, her obstinacy, her loyalty and devotion to those she loved. He wanted her in his life and not just in his bed. That was why it had plagued him to see her care of those at Abbernathy. He had wished for her to feel that same sense of belonging, not just to the people of Brackenmoore, but to him. Mostly to him.

Was Kendran right—that she had felt something for him—though he hesitated to believe it could have been love? Unfortunately, no matter what her feelings might have been, he had surely killed them.

His fist hit the wall and he immediately drew it back to rub his scraped knuckles. There was nothing to be gained by hitting walls, or going over and over the difficulties in his mind. He suddenly realized that he must speak to Raine, try to make her see that he was sorry, that he wished to be a real husband to her, to put her and his child first.

Would she accept his offer? Benedict's gaze swept the chamber again. It was as if he could make some sign or answer materialize there simply by willing it.

There was no sign.

The answer could be found nowhere but in himself. It was his own fear of rejection that prevented him from going to her. Benedict squared his wide shoulders. He was many things—thoughtless, too driven and even obstinate—but he was not a coward.

Devil take his pride, for it would be cold comfort in the years ahead. Rounding on his heel, Benedict left the library. He would have it out now. Anything was preferable to this agony of loneliness and indecision. When he entered Raine's chamber and found it empty, he felt a lag in his determination to have all settled. But only a slight lag. The faint hope that she might still have some gentle feeling for him drove him on.

He called for Maeve. That wise soul seemed to read his intent the moment she entered the chamber, and he could not help seeing that she was pleased. He ignored this, asking, "Have you any notion of where my wife has gone?"

She nodded. "Aye, my lord, I saw her pass through the hall some time ago. She was wearing a cloak, thus I assumed she might be taking a walk."

He nodded and left without answering the questions he saw in her gaze. He made his way directly to the stables and collected his stallion. He wished to speak to Raine before talking to anyone else of this matter. This was their relationship, and should have been something they addressed together since the beginning.

It was only when he was unable to find Raine about the castle grounds or at the beach that he began to grow concerned. Returning to the keep, he had it searched from top to bottom. It soon became apparent that she was not there.

With a growing sense of unease he questioned Aida, who could do little but sputter incoherently past her tears. Trying his very best to be calm with her in spite of his own anxiety, Benedict learned only that there was nothing missing from Raine's belongings but the garments she had been wearing.

The suspicion that had begun to insinuate itself into Benedict's mind was untenable. Yet it would not go away.

Was it possible that, even after giving her word that she would not run away again, Raine had done just that? His chest ached at the very thought. But would she leave without William? He could not credit it. Yet she was gone.

Raine had been angry with him after the things he had said to her, the despicable way he had behaved, shouting and thrashing about the library like a madman before ordering her out. He clearly recalled the one request she had made on agreeing to come back to Brackenmoore—that there would be no more orders.

Again he was beset by a pain in his chest, this time in realizing just how wrongly he had behaved. How could she be blamed for leaving, under the circumstances?

Yet even as he thought this Benedict knew a sense of doubt. Raine had given her word. Was it not true that no matter how difficult or untenable keeping her word might be, as in the case of protecting Will even if it meant marrying a man she did not love, she had done just that?

A great wave of fear swept over him, as he was suddenly and painfully certain that she had not run away. Something had happened to her. Or, God forbid, someone had taken her. As soon as the thought entered his head Benedict knew that was exactly what had happened. The castle and grounds had been searched. If she were the victim of an untoward accident there would have been some sign of it.

Who would have taken her? A picture of Denley Trent as Benedict had last seen him at Abbernathy rose in his mind. The man was crazed, convinced for no reason that Raine was betraying him by her marriage to Benedict.

With a cry of rage, he spun around, the guilt of his own fault in this riding hard upon his heels. He had been nothing short of a fool himself to underestimate the man. Obviously that bumbling air had too easily distracted him from Trent's rigid and unwavering determination to have Raine at all costs. No more would he play the fool. This time Denley Trent would pay with his life. And if he had harmed her in any way? Benedict's stomach clenched at the thought.

If he had, only God could help him.

Benedict garbed himself for travel, then hesitated only to inform his steward of his departure. Understandably, the man was horrified by his cryptic explanation of where he was going and why.

"My lord, there will be no one of the Ainsworth blood here. I cannot recall such a thing ever occurring."

Benedict met his troubled gaze. "Kendran was to return on the morrow. You must send for him. Beyond that I can do naught but find Raine. She may be in grave danger."

Benedict then left the keep without a backward glance. For the first time in his life Brackenmoore did not figure foremost in his mind. All he could think about was getting on a horse and finding his wife and their child.

Only as several of his men and William's entered the stables and began to saddle their horses did he realize that the steward or possibly Maeve must have ordered them to accompany him. Benedict made no effort to slow himself to accommodate their preparations for the journey. But he was pleased to find them right behind him as he passed through the castle gate.

The journey to Trent's holding passed in a blur of anger and impatience. Benedict was grateful that William's men had accompanied him, for they knew the most direct route there and were willing to keep up the pace he set in order to rescue their mistress.

He could not hide the agony he knew was written on his face. There was no point in attempting to disguise his feelings any longer. Raine meant more to him than his dignity or even his position as overlord. Nothing mattered but that he find her.

They arrived at the wood-frame house in the heavy darkness that presages dawn. Benedict leapt to the ground before his horse had come to a full halt. He strode to the door, pounding upon it with a tightly clenched fist. "Trent!" he bellowed.

The door was opened after only a short time by a sleepy-eyed serving man, who peered out, his gaze clearly still adjusting to the glow of the lantern he held high. When he took in not only Benedict but also the men who had moved to stand behind him, his gray eyes rounded. He stepped backward, making to close the door. Benedict pushed past him, demanding, "I will see your master now."

"But—"

"Fetch him, 'ere I order my men to burn this pile of tinder to the ground."

The man rushed behind the curtained partition at the far end of the room nearest the hearth. A moment later he heard Denley exclaim, "Tell him I refuse to see him."

Benedict followed the serving man. He found himself

in the bedchamber. Trent was sitting up, glaring at his servant. A woman huddled at his back, her eyes wide. Her hair, which hung about her in a golden-brown tangle, did not disguise the fact that she was not uncomely. The fear in her gaze made Benedict hesitate. He had no wish to terrorize anyone but the man who had taken his wife. That need pushed him on.

He strode to the bed. "Where is she?"

Trent stared at him in puzzled amazement. "You mean Raine?"

Benedict bent over him, his heart beating like a drum in his chest. "Of course, Raine, but you know that better than anyone."

Denley stared at him in utter horror. "I do not have her." There was no mistaking his fear and shock.

Utter despair pierced Benedict as he realized that the man was telling the truth.

If she were not here... Dear God, where could she be? A great yawning chasm of anguish and uncertainty opened up inside him as he realized that he did not know what to do, where to go.

He had been so sure, had convinced himself so thoroughly that it was her cousin who had taken her. No other possibilities had even entered his mind. He ran a trembling hand over his face.

Denley spoke up quickly. "I swear it is true, Ainsworth. I have not seen her."

Benedict heard him as if through a wall. It was all he could do to form a sensible reply. "I believe you." Now that he knew Raine was not with her cousin, he had lost interest in him. He could fully focus on nothing save his own pain and dread.

He turned and left the hall without another word.

Mounting his horse, he looked out over the road before him, his mind a whirl of torment.

Raine!

Raine knew not where she might be, for the round, stone, windowless chamber was in no way familiar to her. That did not astonish her greatly, however, for it had taken a short time to reach it and she was not acquainted with the area about Brackenmoore. She was surprised that Denley was.

The room bore no furnishing but the bed, which was made of a heavy wood frame and an ancient fur. The rush-strewn floor offered up no secrets.

It was not until the third day of her imprisonment that Raine saw another human being. Previous to that her food and water had been passed to her through a narrow aperture in the heavy oak door, which could only be opened from without. All of her cries for Denley to speak with her had met with silence.

Thus it was with some surprise on the morning of that third day that she saw the door itself open. Quickly she rose from the narrow bed. Even as she searched the bare chamber for the hundredth time in the hope of finding a weapon of any sort, a man stepped inside, closing the portal after him. He was a strange man, his shape distorted in a way she had never seen, his shoulders and chest incredibly wide for his stature, his shoulders uneven in height. His face was equally distinctive, his head large, as was his nose, his wide mouth crooked. It was his eyes that she found most arresting; wide and fine, they were of an amazing and beautiful sea green.

The shock she felt at seeing not her cousin, but this squat, misshapen figure standing there in a long robe could not be measured. It was a very long moment before she found her tongue. "Who are you and where is Denley?"

The man frowned. "I know not who this Denley you call for might be." He pointed to his own disproportionately wide chest. "I am Alister Harcourt, lord of Treanly."

"Alister Harcourt?" Her brows knit in confusion. "I have heard the name through my husband, but do not understand why would you bring me here. I do not even know you, sir."

He shrugged, his heavy-featured face cruel. "That you would even wonder why I would seek revenge only serves to further convince me that I have done what is right in taking you from your husband."

Even as Raine saw that cruelty she could not help noting that his unusual eyes bore an unmistakable trace of pain. But she was in no position to worry on this, as her own safety and the safety of her unborn child might well hang in the balance. She spoke as gently as her pounding heart would allow. "Please, my lord, you speak in riddles."

He shrugged those uneven shoulders. "Do I? Why would you be so surprised that I might take the righting of the wrongs done to my family into my own hands?" He raised one amazingly large hand and closed it into a fist. "Do you think that the wrongs done me are of such little import that you cannot imagine I might wish to take my own revenge for them?"

Raine ran her hands over her face as she tried to think. The last thing she wished to do was insult her captor and further enrage him. Yet she knew his need for vengeance was not justified. Benedict had told her what had occurred with Tristan and Lily. She also knew that Benedict had been reluctant to reveal the whole truth to this man because of his desire to protect those he loved from gossip and scandal.

Raine hesitated to tell her captor the facts as she knew them. She was not sure that revealing their secrets would change anything, for she did not believe the man was in any state to heed anything she might say.

She looked up at him, her eyes unconsciously pleading. "What do you mean to do with me?"

His piercing green gaze raked her. "That, my lady, I have not yet decided. Suffice it to say that whatever I decide, I wish for it to make the most painful impact possible upon your husband. He will be suffering even now at the loss of his lovely new bride, but not nearly as much as I would have him suffer." His voice became rough with emotion. "He will know the agony I have known in the death of my brother."

Again Raine was aware of the pain in him, and earnestly told him. "I know that my husband is very sorry for your loss."

His expression hardened. "Sorry for my loss? He has done all he can to set my very existence aside, to appease me with lands and money." He glared at her. "Do not think that I am blind to the fact that it was he who convinced King Edward to become involved in this matter. His influence with this court is no secret."

What he said about Benedict's having asked the king for aid was true, and there was be nothing to be gained in denying it. Yet the man did not understand that Benedict had not been attempting to misuse him, only to protect his own family. Benedict had said that Harcourt had brought his troubles with Tristan upon himself, and Raine believed him completely. Her husband had proved honest no matter what his other faults might be.

Her captor went on coldly. "Your husband will suffer the loss of you as I have my brother."

She would not attempt to disabuse Alister Harcourt of his erroneous notion that she would be greatly missed by her husband. The fact that she was gone, and with her his babe, would pain him, for the child meant much to him. And for that reason, if no other, she must get through this intact. Although Benedict felt no love for her, her own feelings for him made the notion of his suffering over the loss of the babe too distressing for her to contemplate.

Somehow she would survive.

Studying the misshapen man before her, Raine thought about the agony he had suffered. Clearly he had loved his brother, no matter what his character. Sympathy stabbed at her heart. She faced him. "Pray believe me, my lord, I am sorry that you lost one whom you loved. I have only just recently lost my own father, and I understand how hurtful it is to know that you will never meet him in the hall, never hear the sound of his voice, his laugh, never feel an arm about your shoulders. It is painful to understand that he is gone for always."

He looked at her for a long, long moment. "Do you think my grief as paltry as that? Do you imagine that I would go to such lengths simply because I miss him?" He lurched toward her, and Raine took an involuntary step backward. "I do not miss him, my lady Ainsworth."

For a long moment she could think of nothing to say, for words seemed meaningless in face of the agony she saw in his eyes. He watched her in return, then finally turned his back on her, going to the door to lean his forehead against it. He spoke harshly to someone without. "Trevor."

Raine saw the slump of those shoulders, felt the pain of all he had said sink into her bones. Acting on impulse, she went to him, putting her own slender arm about those wide shoulders.

He stiffened and jerked back, even as the door swung open. In the next moment he was gone, but not before Raine had seen the unadulterated longing in those green eyes.

She stood staring at that closed door, her heart heavy with sadness. That longing had had naught to do with any masculine need, but something deeper, and she thought perhaps far more terrifying to a man bent on revenge.

Perhaps, she mused, there was some way to make him see that Benedict had meant him no harm. Benedict had taken so many under his wing—herself, William, his ward, Genevieve, his brothers. He would never misuse a misshapen, sad man like the one who had just left her.

Would Alister Harcourt ever believe that? Yet what would happen to her, to her babe, if he did not? Her hand went to her belly protectively. This situation had made her realize that she loved her child, wanted it with every fiber of her being. Even if Benedict did not love her, her love for him meant that the babe had not been conceived in pain and misery, but in love.

The child must survive. It was living proof that she and Benedict were indeed something to one another, if only on her part.

There was one thing that did give her some cause to hope. Clearly Alister Harcourt had not yet decided what he intended to do with her. Perhaps, if he delayed long enough over his plans for vengeance, she could escape. The possibility was remote, of course, given where she was being held, but she had to cling to it.

She could not allow herself to believe that Benedict might come for her. He would have no way of knowing where to search.

Benedict pushed on through the night, his mind so filled with confusion and pain that he hardly knew what to do. He knew only that he must go on, must find Raine and bring her home, beg her to forgive him for all the hurt he had brought her. He had refused to give of himself, time after time, and all for the sake of protecting his own closed heart.

In the early morn, when Brackenmoore Castle at last came into view, Benedict felt no rise of happiness or relief. He felt numb, dead inside, as he had never before felt in his life. Even when his parents had died he had had his brothers to live for, their needs to pull him through the pain.

As Raine had said, they were now men, with their own lives to live. They no longer needed him as they had. And the two people who did need him most—his wife and his child—were gone, leaving this emptiness that would never be filled without them. For he realized that even more than they needed him, he needed them. And he had no idea of where to even begin to look for them.

The moment he arrived at the keep, Kendran, with a white-faced William in tow, hurried out to greet him. His expression was grim as he held out a roll of parchment. "This arrived not more than hours after the steward summoned me home. After overhearing your conversation with Raine that night and realizing your troubles with Alister Harcourt, I took the liberty of reading it.''

Benedict felt dread wash over him anew, the sickness of fear in his heart telling him what Kendran would say even before the words were uttered. ''He has her, Benedict. It is he who has taken Raine.''

Benedict threw back his head and shouted incoherently into an indifferent and cloudless blue sky, which surely should weep as he did inside. Frustration and pain gave him the voice of a caged beast. When he could speak, he said only, ''Tell me.''

Kendran went on, his face grim. ''He sends you a challenge and says that he will not release her unless you meet with him in mortal combat. You alone are to come to the tower on Mayberry Knob or bring about her death.''

Benedict's heart felt as if it had turned to ice in his chest, and in that instant an unexpected and deadly calm settled over him. ''Aye, I will meet with him.'' He rubbed the hilt of his sword with a now rock steady hand. He would meet with him and Harcourt would die.

William stopped him with a hand on his arm. ''How do you know that he has not already hurt her?''

Benedict looked down into those frightened green eyes, feeling love well up inside him for this new brother of his. ''I swear to you, my brother, that has he done so, I will cleave Treanly to the ground and all there will know the sorrow that is ours.''

With that he turned and called for a fresh horse. When his men moved to do the same, he halted them. ''Nay, I will go alone.''

Raine was somewhat surprised when the door of her prison opened the very next day to again reveal Alister

Harcourt. His expression was no less angry or resentful than the previous day, but something, some unknown sense, told her that he was not here to further berate her.

So why had he come? She could not prevent herself from asking. "Why are you here, my lord?"

He answered immediately. "Why did you place your arms about me yesterday?"

She shrugged, surprised at his question. "Simple human kindness."

His face bore an oddly restless and confused expression as he said, "What you call a simple human contact is as foreign to me as the moon." His lips twisted with pain and anger. "You assume that I miss my brother. You have no notion of my feelings for him. You see my horrifying form. Until yesterday Maxim was the only one who had ever touched me in my memory, though it was most oft in anger. He loved me not well, was perhaps not capable of such. He did not pity and fear me, but treated me with the same contempt as anyone else, was more likely to club me about the shoulders than hold them. But he was not afraid to touch me, as all others have been until yesterday."

Raine hardly knew what to say to a man who had never been touched except in anger. "I am not afraid to touch you, my lord, and I know others who would not be so."

He frowned at her fiercely. "Did you think it would gain your release?"

Surprise made her answer with complete candor. "I did not think such a thing, but if I had considered that showing a small amount of human compassion might gain my release, I would have done so."

He seemed completely taken aback for a moment before his features hardened. "And you would have me believe that you did not think that?"

She shrugged. "Believe what you will. I do not hold out any real hope of convincing you of anything. I want only to return to my husband." She heard the yearning and misery in her own voice as she finished, but did not care. She did love Benedict and would hide it no more.

At that moment there was a pounding at the door and a man's voice called, "My lord, a rider approaches."

A trace of uncertainty entered those green eyes for a brief moment before it was covered by a mask of anger. "Ainsworth has answered my challenge to combat, at last."

Raine's heart leapt. So he had sent word of her capture to Benedict!

Harcourt reached out and took her by the arm as he cried, "Open the door." She made no effort to resist him as he then swept through the open door and down a winding stone stair. She knew who the rider would be.

She was hampered only by the slower gait of the man who held her, for she wanted to fly down that stair and into Benedict's arms. That this poor man had no hope of besting him in a contest of arms she did not doubt.

Then, suddenly, Raine knew that she must try to prevent Alister Harcourt's death. It was true that he had done wrong in taking her, but so much wrong had been done to him in his years upon this earth. She had no wish to see his life end because of her.

But she did not know how to stop what was about to occur. He had sent his challenge and Benedict had answered.

Unless perhaps she could convince her husband that he must not do this, must walk away from this fight, for not only Alister Harcourt's sake but their own. To begin afresh here they need leave no trail of blood behind them.

For beginning afresh was just what she intended to do. She would set aside her pride and tell Benedict of her love for him. What he chose to make of that was up to him. This whole incident had shown her that life was too short to hold back. She would not raise her child in an atmosphere of resentment and fear, even if that fear were only of her own feelings.

When they reached the bottom, Harcourt threw open the door and pulled her out with him. They were at the base of a tall, narrow tower situated in a grove of trees, their new leaves still not fully grown.

As she searched for Benedict she saw him ride out of the forest to her right. Her gaze drank in the sight of him even as she saw fatigue in the lines about his beloved mouth, the dark circles beneath his eyes, eyes that found hers instantly. His relief at seeing her eased those lines and brought a look of determination to those features as he slid to the ground and reached for his sword. "Come then, Harcourt. I am here."

Alister Harcourt pushed Raine away with a growl. "And about time it is, Ainsworth."

As they approached one another, she tried to think, for she could not allow this to go forth. Tired though he obviously was, Benedict would make easy work of disposing of his opponent. She called out, "Do not go on with this. More death will solve nothing."

They paid her no heed. Raine ran her hands through her hair in utter frustration. Desperately she moved to stand between the two of them, her eyes holding Benedict's. "Please, my lord, do not do this. Let us have an end to this feud. I would not have you kill this man in my name. He has done me no real harm.''

Benedict shouted, ''No harm, Raine? He took you from me, meant to kill you if I did not answer his summons.''

She looked at Harcourt, pleading with him, praying that he would swallow his pride and answer with what she knew was the truth. ''My heart tells me that he would not have killed me. You would not have, would you, my lord? I beg you speak true. Your death aids no one.''

She could see the indecision on his face. Turning to Benedict again, she said, ''Please, my lord husband, put down your sword.'' She could see the warring emotions on his face, the rage that drove him on, needing some outlet, needing the spilling of blood in order to be appeased.

Yet knowing this, she whispered, ''Please, my husband, if you bear me any goodwill at all, do not fight him.''

Then, as his gaze remained trained on hers, an outraged cry filled the stillness. ''You will not cheat me of my revenge, Ainsworth.''

Benedict watched as his beloved Raine, unkempt but apparently unharmed, spun around to face Alister Harcourt, who was moving forward with hatred and purpose. To Benedict's utter horror she leapt to block his path, her gaze now holding his.

Benedict shouted, ''No, Raine!''

But she did not answer him nor look around as she faced the other man. ''Do not do this, my lord. Killing will not ease the ache inside you. Only forgiveness can do that.'' When he stopped, studying her with both rage and confusion, she moved toward him slowly, holding out her hand, her gaze unafraid and determined.

Again Benedict cried, "No!"

But she did not turn to face him as she said, "Please, my husband. I beg you. This man has known nothing but pain in his life." Then she again said to Harcourt, "Tell him true. You would not have killed me."

The misshapen man seemed unable to look away from her gaze as his eyes dampened. "Nay, I would not have killed you. How could I when you treated me as a human being, me the man who had taken you from all you held dear?"

Benedict could not credit this. He shouted back with outrage, "Aye, you say that now, my lord, but you did mean to when you took her."

Harcourt barely glanced in his direction and spoke with a depth of pain that was shocking. "You ignored me, treated me as all others have. As if I were nothing. Your lady wife saw me as something more even than my own brother, and with no hope of gain."

Benedict was unable to doubt him further. Raine had accomplished in a matter of days what he had not been able to do in all the months since Maxim Harcourt had died. By following the message of her heart she had brought about peace.

His anger slipped from him as he realized that he was as much to blame for this situation as Harcourt. How could he, Benedict, kill him when he had ignored the very instincts that had told him the man was acting out of grief? Long ago he should have gone to him and offered his regret. But he had been too occupied in defending his heart against the woman he loved.

With his anger gone, what remained was regret that he had been so much a fool, and an undeniable sense of love and admiration for his wife. He watched as, with no trace of fear, she placed her hand upon Harcourt's shoulder. And when she did so the man lowered his head, a sob escaping him.

Aware of him as she was, Raine could feel the change in Benedict's demeanor. Loving him all the more for his willingness to show mercy here, she whispered gently to Alister Harcourt, "Pray forgive the wrongs done you, my lord, by all of us. And accept my hand, my friendship, however small a gift it may be, in place of your revenge."

He looked up at her, clearly uncertain. "Your kindness I understand. It comes from inside you. But why would you offer me your friendship?"

"Because you are a man who is in need of a friend, I think." She waved at Benedict, who stood with his sword pointed to the ground. "My husband is a man who befriends all those who come to him in need of care, and for no other reason than that. He befriended me, when I most needed someone, though it took me some time to appreciate his actions as they were meant. His compassion is one of his very best qualities, although not the only one. I would be like him in that respect." She cast Benedict a glance she knew revealed all she had heretofore tried to hide, then turned back to the other man. "You knew your brother. Believe that Benedict would not uphold the harming of anyone if he felt there was another way. He will end this fight with you even though you stole me away from him, and not only me, but his coming child."

She saw the shock that registered in the other man's gaze, and pressed on. "Benedict knows that you are owed an explanation of all that occurred, though 'tis not from him but from his brother. You will have your explanation, my lord, on my honor."

For a long moment he hesitated, then his sword fell. She looked into those fine green eyes, whispering, "Thank you."

Then, with a cry of joy, she turned to Benedict. Before she could take two steps, she was enveloped in his arms, her face pressed to the solid and beloved wall of his chest. She breathed deeply of his scent, sweat and fear and relief, and reveled in it. For he was here holding her close, her husband, the center of her world—her very existence. But after a joyous moment when she felt as if he would never let her go, his arms loosened. As he pulled away she looked up at him, bereft without his nearness.

Benedict dropped his hands to his sides, stepping back, his face full of sadness and regret. She shook her head in confusion. "What is wrong? Are you not happy?"

His misery was clearly unabated by her words. "I am pleased, overjoyed, that you have suffered no harm, but it has been through no credit of mine."

"What are you saying, Benedict? You saved my life." Her hand went to her belly. "The life of our child."

He raised his hands to cover his face, a sob of agony escaping him. "And nearly lost you both through my own folly. If I had not been so bent on doing everything, taking care of everyone myself, none of this would have occurred. I nearly lost the one I love most in my need to keep those I loved too closely beneath my care."

She felt a strange sense of unreality at what he was saying. "Love. Are you speaking of your love for the babe?"

He looked up at her, shaking his head as if confused by her question. "Aye, how could I not love my own babe? But it is you I speak of, Raine, my beloved wife. The thought of having lost you nearly drove me mad."

Her heart thudded to a stop as she stared up at him. "You love me? You love me, Benedict?"

His deep blue eyes grew damp, as they seemed to drink in her face. "Aye, Raine, I love you with all of my heart and soul. You *are* my soul."

Joy flooded her in an all-encompassing wave. She held out her arms. "And I love you. Will always love you."

Pain and happiness warred on his handsome features. "But how could you love me when I have not—"

She put her finger to his lips, feeling joy in the simple act of touching him so intimately. "Shh, my love, not now. Let us do no more than love for now."

He closed his eyes, then gently, tenderly kissed her finger. "I love you, too," she whispered, her voice husky with emotion.

Then he was grabbing her to him. Raine closed her own eyes, knowing that this was where she wanted to be for the rest of her life, right here in his arms, her cheek pressed to his heart. There could be no more happiness than this.

Yet as his lips found hers she realized there was more, more than she had ever imagined.

When she thought to look for Alister Harcourt sometime later, he was gone. She felt no worry over this. The time would come to make a permanent peace with him.

This moment was for her and Benedict, and the start of their new life together.

* * * * *

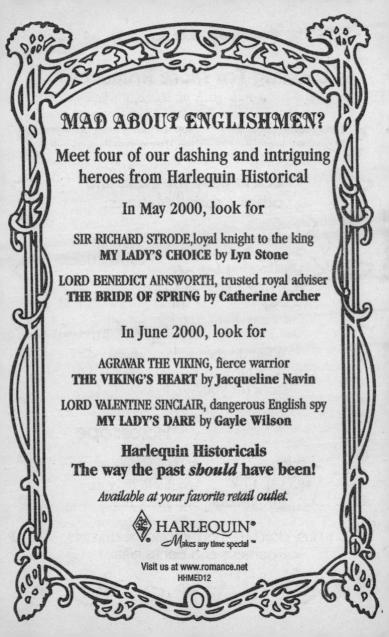

Return to the charm of the Regency era with

GEORGETTE HEYER,

creator of the modern Regency genre.

Enjoy six romantic collector's editions with forewords
by some of today's bestselling romance authors,

Nora Roberts, Mary Jo Putney,
Jo Beverley, Mary Balogh,
Theresa Medeiros and Kasey Michaels.

Frederica
On sale February 2000
The Nonesuch
On sale March 2000
The Convenient Marriage
On sale April 2000
Cousin Kate
On sale May 2000
The Talisman Ring
On sale June 2000
The Corinthian
On sale July 2000

Available at your favorite retail outlet.

HARLEQUIN®
Makes any time special ™